# Coahoma Street

*Jerry W. Moorman*

ISBN 0-9679844-4-0

Farolito Press
P.O. Box 60003
Grand Junction, Colorado 81506

Manufactured in the United States of America
Pyramid Printing and Copy Center
Grand Junction, Colorado
www.pyramidprinting.com

# FOREWORD

To truly understand this novel and the complex social system it portrays, you must realize that the year was 1967. Mississippi schools in the Delta had been racially integrated for only two years; the one and only black student graduated from Princeville High. Racial unrest was growing and white Mississippi was scared. It was a time of great change and people were concerned for the future.

## STORY

This story is about a white, ex-sharecropper's son who went against the grain of Mississippi's social structure and befriended a black girl. Interwoven into the story are other situations involving incest, murder and social snobbery. The time is summer, 1967; the place is Coahoma Street in Princeville, Mississippi. The following explanation of geography and events leading up to the story will, perhaps, help you to better understand.

## GEOGRAPHY

Coahoma Street is located in the black section of Princeville. Princeville is part of Coahoma County, and Coahoma County is situated in the Mississippi River Delta in the Northwestern part of the State of Mississippi. The word Coahoma is a Choctaw Indian word meaning red panther. Early in the history of Mississippi, Choctaws occupied the Delta and were ruled by Chief Sheriff. The Chief had a very beautiful daughter, Princess Coahoma. Whether the county was named for the panther or Princess is a subject for debate.

Early white residents of the area, which was then known as "The Bottoms" or "The Mississippi Swamps," were known as "Swampikes."

Times were good and people needed each other to survive, then slavery was introduced!

## HISTORY

For many years the early economy of the Delta was based on an agricultural system rooted in slavery. After the Civil War, slavery was replaced by sharecropping. Sharecroppers and slaves had many similarities. Both black and white sharecroppers were little more than "legal slaves" tied no longer by physical chains but instead by the figurative chains of economic slavery born of poverty and ignorance. Even though sharecroppers were free to go, most had nowhere to flee nor the education to survive away from the plantation. A few blacks escaped North to a better life; a few whites moved to small Mississippi towns and formed the social strata known as white trash.

Until recently, few people migrated to Mississippi. The latest census revealed that only 14% of people living in Mississippi were born outside the state. During the 1960's, many white Mississippians looked outside their state to a country steeped in righteousness and blessed with a booming economy. When looking within, just the opposite was true. The state was fraught with poverty and viewed by the rest of the nation as a quagmire of racial injustice and intolerance. Faced with a changing way of life, the white aristocracy of Mississippi turned inward and began a campaign of veiled bigotry aimed at preserving their racial and social philosophy. In many ways, the state had once again seceded from the Union.

Powerful white Mississippians longed for the days of the Old South prior to the Civil War. What most of them never knew was that the Mississippi plantation of the pre-war period was largely a manifestation of overactive imaginations and too many viewings of movies such as *Gone With The Wind*. The truth was far removed from the myth. Prior to the war, Mississippi was merely a disease-ridden frontier, with the cotton growing industry still in its infancy.

There were state leaders, however, who helped promote the myth of the "Old South" and were instrumental in forming the racist thread running through much of white Mississippi. There was none more powerful or

iv

influential in his racial bigotry than Theodore G. Bilbo. Starting his political career in 1912 and ending it as a United States Senator in 1947, Bilbo did many things to ensure that poor blacks remained economic slaves. The most reprehensible of his efforts were chronicled in his book, *TAKE YOUR CHOICE: Separation or Mongrelization.* In his writings, Bilbo advocated a separation of the black and white races. He went so far as to introduce his "Greater Liberia Bill" in the United States Senate on April 24, 1939, which asked for federal aid for Negroes who desired to migrate to Liberia. Obviously, he felt Mississippi would be better served by paying blacks to go back to Africa. To understand Bilbo's thinking and reactions of the white aristocracy in this novel, one only has to read an excerpt from his book as published in Poplarville, Mississippi, in 1947.

"The time has come when we must face the facts. The color line has preserved a white south, but it has not prevented a partial mixing of the races. Some 3,000,000 mixbreeds with a mixture of white and black blood are today classified with the Negro race. With these millions of mongrels around us, we see the evidence of the historical truth that the blood of the two races living side by side will eventually mix. In the presence of millions of mixbreeds, the White South looks backward through three hundred years of contact with the Negro, and feels that the color line, however strongly supported, does not offer a guarantee that the white race is to survive. . . . Amalgamation will make America negroid, destroy race, culture, and hope for the future. Separation will make America white, guarantee the preservation of the white race and the maintenance of our white civilization."

To go against this type of thinking in Mississippi during 1967 was to go against the white power structure. Such an undertaking could have only disastrous results! So we begin our story.

**Note: The name Princeville along with the characters and events portrayed in the book are fictional.**

v

# 1

Jerry Sanger sat in the main terminal watching the hustle and bustle. To his left was a bank of pay phones; to his right was a small restaurant. His seat was one of several attached together by a frame of chrome-looking metal. The seat's texture was almost soft, kinda leather; the stuff you could pour all manner of food and drink on without ever soaking in. Very efficient stuff!

Sanger was busy thinking as he watched strangers flow by. It was only about 6:30 a.m., and the place was already getting busy. He had been there since 10:50 the night before. It was early May, 1967, and he had graduated from high school just last night. He hoped he wouldn't see anybody he knew. That wasn't likely, however, even though he was sitting in the busiest part of the Memphis International Airport. It would be really embarrassing if anyone knew his real reason for being there. He wasn't really worried though; he had been in the airport many times before and had never seen a person he knew. It wasn't exactly the sort of place where his kind hung out.

Sanger occasionally drove the 75 miles from his hometown to the airport. To him, it was the most exciting place in the world. It was always busy 24 hours a day. People were scurrying around, rushing from one place to another, as if they were on some kind of mission from God. It was also a very private place. Even with all the people around, you were always alone. Anonymity was the order of the day; very few made eye contact or spoke. Sanger liked that; he would sit for hours and try to guess where this person or that one was traveling. Since he, himself, had never been further from home than the airport, he imagined that all destinations were full of intrigue and excitement. Yeah, he liked the

1

airport, but that wasn't the real reason he was here so early in the morning.

This occasion for his visit was hiding out. Not from the law or anything like that. He was, in fact, hiding from the rituals of graduation and the ridicule for not fitting in. In polite Southern society, high school graduation was quite an event. First there was the really exciting (translation: boring) ceremony involving 135 graduates dressing in their gowns, listening to speeches, being bored silly and finally walking across the stage to get their diplomas. Sanger didn't mind that part; it was the rest of it that bothered him.

Next came the prom and all-night partying. Required dress: tux; required companion: a female in formal evening gown; required activities: drinking, dancing, drinking, drinking, and staying out all night. Several of these things were not on Sanger's reality checklist. First, he could not afford a tux; second, he couldn't get a date that would want to go to the prom in his old beat up Ford; third, even if he could sweet talk some innocent young thing into going with him, he could not afford the cost of the date. The corsage alone would cost more than he had, not to mention feeding her. Drinking was not an activity in which he engaged. Of course, he could stay out all night!

To avoid the embarrassment of not having a date, etc., Sanger made up a story about partying with some friends in Memphis. Since that was obviously a lie, he had to hang out somewhere. The airport was perfect; nobody asked questions about a teenager in the airport all night. If people noticed, they would assume he missed his flight and was waiting for another.

Sanger looked up at the WELCOME TO THE MEMPHIS INTERNATIONAL AIRPORT sign. "I've about worn out my welcome," he thought. "Time to head home."

About the time he looked down from the sign, three small black children ran by. Their mother hurried in her pursuit of the excited kids. The mother had obviously spent considerable time dressing them. The little boy had on dress pants, white shirt, and a tie. No doubt unused to the tie, he continuously tugged at it as he ran. The two little girls looked like

2

princesses. Close in age, each was dressed like the other in a pink dress with frilly white lace around the collar, sleeves, and bottom. Their smiles were so big, you would think it was Christmas morning. In their excitement, the children accidentally collided with a white couple just to Sanger's left.

"Please excuse them." The mother smiled at the couple. "They see their grandmother up ahead and weren't watching where they were going."

The couple did not respond to the mother; they merely gave her an angry look as she quickly followed the path of the kids.

"Stupid niggers!" The man spit the words at his companion as their eyes continued to send hard stares after the rapidly moving children. "They're takin' over this whole end of town."

The woman was very angry. "They ought to change the name of this part of town from *Whitehaven* to *Blackhaven*. Nothin' but niggers everywhere you look."

Even though he had spent his whole life in Mississippi, Sanger never shared the couple's attitude. Every time he heard the word nigger used, it reminded him of the hatred it represented. He realized, however, that blacks were not the only target of hatred. If you were poor and lived in the South, oftentimes you were the target also, regardless of race. Sanger had been on the receiving end of it countless times himself.

Thirty minutes later, Sanger was driving his old Ford south on Elvis Presley Blvd. The engine sputtered a bit as it warmed up after sitting idle all night. The old car had been like a faithful companion for several years. The blue paint was terribly faded by the Mississippi sun. The interior had more duct tape showing than upholstery. If you drove too fast, the front wheels wobbled. Not exactly a babe magnet, but it kept going day after day. It had never left him stranded. A fancy Ford Mustang it wasn't; but then again, who in his neighborhood could afford a new sports car?

Coming up on the left was Graceland Mansion, home of the street's namesake. He continued past the King's place and on down the street.

3

As he drove south, Sanger kept an eye open for a green building on the right with a large bullfrog painted on its side. That would be Bullfrog Corner. Once there, he would have to turn right and cut over to State Highway 61. Highway 61 would take him home. Home, by the way, was Princeville, Mississippi.

About then, the frog's image came into his peripheral vision. The building was coming up on the right. Sanger figured it must have been dreamed up by some crazy hippie on LSD. What other explanation could there be for such a visual atrocity? I mean get real, a giant frog?

After turning at the corner and spending another fifteen minutes driving across rolling hill country that was rapidly becoming residentialized, Sanger could see the stop sign up ahead. As he applied the brakes, he could hear their usual squeaky protest. Someone had shot several holes in the sign that allowed the sun to shine through. Welcome to Highway 61, the start of the journey to the Kingdom of Rednecks.

A hard left turn at the sign and an hour or so of driving would put him right smack in the middle of his hometown. Hopefully, they hadn't moved it during the night!

He traveled south on the highway out of Tennessee and across the state line into Mississippi. His destination of Princeville lay due south. It was situated in the Northwestern part of the state 15 miles east of the Mississippi River in the heart of the Delta. Prime cotton country sat as its neighbors on all sides.

Princeville was pretty much your typical Mississippi Delta town. As a town it hadn't changed in the past twenty years.

If you ask the local Chamber of Commerce to describe the town, you would get the following propaganda:

> The City, founded by John Prince in 1848 and presently encompassing approximately 14.18 square miles, is located in Northwest Mississippi, approximately 75 miles south of Memphis, Tennessee, and 150 miles northwest of Jackson, Mississippi. It is

one of two major trade centers in the State's Northern Delta and the major city and county seat of Coahoma County, whose Western boundary is the Mississippi River. Located at the head of the Sunflower River's navigable waters, it is one of the largest cities in the Yazoo-Mississippi Delta and serves as the area's commercial and industrial center.

For years the population has remained about 20,000 with very little, if any, growth. The people are a mixed lot. The majority race is black with a healthy dose of Italians, Lebanese, Chinese, and of course, plain ole redneck WASPS.

Unlike most democracies, however, the majority doesn't rule in Princeville; the minority does. As with most small Southern towns, a select few rule and control the many.

Because of the rigid social structure, Sanger didn't much like his hometown. He never had. Only the accident of birth had put him within its boundaries. He knew that if you were numbered within that select few that controlled the town or found favor within their ranks, Princeville could be a good place. If you didn't, then Princeville became a place that had to be survived until you could find a way out.

As he drove toward home, Sanger thought about his hometown and the South in general. The South is not really understood by many. To really know it, you have to live it. Sanger lived it every day of his existence. He understood the South and its many personalities. When he thought South, he meant the real South: the South where it was hotter than Hell in the summer and colder than a well digger's ass in winter; the South where if you were white, you were in the minority and if you were black, you were treated like something to be scraped off the bottom of your shoe; the South that lies east of the Mississippi River and south of the Tennessee line; the South that is populated with people living in three-room "shotgun" houses with no indoor plumbing.

That was the South that Sanger knew, and that was the South in which fate had placed him. Even though he had spent all 18 of his years there, he never felt at home. Someday, he knew fate would send him in another direction to another place. He just hoped he wouldn't have to wait forever. Little did he know that fate was just around the corner.

The old Ford continued its path down an almost empty Highway 61. Probably too early for most folks. As state highways go, 61 is terrible. It is merely a two-lane wide strip of bad asphalt running straight south through the middle of some of the flattest land you ever saw.

Sanger could see swampy land on his left and some kind of cotton or soybean field on the right. A plant expert he wasn't. Every once and a while there was a service station and a few assorted buildings bunched together on the side of the road. Each was usually defined by city limit signs on each end and a speed trap in between. A person with good eyesight could see from one end to the other.

About 40 miles south of Memphis, Sanger passed through the first real town. Named Tunica after the county in which it is located, the place is a typical example of a small farming community. There are hundreds of others like it scattered throughout the state of Mississippi. As he looked at the awakening town, he passed the Blue and White Cafe/Service Station on his right and a small ice-cream drive-in stand on the left. He had to hit his brakes as an old black man (probably heading to the fields for a day's work) eased his dilapidated truck onto the highway.

With a black population of almost 70%, Tunica is in one of the poorest counties in the state. When you're one of the poorest counties in the poorest state, that's really poor. Another of Tunica's distinctions is its number of millionaires. Even given its poverty ranking among other counties, Tunica still has the highest per capita number of millionaires in the state. Go figure!

What a town Tunica was! If you wanted your head busted or your rear end kicked, come to Tunica on Saturday night. Yeah, Sanger knew all about the place.

Several years ago, as a young teenager, his father had sent his brother and him there every weekend to stay with their grandparents. His father thought it would keep them off the streets and out of jail. Little did he know that he was throwing the rabbits into the briar patch.

6

Passing the southern city limits sign, Sanger saw a mileage sign up ahead. Even before he got close enough to read it, he knew what it said: *Princeville 35 miles*. A couple of speed traps and about 45 minutes later, the outskirts of Princeville raised its ugly head.

After fighting the old Ford down some of the straightest road in the world, Highway 61 began a sweeping turn just as it entered Princeville. After traveling 75 miles from Memphis due south, 61 was now headed directly west. Coming up on the south side of the highway was the local Holiday Inn. It was the first franchised motel and had helped start the national chain.

Immediately on the right almost directly across the highway from the Holiday Inn was a drive-in type hangout called the Ranch. The in-crowd of local teenagers (kids with money) goes there every night to meet and discuss the latest happenings in town. The Ranch is quite a study in Southern entrepreneurship. Once you pull in and park your car (all the rich kids have new cars), you simply honk your horn. With that signal, a young black boy comes running up to take your order. Never a young white boy; always a young black boy. His job is to take your order plus a healthy dose of whatever kind of humiliation you want to lay on him. Apparently the system works; everyone (except the black boys, of course) seems very happy and content with the arrangement. Even though it was still early morning, Sanger kept an eye out for young black boys running across the road.

Continuing west on 61 (called *State Street* in town), he passed the old Chinese grocery on the left and the string of black honky-tonks on the right. Most of it looked pretty much the same as it had probably looked for the past 20 years.

A little further along, Highway 61 is intersected by Highway 49. As 49 ventures north through town, it becomes Desoto Street. Sanger turned right on Desoto and headed for his neighborhood, Coahoma Street. When the car reached the Fourth Street intersection, Sanger turned right. He was now headed into the heart of the black section of town. Coahoma Street was only a few short blocks of dilapidated housing away.

Coming up was the Coahoma Street intersection! Before he went home, though, he decided to cruise by his place of employment for the summer. Starting bright and early Monday morning he would be a proud employee of the COCA-COLA BOTTLING COMPANY. Sanger figured he would probably hate the job, but in reality he had little choice. Because he needed money, he needed a job. He figured he would hang around with the Coahoma Street Gang until the end of summer, then take whatever he had saved and maybe head out West. He had heard that Colorado was a nice place.

# 2

If you don't want the money for the bottles, shove off and quit wasting my time. Just take your business down the street." As Sanger talked, sweat ran down his face and under his collar. "It must be in the 90's already," he thought.

"You tryin' to screw me, man." The black teenager stared at his feet while he talked trying to avoid eye contact with Sanger who was looking down at him from the loading dock.

"You know I can't buy bottles with chips busted out." Sanger sorted bottles as he talked. "The boss'll have my skin."

"O.K., O.K. Gimme the money." The young black boy wasn't really mad at Sanger; he was just trying to get all the cash he could.

"Another afternoon in paradise," thought Sanger as he tossed a chipped bottle that had avoided detection into the trash dumpster. For the past month he had been working on the loading dock at the Coca-Cola Bottling Company on Fourth Street. In addition to loading trucks, he also bought bottles. That was his responsibility because he was in charge. Only the guy in charge could handle money. It didn't matter that he was only eighteen; the only thing that mattered was that he was white. You had to be white to be in charge. Since he was the only "white" working on the dock, he was automatically in charge. What a deal!

While bent over examining bottles and contemplating the quality of his employment, Sanger looked up just in time to see an old green Chevy pick-up truck turn off Fourth Street and slowly roll across the gravel drive toward the loading dock. To say the truck looked like someone had whipped it with an ugly stick was the understatement of the day. It looked even worse; his mind just couldn't come up with an appropriate analogy at the moment.

The truck didn't warrant any special attention, though; he probably saw a dozen every day just like it. They always belonged to a black honky-tonk or grocery store owner. The driver came to the Plant to buy "pop." Pop was what the black folks and Yankees called all soft drinks.

As the truck pulled alongside the dock, Sanger looked up from the bottles he was busy sorting. "More work," he thought. Buy bottles, sell Cokes, load trucks all day long—10, 12, sometimes 14 hours. Boy, graduating from high school had really launched him into a great job.

Trying to focus his mind on the job at hand, he looked at the truck. The door was being forced open with a protesting squeak. The driver finally won the battle with the door swinging completely open. As the driver climbed out, Sanger saw that it was a well-dressed, light-skinned black girl. Some of his less sophisticated friends would have referred to her as a high yellow nigger.

He couldn't help but take a second look. She was probably the prettiest girl he had ever seen. It wasn't exactly her body or her face or the color of her skin; it was something else, something about the way she looked. Whatever it was, he couldn't take his eyes off her as she walked over to where he was working.

"Hi." The girl made eye contact with Sanger as she approached the dock. "Can you help me?"

Sanger hardly heard what she had said. He was too entranced by her face. Really, it was her eyes. They were either green or grey; he couldn't tell which.

"Uh . . . sure." Sanger was almost embarrassed by his reaction. If his dark brown complexion could have turned red, it would have. He was thankful for small favors!

10

"What can I do for you?"

"I need ten cases of Cokes for our store." She unfolded a list and handed it to him.

He was surprised she hadn't asked for "pop."

Sanger's mind went into overtime as he hurried into the Plant to get the Cokes; he couldn't help but think about her. No girl had ever had that effect on him before, especially a black girl. If she were white, he'd have been trying to find out where she lived. Since she wasn't, he knew the best thing to do would be to concentrate on work and forget anything else.

Much to his pleasure, she was smiling at him as he came rolling the Cokes back out on the dock.

"Thank you very much."

"Damn, she was pretty," he thought as she stood there in the sunlight talking to him. He tried to slow down his movements as he finished loading the cases into her truck.

"Where's the man I pay?" She was still smiling.

"You can pay me." Sanger talked, but his thoughts extended beyond the words coming out; he could have looked at her all day. Her face seemed to be framed by the sun at her back.

"But." Her voice quivered a bit in hesitation as she began to protest. "They don't usually trust cash to a bl . . . ." She stopped speaking right in the middle of the word. Surprise was etched across her pretty face.

Sanger thought he detected a blush. He knew now that she had thought he himself was a light-skinned black. It wasn't a difficult mistake to make. First of all, no whites ever worked on the loading docks. With summertime temperatures running over 100 degrees, most couldn't handle the intense heat. Secondly, his skin was very dark, considerably darker than hers. Since very early in life, people had made fun of him for

11

"looking like a nigger." The hot Mississippi Delta sun sure hadn't lightened him up any; it just added to the problem.

She realized her mistake when he said he could take the money. Blacks weren't allowed to handle cash. Only white folks could do that. A shy smile began to tug at the corners of her mouth.

"That's O.K." Sanger's face lit up with a big grin exposing a set of very straight and very white teeth set in the midst of a chestnut-colored brown face. "I thought you were white at first."

They both looked at each other and laughed. About that time she remembered she was talking to a "white" man. Making jokes with a white person was not usually a good idea for Southern blacks. She quickly busied herself fumbling for the money in her purse, purposefully avoiding eye contact with Sanger. Instead, her eyes were directed at the ground. She was so nervous that she dropped everything. Coins hit the edge of the loading dock and bounced erratically onto the gravel lot. Her wallet went in another direction with all the usual girl stuff spilling and bouncing about.

As he stooped to help her recover the contents of her purse, she hurriedly handed him the money. "Thank you." He could barely make out what she said.

As he turned to take the money to the office, he could hear the old truck fire off. Before he was in the Plant, she was pulling out onto Fourth, obviously heading for home.

"Yeah, just another day in paradise." Sanger glanced up at the metal overhang above his head. He thought he could actually see the heat waves on their way down to engulf him.

Later that morning as he was sorting bottles—Tab in one case, Sunrise in another, the three Coca-Cola sizes in others—a bottle rolled off the dock onto the gravel drive. As he stepped down to get it, Sanger's eyes passed over something on the ground. It was hard to see as it balanced against the concrete base of the loading dock. Bending down to pick it up, he could see that it was a driver's license.

12

As his eyes adjusted from the sun's glare, the name on the front of the license came into focus: Eloisa Jones. The address was only a few blocks from the Coke Plant. Since there was not a photo on the Mississippi driver's license, Sanger could not determine for sure who the girl was. He had a good idea, though. There was only one person he could remember today who had dropped everything out of her purse onto the parking lot.

The best thing to do would be to turn the lost license into the office and have them give her a call. That would be the best thing to do. If he did that, though, he probably wouldn't see her when she came back to pick it up.

"So what," he thought. "Why should he want to see her? She was just another black face in the crowd." That face, though, kept edging its way into his mind.

After a little more thought, Sanger decided to drop the license by after work. It was kinda on his way home—just in the opposite direction. He'd simply run it in and leave. No big deal! What harm could it do? He would do the same thing for anybody. Sure he would!

The day seemed to drag from that point on. It appeared that the stream of bottles to buy and of trucks to load was endless. One after another, they just kept coming. Finally, about 6:00 that evening, the tenth and final truck was loaded for the next day's routes. At last it was time to punch out and go home. Just one short stop to make first.

———————————————————————————————

The address on the driver's license indicated that Eloisa lived at 512 Choctaw Street. Sanger knew about where that was. He thought Choctaw intersected Coahoma Street somewhere around Eliza Prince Elementary School. If he could get on Choctaw, he figured he wouldn't have much trouble finding the address.

Usually after work, Sanger crawled into his old '56 Ford and headed home. After a quick shower and supper, he would wander over to Coahoma Street and hang out with the gang. Not tonight, though; tonight he was out to do a good deed. What a nice guy he was!

13

To get to Coahoma Street, he turned his old Ford into the alley that run south away from the Plant. It meandered past a few old broken down houses and emerged on Coahoma. This part of Coahoma Street was five or six blocks south of the block where Sanger's gang hung out. With the exception of a couple of blocks around where the gang congregated, the entire area was populated by black families. As a matter of fact, this whole section of town was pretty much black. Sanger lived in part of a two-block island of white people in this section of town. His family had lived here for several years now.

As he eased the old car out onto Coahoma, he looked directly across the street at the playground around Eliza Prince School. Like so many other things in Princeville, the school had been named after the Prince family who had originally settled the town. Many years earlier it had been his school in the second grade. Somehow, that didn't really seem such a long time ago.

Off to his left he could see an old grocery store. It had a weathered white frame exterior that extended upward for two stories. The owners probably lived upstairs. That was usually the case, with the people barely scraping a living out of the business.

As he got closer, he could see that the store was on Choctaw. An old sign over the front door identified it as JONES GROCERY. Upon closer inspection, Sanger made the address as 512 Choctaw. Bingo!

Pulling up front, he looked through the old Ford's pitted windshield at a trio of white teenage boys about his age. They kind of swaggered into the old store. It wasn't hard to figure what three white teenagers were doing in a black grocery store. They were underage and wanted beer. Sometimes they would luck out in a black or Chinese grocery and not get carded. It wasn't because the proprietor didn't know they were under age; it was because the owner was intimidated.

By the looks of them, they wouldn't have any trouble paying for the beer. They had arrived in and exited a new Pontiac GTO with mag wheels. Definitely a trio of County Club boys.

Sanger sat in the car for a few minutes. He didn't want the trio to know what he was doing. When he figured they should be about ready to pay for their beer, he got out of the car and headed inside.

As soon as he let the screen door close behind him, he could feel the tension in the old store. Eloisa was standing behind a very worn wooden counter in a defensive posture. One of the County Club heroes was standing in front. Two six packs of beer sat by the old cash register. The other two boys were standing to one side with smirks on their faces. They all looked at Sanger as he walked in. It was obvious that the boy at the counter was annoyed.

"I told you I'm 18." He winked at his friends as he spoke. "I don't have to prove it to your kind."

"I'm sorry." Eloisa was obviously intimidated and angry at the same time. She glanced at Sanger out of the corner of her eye as she spoke. "You know the law in Mississippi says you have to be 18 to buy beer. If you won't show me some identification with your age on it, I can't let you have the beer."

"Hey! Look here." The boy at the counter directed the comment to his two friends. "We got a nigger quotin' the law. Next thing you know she'll be claiming to know how to read." The boy smirked as his two friends roared with laughter!

"Look you high yellow bitch. Sell us the beer or we'll just take it." With that statement, he threw some money at Eloisa and picked up the beer. Turning to leave, he found himself looking squarely into Sanger's dark and by now angry face.

Sanger knew all three of them by name. They were part of the "in group" a year behind him in school. This was the bunch with the big houses, rich daddies, and in general silver spoon attitudes. They were the offspring of Princeville's elite.

The one with all the mouth was Jim Prince, *Prince* as in Princeville. His ancestors, along with the Clark family, had been the original settlers in what was then known as the "Bottoms." The Bottoms name was later dropped in favor of the more proper Delta. Unofficial history had the Princes cheating the Clarks out of the land. Too bad; unofficial history also portrayed the Clarks as hard-working, honest people. If the Clarks had prevailed, perhaps the town would have been a better place.

Prince's two buddies were Billy Sands and Charlie Merk. Unlike Prince, their surnames could not be found on the list of early county settlers. They could, however, be found on the current membership list of the Princeville Country Club.

"Well, what do we have here?" Prince looked at Sanger with an expression similar to that used upon discovering dog dung on his shoe. "It's one of our recent high-school graduates. Looks like he's already making a career move. I mean with the fancy Coca-Cola Bottling Company uniform and all. What are you doing here, Sanger; come to get yourself a good ole sliced bologna sandwich for supper?"

His buddies roared with laughter again as if on cue!

"Give him a break." Sands's voice was consumed with sarcasm. "You know some of these poor white boys live over here in nigger-town."

"Yeah." Merk stepped a little closer. "This is probably where he does his grocery shopping."

With another big laugh, all three of the boys headed for the door. There was just one problem; Sanger was still standing in front of it.

"You boys forgot a couple of things." Sanger's voice had lowered and taken on an intense quality.

"Oh, yeah?" said Prince. "Like what?"

"First, you forgot to leave the beer; and secondly, you forgot to tell this young lady you're sorry for what you said."

"And what if we didn't forget?" Merk's lip seemed to snarl as he spoke.

16

Sanger reached behind his back to the screen door. He needed to even the odds a tiny bit. Since screen doors are designed to keep the bugs out but let the air in, they have to have an automatic closing mechanism. Someone had figured out a long time ago that a fairly stiff coiled spring with one end hooked to the door facing and the other to the door would automatically pull the door closed each time that it was opened. To make it easy to remove the spring and prop the door open for deliveries and such, the spring was attached to cup hooks on each end. Sanger unhooked the door spring and bent it double with both ends held in his right hand.

"I sure hope that's not the case." Sanger watched the three boys; he could tell they were weighing the odds.

"Hey, Sanger. We were just kidding around." Prince put the beer back on the counter.

As Eloisa handed him back his money, he halfheartedly said, "sorry."

When the three of them were through the door and outside, Prince yelled back, "Sanger, we'll see you again real soon; count on it."

Sanger, didn't respond; he just sent a cold hard stare their way. "You're right," he thought. "Anytime I see you jerks will be too soon."

Eloisa was looking at him as he turned around.

"Regular customers of yours?" His face lit up with a face-splitting grin as he looked at her pretty face.

"No, and I hope they never get to be. Are they friends of yours?" As she asked the question, Sanger noticed that she would never look him in the eye.

# 3

H ey, Sanger! Where you been, pulling your pud?" Steed spoke as he tried to find a song on his ever present radio. "You're usually here a helluva lot earlier than this!"

Steed was one of the unofficial leaders of the Coahoma Street Gang; unofficial being the operative word. Actually, everything was unofficial about the Coahoma Street Gang, even the way it got its name. One day Travis, another gang member, had called in a request for a song to the local radio station. When they asked him who it was for, he said, "The Coahoma Street Gang." It stuck from that day forward.

In reality, Coahoma Street just happened to be the name of the street where Sanger and his friends had always hung out. By virtue of their numbers, the group was referred to as a gang. Steed was an enigma in the gang. He was the only one who wasn't dirt poor. It wasn't that he was really rich; he wasn't. It was just that both his parents had pretty good jobs and didn't mind sharing the proceeds with him and his two brothers. Consequently, he always had cash in his pocket.

Steed had also been the one to come up with the official mark of the gang. Since every gang usually had a tattoo or colors or something to identify members, he figured the Coahoma Street Gang needed something. Deducing that his parents wouldn't be real high on a homemade tattoo, another idea hatched in his mind. He decided a burn scar would be pretty cool and at the same time impress the ladies. After much discussion, a more or less consensus was reached. Each gang member would be burned on the top of the left arm with the heated cap of a Zippo® cigarette lighter. If a Zippo® lighter was used each time, then every member would have an identical rectangular burn scar on his left arm.

Every gang member went through the burn rite except Sanger. When it came his turn, he told them that they were "friggin' crazy." Since it was generally acknowledged in the gang that he was the "egghead" or smart one, his individualistic behavior was nothing new. After all, he was the only gang member who didn't smoke or drink.

It was decided that Sanger could still be in the gang regardless. With his individualistic attitude, they figured he didn't really care very much. As Culligan had phrased it, "Sanger probably doesn't give a rat's ass one way or another." Since it wasn't really a gang anyway, everybody said it would be O.K. Sanger didn't have to be burned.

The Coahoma Street Gang really wasn't a gang, not in the traditional sense of the word. It didn't stake out its turf to justify assaulting people who mistakenly ventured into its part of town. It was simply nine guys who, for lack of something better to do, hung out under a streetlight on Coahoma Street. All their spare time was spent there "hanging out." "Hanging out" meant that they sat around on the curb and talked, seeing who could fabricate the biggest lie.

Princeville was an interesting town. Like most small Southern towns or large Southern towns or any Southern town, the town was basically divided into two zones: the white zone and the black zone. As with all such divisions, however, there was also a DMZ or neutral zone. This was the area where less affluent white folks lived in the same neighborhood as more affluent black folks. Don't get confused, though; even these white people were still higher on the social pecking order than their black neighbors, just not very much higher. It was in Princeville's DMZ that Coahoma Street was located.

The turf of the gang was a two-block section of Coahoma Street. It lay north of Fourth Street and south of the railroad tracks. If you put it in a category, you'd probably describe it as better than a slum but still a bad neighborhood. It wasn't exactly the kind of place you'd choose to raise your family; not if you had a choice, that is.

Unfortunately, the Coahoma Street Gang didn't have a choice. This was their home, like it or not. And like it or not, these were the surroundings that molded their attitudes and feelings.

The gang always gathered under the streetlight in the center of their two-block area. To show that it was their place, each gang member chopped his initials into the asphalt street with a hatchet. As grafitti goes, it was very difficult to paint over and impossible to wash off. It made them proud; it announced to the public who they were.

If you looked directly across the street from the gang's gathering place, you would see a dingy alley walled by overgrown, unkempt bushes. Directly behind the streetlight was another alley that ran east about one hundred yards then intersected yet another alley. These alleys always provided ready avenues of escape.

South of the streetlight was a row of shotgun duplexes. Each duplex had three rooms, with all the rooms lined up one behind the other. Poor, white trash families occupied these. And finally, to the right (north) of the streetlight about 50 yards away ran the railroad tracks. The tracks were on an elevated section of ground and shielded from view anything beyond.

The Coahoma Street neighborhood was merely a small island of poor, white trash surrounded by a sea of blacks. If you ventured more than 500 yards in any of three directions, you could find yourself in serious trouble. The fourth and only really safe direction to go carried you in the direction of downtown.

In addition to Steed, Sanger, and Travis; the Coahoma Street Gang included Wilkerson, Culligan, Sampson, Parker, Jake, and Sanger's older brother, Jay. Sampson at 20 was the oldest gang member, and Travis at 16 was the youngest. Sanger at 18 was in the middle.

Sanger had been born 35 miles north of Princeville close to the town of Tunica. His parents had been sharecroppers at the time of his birth and lived in a tenement shack out in the country. Because he had been born in the dead of winter, during a time of high water, his mother could not be taken to a hospital. Like his brother, Jay, he had been born at home.

21

The Sangers were a poor family but a proud one. His father took great pride in the family's good name and reputation for honesty. When Sanger was about five years old, his father left the farm and moved the family to town. They had been in Princeville ever since.

Sanger knew that his family was poor, but that never bothered him. He had a good clean place to sleep, plenty of food to eat, and a car of sorts to get him around. He also had the Coahoma Street Gang to hang out with. Sure, he could use a newer car, a fancier house, and richer food to eat; but he figured he didn't really need those things right now. They would come later in his life; he really believed that.

Right now, all he needed was Coahoma Street and his gang. He knew it wouldn't last forever like it was. Before too much longer, the Coahoma Street Gang would just be a memory. Sanger wanted to enjoy it while he could. Everybody knew that this would probably be the last summer for the Coahoma Street Gang. It was June, 1967.

Sanger, his brother, and Sampson had just graduated from Princeville High School. Parker, Jake, Wilkerson, and Steed should also have graduated but didn't quite make the grade. They would graduate next May in Culligan's class, if they were lucky. For all practical purposes, Travis would be the only one with any length of time left on Coahoma Street.

It was a given that each would leave at the first opportunity. For most of them, that opportunity was just around the corner. After all, Princeville wasn't really a very good place to live. It was merely a place to be tolerated until such time as you could get the hell out. Toleration for most of the Coahoma Street Gang was wearing very thin. Bailout time was drawing very near.

# 4

Jim Prince and his buddies had left Jones Grocery and headed to another one over in the Upper Brickyard. The Upper Brickyard was another poor black neighborhood in a different part of town. They had gotten lucky there; the old Chinese grocer didn't have the courage to ask for identification.

"Here, here! Have a beer!" Prince was in a good mood as he crawled back into the driver's seat of his new GTO. "Since we got Bud and it's the one; let's go have some fun." Prince keyed life into the GTO and floored the accelerator as he left the grocery parking lot. The rear end of the car fishtailed from side to side on the loose gravel surface. With a loud squeal, the tires connected with the hard asphalt surface of the street.

Since the beer was in Sands' lap, he ripped one out of the six pack and handed it to Prince. "Hey, Charlie, you want a beer?"

"Do niggers like watermelon?" They all laughed as Sands passed a beer back to Merk.

"Boy, that Sanger is a real dickhead, ain't he?" Sands muttered between swallows of beer.

"Yeah," Prince snarled as he spoke. "But he's gonna get his ass kicked one of these days, and I'm gonna be the one doin' the kickin'."

"Y'all better be careful when you start tryin' to kick Sanger's ass." Merk had leaned up from the back seat as he spoke.

"What's to be careful about?" Prince was looking at Merk in the rearview mirror as he responded. "We'll just catch him alone in our part of town some night, and then the three of us will kick the crap out of him. Without something in his hand, he won't be so bad."

"You do it like that and you'll have that whole Coahoma Street Gang on our case." Merk seemed to have a tinge of fear in his voice as he talked. "You'd better figure out another way."

"Oh, I really give a flyin' crap about the big, bad Coahoma Street Gang!" Prince laughed as he spoke. "Most of 'em can't make a fist without written instructions."

"Most of 'em ain't all of 'em." Merk would not yield his point. "There are three or four of 'em that can eat our lunch without breakin' a sweat."

"Charlie's right," interrupted Sands. "Remember last summer, when we all had to go to County High for summer school?"

"I remember. What about it?" Prince glanced out his side window at the shabby houses passing by as he responded.

"Well, Sanger's brother, Jay, was there too." Sands' voice took on a sound of awe. "One day outside, Mark Gibson was shoving some kid around. You know how Gibson is, always usin' those big muscles of his to scare some slob shitless. Well, as usual, he also had diarrhea of the mouth. He was telling everybody what he was goin' to do to the kid and askin' if anybody there thought they could stop him. Me and the other guys were having a good laugh about it, when all of a sudden Sanger's brother stepped out of the crowd. He just kinda grinned and said yeah, he could."

"As Gibson walked up to Jay, without another thing being said, Jay hit him. Damn, man, I don't think I've ever seen anybody hit like that. Gibson went down hard with just that one punch. To top it off, Jay had used his left hand—and he ain't even left-handed!

"And you know what's worse? Jay kept messin' with Gibson for the rest of the day. Everytime he'd see him, he'd push him or slap him or something. By the end of the day, Gibson was just a big musclebound crybaby. Yeah, I'd be real careful about screwin' around with Sanger because when you do, his brother Jay ain't gonna be far away."

"Well, I don't care how bad the Sanger boys are." A false sense of confidence had crept into Prince's tone. "I'm gonna find a way to take care of that prick Sanger. Nobody does what he did to me and gets away with it! Maybe I'll get my old man to have their old man fired. Wouldn't that be a kick in the pants?"

"Yeah." Merk and Sands joined in like back-up singers. "That would be a real kick in the pants!"

Prince took a swig of beer and then laughed. "Hey, that's enough about the Sanger assholes. Let's cruise out to the Ranch and see what's goin' on. Maybe we'll get lucky!"

# 5

Jim Prince turned his car into the small street that would take him up the incline that most referred to as Nob Hill. The neighborhood was just ouside the city limits on the way to the Country Club. His family had lived there all of his life. As he topped the hill, he could see his house coming up on the left. Like all the rest in the neighborhood, it was huge. Turning into the circular drive he looked at the house's facade. There were six two-story columns across the front with large double doors in the middle. To the right of the front doors, he saw that the light was on in the living room. As he glanced at the dash clock, he noted that it was almost 9:00 pm.

There hadn't been much goin' on out at the Ranch so he and his friends had polished off the beer and then decided to call it a night. That was pretty typical of a weeknight, though; there rarely was anything goin' on in Princeville until Friday or Saturday night. Hopefully, he had stayed out long enough. He didn't want to get home too early.

If he did, then he'd have to listen to his mother and father shouting insults at each other. That was the nightly ritual around his house. It always started about 5:30 every evening. By then his mother would be on her third drink before supper. His father would have made his first wisecrack about her drinking, and then the fight would be off and running. By 11:00, his mother would usually be in bed passed out and his father out of the house somewhere.

Prince sat in the car for a minute eating a breath mint. Even though his father knew that he drank beer, he didn't want to push the point. With his mother being an alcoholic, he knew that drinking could be a very touchy

27

subject with the old man. As Prince walked in the front door, he could hear that he was early. His mother had just finished yelling some obscenity at his father, only the last part of which he had heard. It had something to do with his father's sexual use of Grandma Prince. His father had responded by calling her a drunken slut.

He knew he should be used to it by now, but he wasn't; how could you ever get used to your parents talking to each other like that? If it weren't for the new car and the money his father kept giving him, he would have been long gone. Besides, there were some good points to all the fighting.

Because of it, his parents didn't pay much attention to what he did or where he went. As long as he was home before they got up in the morning, it seemed to be O.K. Plus he knew that his father thought that if he gave him enough money, it would make up for the crappy home life.

Prince could handle it, for another year anyway. After that, he'd be over at Ole Miss going to college. Once he got there, he'd never have to come home. They could kill each other for all he cared.

Well, he did care a little bit. If his father were killed, where would the money come from? If one of them ever did get around to killing the other, he sure hoped his old man didn't get the short end of the stick. He could live without his mother; it was his father that he had to have, at least for the time being.

Prince quietly eased the front door closed and headed up the stairs toward his bedroom. At times like this he sometimes wished he had a brother or sister to bitch to about the old man and old lady.

Naw! Then they'd get a cut of the money. As long as he had money, he could live with anything else.

---

"I've had about all of your drinking and carrying on, Beth, that I'm goin' to put up with." Prince's father, Jackson, had raised his voice and was sending out angry barbs with his eyes.

"Whatta you mean, carrying on?" Mrs. Prince's voice had the raspy sound of one abused by too much alcohol over many years. "Carrying on is what you do with your whores up in Memphis. You think I don't know what's happenin' when you go off to Memphis? You're up there sniffin' around every little bitch that shakes her ass for you. At least I'm a little selective in who I let into my bed."

"Will you watch your dirty mouth; you know Jim could be home anytime." Jackson involuntarily glanced at the door to the room.

"Do you think he doesn't know about you and me?" Beth's laugh had a very artificial sound to it. Obviously, there was no real humor in her speech. "He's known as long as he's been old enough to listen. Lord knows how he'll turn out coming from a bastard father like you and listening to this crap every night."

"Well, he wouldn't be listening to this crap if you'd keep your voice down." Jackson lowered his voice almost as if he wanted to set the example for his wife.

"To hell with you and your holier than thou attitude, Jackson. I'll say what I want to say, as loudly as I want to say it, and when I want to say it—and there's not a damn thing you can do about it! So, why don't you just leave and let me be?"

"I'm about to leave." Jackson stepped very close to Beth. She could feel the warmth of his breath as he spoke. "But I'm sure as hell not goin' to let you be. Not until you quit acting like a slut around town for everybody to see. I've got to live in Princeville, and I don't want people talking about my wife behind my back. If you've got to act like a bitch in heat, the least you can do is be a little more discreet about it. If I have to tell you again, you'll be sorry!"

"Well, just what are you goin' to do, macho man; beat me up? Then what would your friends say?"

"Just keep on pushing and I might do a helluva lot more." Jackson's teeth made a grinding noise as he fought for composure. "I don't know why I ever married you in the first place; I sure as hell never loved you."

"You son-of-a-bitch; you married me because I was three months pregnant and because you saw an easy way to get into my father's bank. That's the only reason we got married and the only reason we stay married. If I could run that bank without you, you'd be old news." Beth threw back her head as she drained the last drop of liquor from the glass.

"Run the bank without me! That's a friggin' joke. You can't even balance your own checkbook. Your father raised his little cotillion queen to be looked at, not to be capable of a day's work. If it weren't for me, the bank wouldn't have lasted a year after the old fart died. But you're right about one thing. The only reason I keep you around is because of your interest in the bank.

"You're lucky your daddy's still looking after you. He knew I'd dump you as soon as he was dead, and he knew that you were too stupid to run the bank. So, to keep you married and to keep the bank goin', he left each of us 50% interest in the damn thing. Now we're stuck with each other until death do us part'."

"Jackson, you really are a bastard!" Beth sat down on the overstuffed sofa crying with her face in her hands. "Just leave and go drink with your buddies at the Club. With any luck, maybe you'll have a wreck on the way and kill your no-good self. I wish you were dead, you son-of-a-bitch."

Jackson Prince stormed out of the house muttering to himself, "Someday, bitch, someday I'm going to put you in the ground and solve all my problems." The house shook as he slammed the front door!

# 6

Jackson Prince went to the Princeville Country Club every night. It was there that he found refuge from the constant emotional barrage at home. He wished he could find an equitable way out of his domestic difficulties. He knew deep down inside, though, that only death would separate Beth and him. He had made this bed for himself a long time ago.

---

It had all started some seventeen years ago when he had been 23 years old. His family had a name that everybody looked up to. After all, his ancestors had been among the first to settle on the ground now known as Princeville. They originally laid out the town and named it after themselves. The problem was, however, that by the time Jackson came along, the only thing the Princes had left was their name.

He grew up in a facade of artificial wealth. Sure, the family went to the Club and mixed with Princeville's elite families. But the sad truth was that it had taken everything that Jackson's parents had to maintain the image. By the time he graduated from Ole Miss, there was nothing left.

He returned to Princeville and took a job in one of the local banks. By living with his parents, he was able to use his meager salary to keep the family home up and the facade going. After a year of being the poorest rich guy in town, he knew he had to do something. That's when he started to develop his plan.

It had become painfully obvious to him by now that he wasn't going to get rich working for a bank. If he were going to get rich, he needed

31

to own the bank, or at least be married to the daughter of someone who owned it. He knew just the daughter. Her name was Beth Cotton, and her father owned the biggest bank in town. They had all the money Jackson would ever need.

His plan was simple. They had something he needed, and he had something they needed. Everybody knew that old man Cotton had ridden a freight train into town 30 years earlier. Over the years he had managed to make a lot of money. What he had not been able to do, however, was shake the stigma of his humble beginnings. Even though he could buy and sell anybody in town, deep down inside he felt he wasn't really respected because he wasn't old money.

Jackson could change all that overnight. He had the name; the Cottons had the money. To him, it sounded like a marriage made in heaven. It just needed a little nudge. After a couple of well-placed hints, Jackson found himself the recipient of a Sunday invitation to lunch at the Cottons.

From the very beginning, he and Beth had not hit it off very well. But to please her father, she had started to date Jackson. It was a rocky romance, to say the least. After about three months, Jackson could see that his natural charms were not going to be enough to win Beth's hand. He needed to regroup and try a different approach. Since Beth always seemed to like to drink when they went out, Jackson figured it would be easy enough to get her drunk. If he could get her drunk the next time they went out, his new plan could be put into action.

About a week later, they were invited to a party out at Moon Lake. Moon Lake is about 20 miles northwest of town. A lot of people have weekend places there. As the evening wore on, Beth drank more and more. Usually, Jackson controlled her drinking. He didn't want to risk taking her home drunk and old man Cotton seeing them. But that night he made no attempt to slow her drinking; he actually encouraged it. By midnight, she was totally sloshed.

Jackson thanked the host and hostess and made an excuse for Beth's over indulgence. He told them that he had proposed on the way out to the lake and that Beth was celebrating.

After getting her into the car, he headed down toward Paradise Point. The Point was a place where you could swim during the day and party at night. As a teenager he had spent many pleasurable nights there. A friend of his had a trailer there that they occasionally used for "getting together." Since his friend was out of town, Jackson knew that he would have the place to himself.

Jackson's plan was simple. Once he got Beth drunk, they would have sex and he would try to get her pregnant. With any luck, he would succeed; and bingo, Beth would need to get married.

Well, three months later wedding bells were ringing in Princeville. Ms. Beth Cotton was now Mrs. Jackson Prince, and Mr. Jackson Prince was now the newest Vice President of the Princeville State Bank.

Mission Accomplished!

For the first year of the marriage, the two of them had tried to make a go of it. It was no use, though. Beth's drinking got worse and Jackson became very verbally abusive. On the outside, they kept up the charade. On the inside, they fought almost constantly.

When the marriage was on the verge of collapse, Mr. Cotton got extremely ill. For nearly a year, he hung on to life tenaciously. While her father was sick, Beth spent almost every waking moment at his side. Since her mother had been dead for several years, she was the only family he had.

The illness caused an unspoken truce to be declared between the warring couple. It lasted up until the day the old man died. Two days after burying her father, Beth and Jackson had an appointment with the family's attorney.

"After the reading of the will, I want you out of this house." Beth had spit the words at Jackson the day of the reading of the will. "You know the bank is mine now, and you won't be needed there any longer. I'll be rid of you for good. Your free ride is coming to a screeching halt!"

When the will was read, Beth almost went into shock; Jackson merely laughed. "Let's go home, Dear, and have a drink." His tone was haughty and mocking. They did. She hadn't stopped for 15 years.

---

Jackson turned off the road and headed up the drive to the Country Club. A couple of drinks and a little meaningless conversation would erase the evening's events from his mind. They always did. There was one thing, though. Part of the evening he didn't want to put out of his mind. Part of it he wanted to savor and fantasize about. If only he could figure a way to do it and not get caught. Yeah, if he could only put her in the ground; it would solve all his problems. If he could get away with it!

# 7

After the night of the run-in with the Country Club boys, Sanger found an excuse to drop by Jones Grocery almost every night after work. Eloisa told him that she worked alone in the store from 6:00 to 7:00 while her parents went upstairs for supper.

After a couple of weeks of nightly "shopping" at the store, Sanger and Eloisa had become friends. Each night he would linger a little longer and talk to her. At first, Eloisa was very shy and nervous. Sanger would do most of the talking and she most of the listening. He always spoke softly and smiled a lot.

After a few days, Eloisa began to talk back and smile a little nervous smile that, to Sanger, seemed to light up her face. Within a week, she was comfortable enough with Sanger to look at him when they were talking.

Sanger knew that coming to see a black girl every day was a crazy thing to do. He didn't really know why he kept on; he just did. It was almost as if there were some sort of special bond between them. He had felt it that first day in the parking lot of the Coke Plant. With each visit, it seemed to be getting stronger and stronger.

---

"Hi!" Sanger spoke as he walked into the store. "How are you doing today?"

"Hi!" Eloisa smiled at him. "I'm doing just fine. How are you?"

Sanger just smiled at her as he went to the back of the store and got a Coke from the cooler. Every night when he came in, he did the same thing. The routine seemed to make things easier. He'd go get the Coke, pay for it, and then stand around and visit for a few minutes. Each night the number of minutes got longer.

"Why do you come in here every night and buy a Coke?" Eloisa watched as Sanger put the soft drink down on the counter and started digging in his front pocket for some change. "Can't you get them free down at the Plant?"

"Yeah, I can get them free." Sanger handed Eloisa the money. There seemed to be a small electrical shock as his hand touched hers. It caused his stomach to react as he continued. "But they don't taste as good there as they do here."

"Now, just what makes them taste better in this old store than they do at your plant?"

"Oh, I don't know." A mischievous look crossed Sanger's face. "I think the company has something to do with it. Maybe looking at you while I'm drinking it makes a Coke taste better."

Eloisa looked around very quickly to see if anyone else had heard what Sanger had said. "Don't say crazy things like that." She was whispering in a quiet, nervous voice. "If my mama or daddy heard you say that, they'd ship me off to Chicago and make me live with my aunt. Besides, it's not nice to make fun like that."

"Who's making fun?" Sanger's voice took on a serious tone. "Why do you think I came in here that first night and brought you your driver's license? I could've just turned it into the office and been done with it. Why do you think I've been coming in here every night since and buying a Coke? It's because I wanted to see you again."

"But that's crazy!" Shock and fear had crept into Eloisa's voice. "You're white and I'm black. This is Mississippi, not Detroit; things like that aren't allowed around here. You know that."

36

"Things like what aren't allowed?" Sanger tried to keep the anger from becoming obvious. "I just want to be your friend. Is it a crime because I happen to like talking to you?"

"In this town it is," she said. "In Princeville, the only way we could ever be friends would be if nobody knew about it."

"Well then, let's be friends and not tell folks about it." The statement came out as a half-hearted joke. "I won't tell if you don't."

"Why do you want to be friends with me?" Eloisa's tone had taken on a hard edge. "Usually, white boys just want one thing from black girls and it isn't friendship."

"I really don't know." Sanger was genuinely confused. "It's just that ever since I first saw you in the lot at the Plant a couple of weeks ago, I haven't been able to get you out of my mind. It's kinda like you're stuck there. I don't know why. I've never had this problem before. It's just that I have this need to get to know you. Do you understand what I mean? I want us to be friends."

"I guess I do kinda understand." Eloisa had replaced the hard edge with a confused softness of her own. "I sorta feel like that myself. It's just that I've never had a white friend before. I wouldn't know where to start."

"You start," said Sanger, "by simply talking and visiting with each other. You might find out that not all white boys are alike. Some of us do want your friendship."

"But where do a black girl and a white boy go to talk in this town?" The question came out of Eloisa's mouth like an unsolvable riddle. Her tone took on a sarcastic edge. "It's not like we can go down to the Paramount Movie Theater. If my parents ever found out, I'd be in big trouble. They've already asked me what you bought every night when you came in."

"What did you tell them?" Sanger subconsciously looked at the rickety old stairs leading up to the store's living area.

"Well." A smile tugged at the corners of Eloisa's mouth. "I told them you bought a Coke then tried to talk me into ordering more Cokes from you at the Coke Plant so you'd get a bigger commission."

"Wow." Sanger was visibly impressed. "You're a pretty quick thinker. What did your parents have to say about that?"

"They told me to tell you to come see my daddy if you wanted to talk business. If you keep coming in here every night, they're going to get suspicious and come downstairs to see what's really going on."

"I don't want to get you in trouble with your folks; after tonight, I won't come in here anymore." Sorrow had engulfed Sanger's demeanor. "I didn't mean to bother you."

"You're not bothering me." Eloisa's response almost jumped from her mouth. "I've enjoyed talking to you. You're the first white person to talk to me like I'm a person too. I think I'd like to be your friend if there were any way."

"If you want to be friends, we'll find a way." Sanger beamed with the small bit of encouragement. "There's got to be some place where two people can sit and talk without the whole town knowing about it. We'll think of something."

"Wherever it is, it has to be close to the store." Her voice took on a conspiratory tone. "My parents don't let me get very far away. They even want to know when I'm in the park reading."

"What park do you read in?" Sanger's mind began to race.

"It's not really a park." Eloisa's eyes reached out to Sanger's. "I just go across the street to the Eliza Prince School playground."

"Do you go there often?" Sanger had an idea.

"Almost every night. When my parents come downstairs after supper, I usually take a book to the park and read for an hour or so. Since it's still

38

light outside, my parents don't really mind. They just tell me not to go any further than the playground."

"Would you mind if I met you at the park sometime?" Sanger spoke in a very tenuous fashion expecting rejection. "We could talk and get to know each other better."

"I don't know." Eloisa seemed to be struggling internally. "It would still be light. What if somebody saw us and told? We could both get in a lot of serious trouble. People in Princeville would never believe that we were just friends."

"People wouldn't have to see us." Sanger seemed to be visualizing another place as he talked.

"What do you mean? Anywhere that we go on the playground people would be able to see us." Eloisa searched his face for an answer.

"When I was in elementary school, I went to Eliza Prince." Sanger's face still seemed to be in another place at another time. "I remember one time I got in big trouble with Miss Carrell, the Principal, for climbing up on top the building."

"How did you get up on top the school building?" Eloisa seemed intrigued. "Did you climb a tree or what?"

"Naw, I didn't climb a tree; I climbed a ladder in a little room next to the cafeteria around back. It went up on the roof over the section where the cafeteria is. I remember I went up there a couple of times before I got caught. It was pretty neat."

"How did they catch you?" Eloisa's curiosity had been aroused. "Did they see you up there?"

"Naw, they couldn't see me from the ground; there's like a four foot wall around the top. That's why I thought it was so neat. I pretended it was my secret fort. I'd sneak up there; and as long as I didn't stand up, nobody could see me."

"So." Eloisa was anxious for an answer. "How did they finally catch you?"

"The janitor saw me going into the room one day and went and told Miss Carrell. When I came back down, they were both standing there waiting on me."

"I bet she whipped the daylights out of you, didn't she?" Eloisa was grinning.

"You know, I expected her to, but she didn't. She asked me if any of the other kids knew about the room and where the ladder went? I told her that I didn't think so. What she did next really surprised me. She told me that if I would promise never to climb up there again and promise not to tell the other kids about the ladder, then she wouldn't paddle me. I promised, and that was the last I heard about it."

"Why do you think she let you off so easy?" Eloisa was genuinely surprised.

"Well, I found out later that they were required by the fire department to keep the door unlocked at all times so the firemen could get on the roof quickly in case of a fire. They even had to leave it unlocked when school wasn't going on. I guess Miss Carrell figured it would be easier to swear me to secrecy than to constantly worry about little kids running around on the roof."

"You mean it wasn't locked or anything?" asked Eloisa. "You'd think that if you figured it out, other kids would have too."

"Apparently, Miss Carrell thought the same way as you. The next time I went by the door after I got caught, I noticed the janitor was installing some kind of attachment to the door. I think it was a buzzer or something that went off when the door was opened."

"So, what's the moral to that story?" Her tone had turned accusatory. "Are you suggesting that we climb up on top the school building?"

"That's exactly what I'm suggesting." He looked her in the eyes and grinned. "If we were on top the building, there's no way that anybody would ever see us. We could talk as much as we wanted to and not have to worry about what the people in Princeville had to say. We could even pretend that we were in Detroit or someplace like that, if you wanted to."

"I'm not sure I should do that." Eloisa spoke apprehensively. "How do I know if I can trust you? You might get me up on top of the school and then I find out you are like all the other white boys and want something other than friendship. Then what would I do?"

Sanger looked at Eloisa and chuckled. "All you'd have to do is stand up and holler. The whole neighborhood would hear you. The cops would be on us like white on rice. I wouldn't stand a chance. If I were lucky, the cops would get me before all your black neighbors."

"Well, even if I trusted you, and I'm not completely sure I do; wouldn't the alarm go off in the office when we opened the door?"

"Yeah, it would, but it would only buzz as long as we had the door open. Besides, it's summertime; I bet nobody is ever around to hear the alarm. Especially at night!"

"I don't know." Eloisa was obviously not convinced. "If I got caught, it's not any telling what my daddy would do. I'm not sure you're worth the risk."

"Well, you'll never know if you don't. This is the last time I'll come to the store. I don't want to get you into trouble. If you don't meet me, the only thing that I'll ever know about black girls is what I'm told; and the only thing you'll know about white boys is what you're told. After talking to you every day for the last couple of weeks, I don't think what I've been told is the real truth. Whatta you say; you wanna be friends? If you do, meet me on the roof of the school! I'll be there at 7:00 Friday night."

"I'm not going to meet you on the roof of any school." Defiance was seething in her voice. "You're just a crazy white boy. You'd better leave before Daddy looks out the window and sees your car and comes down here to see what's going on."

41

Sanger could see that Eloisa was trying real hard to be angry. He could also see that she wasn't very good at acting. "I'll be waiting for you Friday night."

"The only thing you'll be doing Friday night is waiting." Her retort was not at all convincing. "'Cause I'm not climbing up on that roof."

"I'll be there anyway." He pushed open the screen door as he spoke. When he turned and smiled at her, he thought he saw the trace of a smile on Eloisa's lips.

"What am I getting myself into," he thought as he walked down the store's wooden steps and toward his old Ford. "If any of the gang or my parents ever find out I am seeing a black girl, I'll be in deep stuff. Deep enough to drown in!"

# 8

The summer passed quickly for the Coahoma Street Gang just as the others had before it. Their life was played out like one big street party. Except for Sanger, not many of them thought about the future. Each was content to face whatever life threw at them without making much of an attempt to alter their fate.

One hot weekday in late July, Culligan was hanging out on Coahoma Street by himself. Unlike most of the other guys in the gang, he didn't have a regular job. Occasionally, he had to go to work for his father, but that was hardly ever more than once or twice a week. Today, he was alone and bored. He knew that none of the other guys would start showing up for three or four hours. To pass the time, he decided to walk downtown to the Stag Pool Hall. At least it would be cool, and he could kill time shooting pool.

Since it was so hot, Culligan decided to stay off the asphalt streets and stick to the alleys. Having lived in this part of town his whole life, he knew the alleys as well as he knew his own backyard. Overgrown with bushes and trees, most of them were well shaded and cooler than the streets.

He cut across the street from their streetlight and straight into the alley that started there. It went for a block and then came out on Mississippi Street. As he got close to Mississippi Street, Culligan turned right and started down another alley. This one went behind the houses on Mississippi Street and emerged on South Edwards Street about a block east of the Desoto Street viaduct. He figured he'd get on the sidewalk there and head on down to the Stag.

About a third of the way down the alley, he stopped by an outbuilding in somebody's back yard to light a cigarette. As he flicked open his Zippo® with one hand the way the gang always did, he thought he heard voices. Putting the lighter back into the pocket of his jeans, he exhaled the first draw of the cigarette and listened. There it was again; it sounded like two little kids giggling.

Culligan moved closer to the fence and maneuvered the hedges away from his face so that he could see into the yard. He was curious because he knew that old man Ruber lived there and there weren't supposed to be any little kids around.

He had heard his parents talking about Mr. Ruber one time. They said that ever since his wife died, he had been a hermit and never left the house except to go to work or buy groceries. Other than that, no one ever saw him. Even the men that he worked with said that he wouldn't ever talk to them. He just came to the factory every day, did his job, and went home.

People had given up years ago trying to be neighborly or friendly. All they got for their trouble was silence and a dirty look. Apparently, the loss of his wife had been more than Mr. Ruber could deal with. He retreated inside himself and wouldn't let anybody else in.

Culligan's mother had said that the really sad thing about the whole affair was that Mr. and Mrs. Ruber had two little girls when she passed away. Nobody had seen or heard anything about either of them for years. Speculation was that old man Ruber had sent them off to be raised by kinfolks since he couldn't stay at home with them and work too.

People just left Mr. Ruber alone. His house was old and looked like it was falling apart. All the kids in the neighborhood were afraid to go near it because they thought Ruber was some kind of devil or something. All the tall bushes around the backyard fence made it impossible to see into the yard. It was the kind of place that you walked by every day for years but didn't really know anything about.

Culligan worked himself closer to the fence. By pushing a couple more limbs out of his way, he was finally able to see into the yard. He couldn't believe his eyes. On the other side of the fence were two of the prettiest girls he had seen in a long time. But what were they doing in Mr. Ruber's backyard? If he found them there, they'd get in big time trouble.

Culligan decided to watch them for a while and see what they were doing. He took another drag off the cigarette as he watched.

Both girls looked about his age. He figured they must be from out of town or something. They must be visiting relatives in the neighborhood. What he couldn't understand was how they got into Ruber's backyard and what they were doing there.

The girls were both dressed in what Culligan figured must be their Sunday clothes. Besides being all dressed up, they both had on heavy makeup. It was as if they were both dressed up to go somewhere special.

While trying to get closer to hear what they were saying, he inadvertently made a scraping noise against the fence. When he did, both girls heard it and looked up. They were looking right at him. He thought they were looking at him kinda funny. It was as if they had never seen a boy before in their lives. The expressions on their faces were a mixture of pure terror and uncontrollable curiosity.

Little did Culligan know that these two girls had never really seen a boy before. Their only exposure to anybody (other than their father) for many years had been through the magic of television. They had not actually seen a boy in the flesh since their mother's funeral. That was the last time either of them had been out in public.

"Hi!" Culligan looked over the fence at the frightened girls. They visibly jumped at the sound of his voice. It appeared to him that they were wrestling with whether to run or stay and talk.

"My name is Will Culligan. What's yours? What are you two doing in old man Ruber's back yard? He'll kill you if he catches you back here!"

The girls stared at Culligan for a few seconds, then they looked at each other and giggled. As he stood there watching them, they'd say something to each other, point at him, and then start giggling again.

45

"This is really some weird Twilight Zone kinda stuff," he thought to himself as he stared through the fence at the beautiful but very strange girls. "Really weird."

"What are y'all giggling at?" He was getting pissed off at their attitude. "Is my fly open or something? Come over here so I can talk to you."

The girls both moved closer to the fence, then quickly moved away giggling again.

"O.K. If you won't come over here, then I'm comin' over there and see what's so funny." Culligan smashed the cigarette butt under his foot and moved to the fence.

The fence was the cyclone wire type about five feet tall. He put his left foot about halfway up the wire and climbed to the top. With his right foot on top of the fence, he propelled himself over to the other side. He landed on the dirt only a few feet away from the girls. Even though they still looked scared, neither of them made any effort to move away.

"Hi. Like I said, my name is Will Culligan. What's yours?"

"My name's Alice and Daddy's goin' to be real mad if he catches you in our yard. Daddy says nobody is ever s'posed to be back here and that if we see anybody, we're s'posed to tell him. Ain't that right, Janice?"

The second girl nodded in agreement.

"What do you mean, your yard?" Bewilderment was evident in his voice. "Old man Ruber lives here by himself. Are you two girls visiting him or something?"

"We live here." The second girl, Janice, had spoken to Culligan. "We've always lived here. Our whole lives." Then she looked at Alice and giggled again. They both started giggling.

Culligan stood there in amazement. Even though the two girls looked his age, they both talked and acted like small children. And if that wasn't strange enough, what they had just told him was even stranger. How

46

could they have lived there their whole lives? He'd lived in this neighborhood all his life, and he had never seen either one of them before. They must be pulling his leg.

"You're jerkin' my string, right?" His eyes asked the question along with his voice. "You don't really live here. You're just teasing me. Now really, who are you?"

"I'm Alice and this is my sister, Janice and we do, too, live here. If you don't believe us, you can go home, and we won't play with you anymore! We don't have to talk to you; we can go back inside and watch TV."

Culligan was really confused now. It was obvious that the two girls weren't playin' with a full deck. But it did appear that they were serious about livin' in Mr. Ruber's house. It just didn't make any sense.

"Hi, Janice and Alice." He decided to play along with their silly charade. "What's your last name? I told you mine; now why don't you tell me yours? Do you know what your last name is?"

"Yes, we know." The two girls talked at the same time. "Our last name is Ruber, Alice and Janice Ruber. See, we told you we knew." They both giggled again.

Culligan couldn't believe his ears. Could these be the two daughters that he had heard his parents talking about? If they were, then why hadn't he seen them before—especially if they had always been living there.

"If you've always lived here, then why haven't I ever seen you two before? I've walked by this house a thousand times in my life and never seen anybody except your daddy. Where were you all that time?"

"We aren't allowed to go out front." Janice was holding Alice's hand as she spoke. "Sometimes at night, though, Daddy lets us come out here with him."

"What are you doin' out here now?" Culligan looked at the girl's hands clasped together. "Does your daddy know you're comin' outside while he's at work?"

"We're being real naughty." Alice had a sly grin edging its way out. "If Daddy finds out, we'll git a whuppin'. He told us never to go out while he's at work."

"And he told us never to answer the phone, neither." Janice joined in her sister's explanation. "He said he'd whup us to death if he ever caught us goin' against his orders."

"We got hot in the house." Alice jumped back in the conversation. "We just came out here to git cool. You won't tell on us will you?"

"Yeah, please don't tell!" Janice seemed to be sincerely begging. "If you won't tell, you can come back and play with us some more."

"Yeah, you can come play some more," said Alice.

"Don't worry." Culligan stared at the two girls in amazement. "I'm not goin' to tell on you. You're not hurtin' anything playin' in your own backyard. I'd better go now, though. I imagine your daddy'll be comin' home anytime from work. He'd probably get pretty mad if he knew I'd been back here talkin' to y'all."

"Will you come and play with us tomorrow?" Janice was swaying back and forth the way a small child does when tentatively asking a question. "If you will, we'll let you play with our dolls. You can pretend to be the daddy and we'll be the mommies. O.K.?"

"I'll come again as soon as I can." Culligan used the exaggerated tone he would use with a small child. "But it has to be a secret. Promise not to tell?"

"We promise." Both girls had big smiles spread across their pretty faces.

As Culligan climbed back over the fence, he could hear the two girls once again giggling. Turning to take another look at the girls to make sure he wasn't hallucinating because of the heat, he saw them both waving good-bye like two infants.

This is worse than the Twilight Zone, he murmured to himself as he headed back for Coahoma Street. He had forgotten about the Stag and shooting pool. Weighing heavily on his mind now were those two girls. Something really weird must be goin' on in that house. When he saw them again, he'd ask them some more questions.

# *9*

John Ruber had lived on Mississippi Street in Princeville for the past twenty years. He and his wife, Sara, had bought the place the second year they were married. Four years later, Sara had died leaving him with two small daughters. John had thought about moving several times but always changed his mind.

Even though old, the house was big and still structurally sound. Plus, the girls had never lived anywhere else. It would be very difficult to take them to another neighborhood. There would be the questions about why the girls didn't go to school and who took care of them when he was at work? The good people of Princeville were always trying to mind everybody's business except their own. There on Mississippi Street, the neighbors had learned a long time ago to mind their own business and let him do the same.

The neighborhood was very rapidly being swallowed up by the surrounding black section of town. John knew that it would just be a matter of time before he and the girls had to move; but until he absolutely had to, they were staying here. When he was forced to move, he figured they'd probably move out into the country somewhere.

The girls really weren't girls anymore; they were women, Alice was 18 and Janice, 17. Although they had the bodies of women, their minds were something else. Neither one of them could read or write. They had the intellectual abilities of 10-year-olds.

John thought that the death of their mother had caused them both to become retarded. Since they were both retarded, he had not ever sent them to school. What they needed to know, he figured he could teach them at home. Since they were small children, he had kept them inside of the house most of the time.

When the girls were still babies, John hired an old nigger woman to come and stay with them while he was at work. Once Alice got to be five, he didn't hire the old lady anymore. He figured they could stay at home by themselves. He simply taught them that they didn't answer the phone or go to the door while he was away. He told them that if they did either of those things or went outside, he would know about it and they would be whipped. Since he had beaten both of them on a regular basis for most of their young lives, they were afraid to disobey him. They knew what it meant to be whipped.

So every day at 6:45, John Ruber made sure all the doors were locked as he left the house for work. He didn't have to worry about the windows; he had nailed them all shut years ago. He knew the girls would still be there at 4:15 that afternoon when he got home. John had been doing that now for over fourteen years. Alice and Janice had not been away from home all that time. John got up every morning and went to work at Emhart, a factory that made automatic door closers. While he spent his days operating a milling machine, the girls spent theirs watching TV.

To Alice and Janice, their views of the world outside their house came from the endless hours of television that they watched every day. John never even took them to the grocery store. The furthest either of them had ever been from the house was an occasional opportunity to accompany their father to an outbuilding in the backyard by the alley.

Ruber did everything for the girls. He bought their food, their clothes, their underwear, their hygiene products, even their makeup. To them, he was their world. He told them everything they needed to know.

Because Alice and Janice never had the opportunity to talk to anybody else, they believed everything their father said. If he told them to do something, they did it without question regardless of what it might be. To disobey their father meant a beating. Since when he drank he beat them sometimes for no reason at all, they knew what his belt could feel like. Because of that, they acted more like a couple of slaves than they did two daughters.

Summertime was especially bad for Alice and Janice. In the Mississippi Delta, the summertime temperature could be over 100 degrees on a regular basis with average humidity of 85%. With all the windows nailed shut in the house, they couldn't open any of them to let in air. Consequently, summer days and nights were very miserable for the girls. The only time that they were ever cool was at night when their father would make one of them come into his room. He had the only air conditioner in the house. It was an old window unit that he ran at night while he was in bed.

One Tuesday morning, John wasn't feeling particularly good when he got up. The past night had been the occasion for one of his drinking binges, and he had a bad hangover. As a result, he was not as thorough as usual in checking all the doors to make sure they were locked before going to work.

His main concern that morning was how he was going to tolerate all the noise in the factory with such a throbbing headache. Checking doors had somehow lost some of its importance. Besides, he was pretty sure he had locked them all last night when he got home from work. What John had forgotten was that he had gone out back to the outbuilding after he started drinking. When he came back in, he had neglected to lock the door.

As usual, promptly at 6:45 that morning John walked out the front door and locked it behind him. As he climbed into his old pick-up truck, he was already dreading the next eight hours at Emhart. He had always hated his job; but on days like this, it was almost beyond toleration.

Alice and Janice were still in their room when they heard the front door close and the key turn in the lock. That was always their cue to come out. They were deathly afraid of their father, especially during and immediately after one of his drinking binges. On mornings like this, they never ventured out of their room until they were sure that he was gone to work.

"Daddy's gone to work now." Alice was peeking out the front window of their bedroom as she talked to Janice. "Let's eat breakfast."

Cautiously, the girls peered out their bedroom door. Once they had assured themselves that their father was really gone, they both walked out into the hallway and headed for the kitchen. Each morning for breakfast they had cold cereal. Breakfast was just like the rest of their day. It was always the same. First they ate breakfast; then they cleaned up the kitchen. After that, they both went into the living room to watch TV. TV was the most important part of their day.

The first thing they always did was to exercise with Jack LaLane. It was as much a part of their day as eating. Alice had remembered doing this with her mother when she was very small. After their mother died, Lucy had come to take care of them every day. Since Lucy thought the white man with all the muscles in the tight pants was real funny, she let the girls watch it. After Lucy quit coming, they continued. The daily exercise was the only thing that kept them from being overweight. After the exercise show, they watched soap operas until lunch. After lunch, it was more soaps and then game shows. At night they went to their room after cleaning up the supper dishes.

Today was different, though. By the time the girls went back into the kitchen to prepare their usual sandwich for lunch, the temperature outside was already over 100 degrees. They were both sweating very heavily. It was going to be another very uncomfortable day for them.

As they were finishing lunch, Janice happened to look over at the back door. It looked funny to her. Something was different about it. Janice got up from the table and walked over to the sink. After putting her plate in the sink, she went to the back door and just stood staring at it.

"What are you doin' by that door?" Alice was finishing the last bite of her lunch and talking with her mouth full.

"Daddy left the door open." Janice continued staring at the door as she spoke. "He forgot to pull it to."

Alice quickly got up from her place at the table and hurried over to where her sister was standing by the back door. "Daddy never left the door open before." Alice was standing by her sister and also looking at the partially ajar door. "I wonder if he did it on purpose. Maybe he did it so we could go outside. I bet it's cool under the big tree out there."

"You know Daddy don't let us outside 'less he's with us." Janice's attention was still on the door as she talked. "If we go out under the tree, he'll whup us."

"Maybe it's magic." A glazed-over look had appeared on Alice's face. Obviously, her mind had drifted into fantasyland. "Maybe magic opened the door. Maybe our fairy godmother did it. She wants us to go outside."

"I don't know." Janice looked worried. "If Daddy finds out, we're gonna be in big trouble."

"We won't tell him." Alice was pleading with her sister. "It's so hot today. Maybe we could go out under the big tree just for a little bit."

"I'm scared." Janice was not convinced they should break such a big rule. "Daddy'll whup the daylights out of us if he finds out."

In all their years, this was the first time that a door had been left unlocked. It wasn't as if they couldn't have gotten out of the house before. They could have; all the doors could be opened from the inside. It was just that they were so afraid of their father that they hadn't dared open a door while he was gone.

In addition to the unlocked door, there was something else at work here. Alice had been getting braver and braver lately. She knew from watching TV that when you got to be 18 years old, you were grown. When you were grown, you could do stuff yourself.

Then there was something else. The girls probably weren't really retarded, not mentally anyway. Sure, they were socially retarded, but who wouldn't be if they had been kept locked up in a house for their whole lives.

Even though they couldn't read or write, the girls did have a certain level of intellectual development brought about by the years of endless TV. This intellectual development had begun to manifest itself lately. The girls had actually begun to question their father and some of the things he made them do. So far, they had not mustered the courage to question him directly; they did, however, talk a great deal between themselves.

"Come on." Alice said as she pulled the door all the way open. "Let's go sit under the big tree."

"O.K." Janice gave in. "But only for a little bit. We've got to come right back in so Daddy won't catch us."

---

After that hot Tuesday, the girls began to sneak outside every day after lunch. When their father didn't catch them the first time, they figured that it must be alright. With each trip into the backyard, the girls became more and more confident. If you were to pass by and see them, you'd not think anything of it except that they were two very pretty girls out for a little fresh air.

Because going outside was such an adventure for them, they started dressing up for the occasion. Each one would put on her prettiest dress and then take great care in applying makeup to her face.

Since the girls were small, their father had bought them makeup and told them to wear it. Because there was no woman around to teach them the proper methods and techniques for applying the makeup, the girls learned from TV shows and commercials. As a result, they both always wore their makeup very heavy. With the exception of that one thing, anyone passing by would have taken them for a couple of normal teenage girls.

# *10*

Sanger stood in line behind three black workers waiting for his turn to punch in. It was two minutes before 7:00 on Friday morning. Time to get another day started at the ole Coke Plant. The time clock was located in a small, glassed-in alcove in front of the main office. When four or five guys were trying to punch in at the same time, it got very crowded.

Standing next to the time clock was an old-fashioned Coca-Cola machine. Its mechanism had been altered so that you could get a Coke out without depositing money. Its purpose was to provide cold Cokes for the employees and any visitor that wanted one.

When Sanger had first gone to work at the Plant, he thought it was pretty neat that he could have all the free drinks he wanted. With the temperature usually running over a hundred degrees on the loading dock, a guy could get real thirsty. His first day on the job, he drank ten Cokes. That night he got sick. All the sugar and caffeine had really done a job on his system. After that first day, Sanger vowed never to drink Cokes on the job again. Instead, he started taking three salt tablets a day and drinking water when he got thirsty. He hadn't had a problem since.

As Sanger was putting his timecard back into the slot of the metal rack where they were kept, he heard someone tapping on the glass. When he glanced over toward the main office, he could see the Plant manager, Martin, motioning for him to come into the office. "What now," he thought.

"Hi Jerry." Martin started talking as Sanger opened the office door and was halfway in. "Looks like it's goin' to be another hot one out there today. You ready to go get 'em?"

"I'm always ready to go get 'em, especially on payday." Sanger's ever present smile was already in place.

Even though Martin could be a pain sometimes, Sanger basically liked him. The Coca-Cola Company was Martin's life so he thought it should be everybody else's too. Sanger didn't exactly share his enthusiasm for the company, but he did admire Martin's dedication. Martin had given him the job there and then gone out of his way to help him settle in.

"Jerry, I just wanted to let you know that you're doin' a good job out on the dock." Martin had assumed his authoritarian but benevolent personality. "Since you've been out there, our bottle losses have dropped from 300 cases a week to almost nothin'. Having a white person on the dock has really made a difference. The boys can't get away with stealin' anymore. I also wanted to tell you that you can stay here as long as you want. There's always a job at the Coca-Cola Bottling Company for you."

"Thanks, Martin. I appreciate that." Sanger looked down at the dirty linoleum floor as he replied in an almost embarrassed tone. "I just try to do my job out there." He started to say something about the "boys" stealing but didn't. Martin probably wouldn't have believed him anyway. Besides, why spoil Martin's good mood? He had so few of them.

The truth about the bottles was that most of the 300 missing cases a week were not the fault of the black guys; it was, in reality, the fault of the white guys.

After Sanger had been on the job a few days, he started noticing that a couple of the route salesmen would tell him they had a certain number of empties on their truck. When he checked them, however, he could not make his count equal theirs. After calling them on it a few times, they started giving him an accurate count.

Almost as if magic had occurred, the bottle shortage situation on the loading dock disappeared. Sanger got credit for stopping the blacks from stealing. In reality, though, he had stopped the white route salesmen from lying and inflating their empty bottle count.

"Well, guess I'd better get with it." Sanger smiled at Martin again. "We've got to unload and load 12 trucks today. I want to get started so we don't have to stay late tonight."

About that time the secretary, Lorene, looked up from her work. She had been working at the Coke Plant for several years now. Sanger had known her for most of his life and had gone to school with her daughter, Beth Ann. Her husband had even given him his first baseball glove when he was very small. Sanger liked Lorene; she was a pleasant addition around the office.

"I bet you've got a date with some pretty little blond tonight, don't you?" Lorene's voice was laced with mischievous intent and accompanied by a grin. "If you don't get those trucks loaded on time, you'll be late and she'll get mad at you. Am I right or what? What's her name?"

Sanger didn't want to lie to Lorene, so he just looked at her with a big smile on his face. "I can't tell." He assumed a joking tone of voice. "It's a secret. If my regular girlfriend finds out, she'll kill me. She thinks I'm goin' fishin' tonight."

Lorene laughed and turned her attention back to the bookkeeping she was working on. Sanger turned toward the door to head out.

"Remember what I told you." Martin was talking to Sanger's back. "You've got a career here with Coca-Cola as long as you want it."

Sanger snickered under his breath as he walked out into the Plant. "Martin," he thought, "if I figured that I had to work here for the rest of my life, I'd go out right now and commit suicide."

Dummy was the first person Sanger saw as he walked out into the Plant. Dummy was the senior employee at the Princeville Coca-Cola Bottling Plant. He had started to work there almost fifty years earlier when the Cokes were delivered in a horse-drawn wagon. Now all these years later, he was still working—at minimum wage.

Dummy, of course, was not his real name. Everybody had always called him Dummy because he was deaf and could not speak very well. His real name was Roosevelt, but few people ever took the time to find that out. Over the years, Dummy had learned to read lips after a fashion.

If you exaggerated your lip movements and spoke very slowly to him, he could understand most of what you said. Dummy could also read. Where an old, black deaf and dumb man learned to read in Princeville, Mississippi, was anybody's guess. Sanger figured that he had probably taught himself over the years.

Sanger liked Dummy and the feeling was mutual. Given the fact that Dummy was probably somewhere on the back side of 70, he was not real concerned with other people and their opinions—even the boss. If he didn't like you, he made no attempt whatsoever to hide it.

Dummy pretty much did as he pleased. Martin tolerated him because there were some things in the old plant that only Dummy knew how to do.

Dummy was no dummy, though; he would not teach anybody how to do his job. Anytime anyone asked or came around, he'd simply put his hand in the air and wave them off with a disgusted grunt.

Today as Sanger came out of the office, Dummy was standing there shaking his head in a negative gesture like he often did. Apparently, he had been reading Martin's lips as he talked. As Sanger walked up to him, Dummy put his fist down in front of his own crotch and used his hand to simulate masturbation, then pointed to Martin. That was Dummy's way of saying "screw him."

Sanger just laughed. "You got that right." Dummy was still laughing as Sanger walked by him on into the Plant.

The inside of the Plant had already started to get noisy. The bottling line had started up and bottles were clanging together up and down the long conveyor belt. The unmuffled engine of the forklift could be heard in chorus with the clanging of the glass. Loud voices could be heard everywhere as workers competed with the manufacturing sounds to be heard.

Everywhere you looked, pallets of empty bottles or pallets containing filled bottles of Coke sat stacked to the top of the building. Each pallet held 30 cases of drinks, six cases to a layer and five layers high. In most parts of the Plant, the Cokes were stacked five or six pallets high.

Sanger knew from personal experience that this could be a very dangerous place. His second day on the job he had been standing in an area of the Plant where the pallets were stacked six high. All of a sudden, some sixth sense had made him look up over his head. As he did, he could see the top pallet start to move. When it started to move, he started to run. He barely made it out of their range before the first cases hit the floor. It had taken him and the "other niggers" almost two hours to clean up the mess.

The morning went as typically as Friday mornings usually did. Fridays always were busier with people buying drinks for the weekend and others selling bottles to get a little extra spending money. Between buying bottles and selling drinks, Sanger helped the other two guys on the dock load the trucks for Monday's routes.

By 4:30 that afternoon, all the trucks for Monday were loaded with the exception of one. They were about halfway through it when Sanger looked up toward the street. Coming across the parking lot was one extremely large black woman. From the look on her face she had something very serious on her mind. Sanger hoped it didn't have anything to do with him.

He stopped loading the truck and walked over to the edge of the dock to see what the woman wanted.

"I's wants to talk to Bughead." She started speaking as soon as she was close enough for Sanger to hear. "Tell him to come out here!"

Sanger looked around to see if Bughead was out on the dock. He was one of the other two men that was helping to load the trucks today.

"Paul." Sanger yelled out to the other worker on the dock. "Where'd Bughead go?"

"He's gone in the Plant to git some dranks." Paul spoke as he hoisted a case of 16-ounce Cokes to the top of the truck's holding bin. He's gonna be rite back out."

Sanger turned back to the woman to see if she had heard what Paul had said.

"I's'll jest wait rite here." Her voice was seething with anger as she spoke.

About that time, Bughead came back out of the Plant pushing five cases of orange drinks on a two-wheeler. When he saw the huge, angry black woman that was waiting for him, he almost stumbled and toppled the cases of soft drinks.

"Bughead, you no-count, bug-eyed, egg-suckin' fool." She spit out the words so vehemently that moisture from her mouth struck him on the chest. "I's been 'spectin' to see yo skinny ass all week. You forgit 'bout owin' me two dollars?"

"Betty, I wus comin' round to see you soon as I quit work today." Bughead took a step back hesitantly in response to the woman's tirade. "I's gits paid after work."

"Youse better come 'round or I's gwine to cut you so bad yo mama won't know who you is." The black woman's eyes seem to open wider as she barked the words. "The next time you want some lovin' on credit, don't come cryin' to me. I's messed with yo ugly self fer the las' time."

The gravel in the parking lot almost seemed to quiver as the woman turned sharply and stomped away. Sanger felt sorry for Bughead if he didn't go by and retire his debt after work.

The rest of the afternoon was spent with Sanger and Paul giving Bughead a hard time about buying his lovin' on the credit and then not wanting to pay his bill. They both told him that if she turned him in, it would ruin his credit rating. The credit report would read that he was behind in his payments to Betty, "the Dealer in Love." They thought it was a lot funnier than he did.

At about 5:30 the guys on the dock punched out and drew their pay for the week. Each of them was given a small manila envelope. Inside, they found a slip of paper which listed hours worked and deductions withheld. Also inside was their pay in cash.

Each Friday after work, Sanger always hung around after being paid so that he could help the black guys double check their pay envelopes to make sure they hadn't been shorted. Bughead must have been in a big hurry; he was the first one of the guys to come over to Sanger.

"Hey, Jerry." Bughead was holding out his envelope to Sanger. "Will you check my money for me? I's worked a lot of overtime las' week. I wanna make shore the man ain't cheated me."

"I'm sure that if Mr. Martin made a mistake, it wasn't on purpose." Sanger reached out his left hand and took the pay envelope from Bughead.

Sanger took out his pencil and quickly figured Bughead's hours times minimum wage plus the time and a half rate for overtime. He then handed the envelope back to Bughead. "Everything's O.K.; you got what you were supposed to. Now go pay your bill; and tonight, Bughead, if you have to buy anything on credit, don't buy it from a woman that outweighs you by 50 pounds."

"Thanks, Jerry." Bughead walked away smiling.

After helping several more of his black friends double check their pay envelopes, Sanger was ready to head for home. He wanted to get a quick shower and eat. He had less than an hour to go before his Friday night appointment.

---

The old Ford came to life with a roar as Sanger sat wondering if he was doing the right thing tonight. After all, it could mean real trouble for both of them if anybody found out. Was his curiosity about this light-skinned black girl really worth the risk? Maybe his question would be answered tonight!

Sanger was careful that no one saw him as he went around to the back of the school. He had parked the old Ford around the corner from Eliza Prince so that it wouldn't be conspicuous.

When he got to the back of the school by the cafeteria, he saw that it still looked pretty much the same way it had when he was a student there. One thing you could count on about schools was that they hardly ever changed. Sanger guessed that it was easier that way.

He cautiously approached the door to the little room by the cafeteria. It looked exactly as he had remembered it. Sanger hoped that the school was still required to keep it unlocked.

As he stood facing the door, Sanger reached out with his right hand and turned the knob. Much to his relief, he felt the cool metal turn with the pressure of his hand. Sanger paused before pulling the door open. He knew that some sort of alarm was attached to it; he just hoped that it was the type that he had explained to Eloisa. With his left hand on the door for extra support, Sanger eased the door part of the way open. As he did he cringed, halfway expecting some sort of blood curdling alarm to let loose its warning signal. Much to his relief, there was no sound except the creaking of hinges left too long without oil.

Sanger pulled the door open far enough to slip through the opening. While slipping his body through the opening, he looked overhead for the wires that would be necessary for an alarm system. Sure enough, there they were. He hoped they didn't go any further than the principal's office. If they did, trouble would be starting a lot sooner than he had anticipated.

The room inside was pretty much as he had remembered it. Since it had to be kept unlocked all the time, there was nothing stored there. The only thing in the room was the metal ladder leading up to the roof.

Sanger climbed the ladder. Once at the top, he pushed open the trap door that opened onto the roof. Cautiously, he poked his head through the opening. It, too, was just as he had remembered it.

He was careful as he climbed out onto the roof that he didn't raise his head above the short wall surrounding the roof. Since it was still daylight and would be for a couple more hours, he knew that people were out in their yards. It wouldn't take long for someone to spot him on the roof if he stuck his head up.

Leaving the trap door open for Eloisa, Sanger moved a few feet away from the opening and sat down. All he could do now was wait and hope that she would make the decision to come.

About 7:15, Sanger heard the squeak of the door below as it was slowly opened. He sure hoped that it was Eloisa. Anybody else would mean that he was in deep stuff.

Slowly, the door was pulled closed again causing it to let out another squeak. Then there was a slight scraping sound from below as a foot was put on the first rung of the ladder.

Sanger breathed a sigh of relief as Eloisa's head appeared in the trap door opening. She looked as relieved to see him as he was to see her.

"I'm glad that you decided to come." Relief was evident in his voice as he watched her climb all the way through the opening. "Be careful that you stay below the level of the wall."

"Don't worry." Apprehension hung heavily on her words. "The last thing in the world I want to do is let someone see me up here and go tell my daddy. I'm still not sure I should be doing this."

"Well, that makes two of us." Sanger seemed to lower his voice subconsciously. "But I still wanted to come see you tonight."

"I wanted to come see you too." Eloisa lowered her voice in response. "As long as we're just talking, what harm can it possibly do? There's no law that says we can't be friends."

"You're right." Sanger was relaxing enough to finally smile. "There isn't a law. We can be friends if we want to and no one can stop us. Come on over and pull up some roof and have a seat. Let's talk and get to know each other a little better."

"What do we talk about?' It was evident by her voice that Eloisa was still trying to convince herself that this was O.K.

"Well, the first thing I'd like to know is what you read every day when you come over here. It must be some kind of interesting book to get you to read so much."

# *11*

It was Friday night and the Coahoma Street Gang was gathered under their streetlight. Part of them, anyway. Jake was working, Jay Sanger and Sampson were off with their girlfriends, and nobody knew where Jerry Sanger was.

"Hey, Culligan." Steed was fiddling with his radio as he talked. "Where did Sanger's mama say he was when you went over there?"

"She said she figured he headed over here." Culligan watched Steed try to tune in a station. "He came home about 6:00, got a quick shower, ate, and then left in a big hurry. She said he'd probably show up over here after while."

"He's probably found some willing young thing that he doesn't want us to know about." Wilkerson was sitting on the curb a couple feet away as he spoke. "He'll show eventually with that shit-eatin' grin on his face and say he's just been ridin' around."

"Let's go get a beer." Parker was leaning against his car as he addressed the gang. "Maybe he'll show up at the Ranch later."

---

"Do you really want to know what kind of books I read?" Eloisa seemed surprised at the question.

"Yeah, I really want to know what kinds of books you read." Sanger was looking at Eloisa's eyes as he spoke. "If I know what you like to read, then I'll have a peek at the real you. A poet might even say I'll have "a

67

window into your soul." It will help me know what's important to you and what makes you tick."

"You want to see inside of me, do you?" Eloisa was not smiling. "What if you don't like what you see? What then?"

"That's the risk I take." Sanger's voice was more serious, however, he continued smiling. "But if you never take any risks, you're gonna miss some of the best experiences in life."

"Would you believe that I'm reading a romantic adventure novel set in Hawaii." Eloisa had decided his question was O.K. "Mostly I read stuff like that. It lets me leave Princeville whenever I want to. What about you? What do you like to read or do you even read at all now that you're out of high school?"

"Sure I still read." Sanger tried not to sound defensive. "I like adventure novels and historical fiction about the Orient. Speaking of high school, have you finished high school yet?"

"As a matter of fact, I have." Eloisa was getting comfortable with the situation. "While you were having your ceremony over at Princeville High, I was having mine at Higgins High. We're both in the class of '67, just on different sides of the racial railroad tracks."

"Yeah, that's kinda funny, isn't it?" Sanger had quit smiling. "We both grow up in this two-bit town of 20,000 people, graduate from public high schools the same year, but never meet until the summer after our senior year. And to top it all off, we have to meet on a rooftop so that people won't bother us. Ain't growing up in Mississippi a real trip!"

"It's a trip, alright." There was a sadness in Eloisa's answer. "I'm just not sure it's been a pleasant one. Ever since I can remember, I've always heard that black folks have to learn to get along with white folks if you're going to live in the South. That black folks have their place and white folks have theirs. But every time I've been around white people, my parents tell me not to say any more than I absolutely have to. They say the less you say the better off you are, and try not to sound too educated—it makes white people mad. I never figured it out. How can I learn about white people if I'm not permitted to talk to them?"

"I don't know, either." Sanger realized this was his first insight into Eloisa. "It doesn't make sense to me. All my life I've been told that black people are different than we are. We're the superior race, and blacks should remember their places and stay in them. I shouldn't associate with them; I should stay with my own kind. Anytime that I asked questions, I was told that was just the way it was and we couldn't do anything about it. All my life I've wondered what the big deal was about the color of a person's skin, but nobody has ever been able to explain it to me. If the color of our skin really does make a difference, then I guess we'll find out, won't we?

"You know what's really funny, though? You're a black girl and I'm a white boy; but when you look at the color of our skins, I'm actually darker than you are."

"I've noticed." Eloisa's smile was a nervous one. "That first day when I saw you at the Coke Plant, I thought you were black. I was really embarrassed! I was afraid that I had made you mad. I was really surprised that you took it so well. Most white people, I would imagine, would get upset at being taken for a black."

"You're probably right, but I hope you've figured out by now that I'm not most white people. Besides, when you get as dark in the summertime as I do, you can't take that kind of thing personally. If you did, you'd stay mad half the time. I've had more than one white person take me for a black."

The two continued to talk for over an hour. They were both too nervous about what they were doing to let the conversation lag. Besides, this might be the only chance either of them had to talk like this for a long time.

"It's getting late," Eloisa finally said. "I'd better be going before Daddy comes looking for me. I hardly ever stay for more than an hour or so."

"Could we meet again and talk some more?" Sanger hoped the desperation was not apparent in his voice. "I've really enjoyed being here with you!"

"I don't know." Eloisa had genuine confusion in her voice. "This makes me awfully nervous. Maybe we shouldn't come here anymore. What if somebody saw us tonight?"

"If somebody had seen us, your daddy'd already have been up here with a stick. It's almost impossible for anyone to see you when you get behind the school like this. We could come up here all summer and never get caught if we wanted to.

"We've done the hardest part already." Sanger was uttering a soft plea. "Let's not stop our friendship before it has a chance to get started good. Let's take the time to get to know each other; it may be the only real chance either one of us ever has for a friendship like this. Whatta you say? Let's meet again!"

"O.K." Eloisa smiled at Sanger. "I'll meet you one more time, but that's all. I don't have the nerve to try this all summer."

"How about Monday night." Sanger searched her face for a sign. "Same time, same place?"

"Monday night!" Eloisa agreed with just a hint of hesitation. "But remember, that's the last time."

"Good!" Sanger's smile was so big it seemed to split his face. "You go down first. I'll wait about thirty minutes so that if anybody sees you they won't think anything about it. And . . . Eloisa, thanks for trusting me."

"You're welcome, Jerry. Thanks for looking at me and not seeing just another black face; it's a nice change. I'll see you Monday."

After Eloisa left the school, Sanger waited about thirty minutes before he left, just like he had told her. The last thing he wanted now that they were friends was for somebody to see them and tell her folks. That would put an end to things for sure.

70

As Sanger eased the old Ford across Fourth Street and started down the stretch of Coahoma Street where his gang hung out, he could see that it was deserted. That didn't really surprise him, though; they hardly ever hung out there on Friday night.

Friday night was the time to crawl into one of their old beat up cars and go cruising for a little action. Action in Princeville usually meant anything from talking to some of the girls across town, to drinking beer, racing cars, or fighting.

The preferred action of the Coahoma Street Gang was talking to the girls. Fighting usually came in a very distant last. Besides, talking to the girls was a lot easier. For some reason, the little rich girls from across the tracks liked the boys in the Coahoma Street Gang. It probably had something to do with the psychological high that they got from flirting with danger. They thought the Coahoma Street boys were somehow dangerous.

"Oh, well." Sanger thought to himself as he slowed down at the streetlight where they usually gathered. "The gang is probably out cruising the highway or else down at the Ranch having a beer."

In a way, he was kinda glad they weren't around. He wasn't quite ready for the usual routine of bullshit and grabass. The time he spent talking to Eloisa seemed to temporarily transform him into a different person. It made him realize all of a sudden that there was more to life than going to work every day at the Coke Plant and then hanging out at night on Coahoma Street.

It didn't really make sense to him. How could talking to a pretty black girl have that effect on him? He had talked to lots of girls before, but most of them had held little excitement. Maybe it was the fact that he was beginning to doubt many of the things that he had been taught as he was growing up. If he had not been taught the truth about black people, then maybe he hadn't been taught the truth about a lot of things.

Maybe there was a whole lot more to the world than Princeville, Mississippi, had to offer. For the first time in his life, Sanger began to

71

wonder. Maybe there were better places in the country to live than his hometown.

If a town like Princeville wouldn't allow him the freedom to be friends with as nice a person as Eloisa, then maybe he should try to find a town that would. If such a place existed, then it surely must be a better town in which to live.

Sanger stopped at the corner of Coahoma Street and South Edwards. He debated with himself for a second and then turned left and headed in the general direction of downtown. He could have turned right and driven out to the Ranch, but he still wasn't quite ready to start his evening out with the gang.

The gang wouldn't think much about not seeing him for a while as long as he showed up sooner or later. By now they had grown accustomed to his loner style.

The gang found out early in its existence that if Sanger didn't want to do what they were doing, he just went his own way. He never tried to change their minds or say anything against their activities; he just didn't go along.

They knew that he wasn't mad at them and that he would show up again later. He was always quizzed about where he had been and what he had been doing. Sometimes he told them, and sometimes all they got for their efforts was a grin.

Sanger drove slowly down South Edwards to Desoto. At Desoto, he turned right and went under the viaduct. On top of the Desoto Street viaduct ran the railroad tracks that divided the town between black people and white. He continued up Desoto to Second Street where he turned left.

Immediately on his left was the City Auditorium. Its large grey exterior seemed to radiate old and run-down vibes. Ever since he could remember, all the high-school dances, graduations, and other assorted activities had taken place in that beat-up old building. It in a way represented a lot of what was bad in Princeville.

Sanger could remember going to countless dances in the Auditorium. Almost always, he went with the gang as opposed to taking a date.

When he was in the early years of high school, he hadn't been able to afford a car, so he and the other guys would usually walk or hitch a ride to the dances. Most girls weren't real big about walking on their date, so the gang was almost always stag.

When they got there, they usually stood around and watched the guys with cars bring in their dates. It was almost like pressing your nose to the window of a candy store and looking but never being able to go in.

From early in life, Sanger had learned that in Princeville, Mississippi, there was a very rigid class structure. The first part of the structure divided the population into two general groups: black and white.

After the first division, then there were subgroups within the larger groups. The blacks had basically two subgroups. One was at the lowest possible point on the social pecking order. They were the dirt poor people working for minimum wages or lower.

The second and somewhat higher on the pecking order group was black families like Eloisa's. They were still considered niggers on the social register, but they were considered uppity niggers because of better educations or successful business ventures.

The next level above the uppity nigger on the social scale was occupied by poor, white trash. They were considered above the successful blacks by the mere virtue of the color of their skin.

Sanger knew that this was the level where the Coahoma Street Gang and their families fell. Even though white, in many ways they were treated as poorly as the community's black citizens.

From childhood, he could remember the subtle discrimination practiced against him and other poor white people in town. It was never extremely overt or something you could point a finger at; it was more a feeling you were left with, a feeling that somehow you weren't as good as some of the other people in town.

73

As you continued up the social hierarchy of plantation America, you came to the white middle class. They were the people that owned their homes and lived across the tracks. They weren't rich by any definition of the word; but then again, they had a lot more than the poor, white trash had.

At the top of the Southern social pecking order was, of course, the rich white people and those pretending to be. From their lofty perches, they looked down their regal noses at everybody else.

You could tell them immediately. They would never use the word nigger publicly. They always referred to blacks in public as "nigras." When behind closed doors, though, the word nigra was quickly discarded for the more descriptive "nigger."

Sanger knew that as long as he continued to live in Princeville, he would always be on the bottom. The only ticket out was money, and with the wealth controlled so tightly, his chances of amassing any great amount were slim to none.

Second Street continued on past the City Auditorium and into the heart of downtown. That time of night it was pretty well deserted except for people at the movie theater on Yazoo.

Sanger kicked the old Ford a little as he crossed the Sunflower River Bridge. The bridge was the last point of separation before he passed into the part of Princeville known as the Oakhurst section of town.

Scattered west and north of the bridge, the top two strata of Princeville's society could be found at home snug in the thought that all the niggers and poor, white trash had to cross at least one railroad track and the Sunflower River to get to them.

Once across the bridge, Sanger took a hard left and drove in the general direction of Highway 61. Almost immediately, he came to what used to be the Princeville City swimming pool. It was now owned by the VFW or American Legion or some group like that. The city had sold it to them when the threat of integration had brought about the realization that it might actually have to be opened to blacks.

He didn't know what the selling price was, but he suspected that it was probably in the range of one dollar. Now for a very small fee, anybody could join the organization's club and swim in the pool. Of course, you had to be accepted by the membership committee. The city pool had now become the poor white person's country club.

Behind the swimming pool was Princeville High School. It was from there that he had graduated a little over a month ago. Sanger's class had been the first Princeville High class to graduate with a black in it. The graduates numbered 134 whites and one black.

As the old Ford went by the Cherry Street intersection, the street dipped and passed through another viaduct similar to the one Sanger had passed under earlier. The view on the other side of the railroad tracks told you immediately that you were out of the Oakhurst section and back on the poor side of town.

Coming up on the right was an old Chinese grocery store. It was on the edge of a run-down part of town called the Upper Brickyard. It wasn't the worst black slum in town, but it had to be in the running.

Sanger brought the car to a halt at the stop sign leading on to Highway 61. "What the hell," he thought. "Might as well head out to the Ranch and see if the gang was there." He eased the car into the intersection and turned left.

The Ranch was really hopping as Sanger drove by. He slowed down to see if he saw any of the gang.

All he could make out was the usual collection of Country Club types on the back side of the parking lot. They always parked back there so they could drink beer without being spotted by the cops. Even if the cops did see them, by the time they could work their way through the crowd, the beer had always disappeared or was in the hands of somebody legally old enough to drink it.

The Coahoma Street Gang and anybody else that wasn't a part of the in-crowd usually parked on the front side of the lot right next to the highway. Although it wasn't nearly as socially prominent a parking spot, it was a whole lot easier to get in and out.

Sanger drove on by the Ranch and made a U-turn in the parking lot of the Holiday Inn. He pulled back out on to the highway and then turned into the Ranch. There was an open parking spot right by the section of the drive that went back to the rear of the lot.

The old Ford squeaked to a stop and he killed the motor. Within a couple of minutes, one of the young black carhops appeared by his window. He was a nice kid that Sanger had been seeing out there most of the summer.

"Hey, Slick." Sanger was smiling at the boy standing by his car. "Been gittin' any lately?"

"I is always gittin' it." The boy shot the retort back with a huge smile on his face. "Them girls can't keeps their hands off the merchandise."

"No wonder you're so damn black, Slick." Sanger talked to the young boy like he would to a Coahoma Street buddy—irreverently. "You're full up to the top with bullshit."

As they both laughed at the joke, Sanger asked Slick if he had seen any of the gang tonight.

"They's wus here a whil-a-go." Slick answered in the usual dialect of an uneducated Mississippi black. "They said to tell you to git screwed if I saw you. Said they'd catch you here after while. I 'magin they be back in a bit."

"In a bit, huh?" Sanger scrunched his brow as he pondered the information. "I guess I might as well wait then. Bring me a Coke, will you, Slick?"

Slick headed off back into the building to get the Coke. Sanger watched him as he went.

"This is almost as bad a way to make a living as my job," he thought. Every night the little black guys came to work there at the Ranch. Every night they had to tolerate being called every name in the book.

The dose of shit they had to endure was such that most of them didn't last a month. It was just more than they could take. Slick seemed to be tougher than most. He was into his second month.

While waiting for his Coke, Sanger looked back toward the rear of the parking lot. He could see the front end of a new Pontiac GTO. "The Country Club heros must be out on the prowl tonight," he thought.

As he continued looking, he thought he made out Jim Prince staring in his direction. Depending on how much beer Prince had thrown down, this could get interesting.

Sanger hoped the gang showed up soon. He knew that Prince would never start anything unless he had a bunch of friends with him. Judging from the number of guys in the back lot, the odds could go in Prince's favor in a hurry.

He should probably have gunned the old Ford to life and left, but if he did that, then Prince would have told everybody that he had scared Sanger off. That would have cost him his pride.

Being poor, white trash, he didn't have a lot of things to lose. His pride would not be sacrificed so easily. He may not have a lot of money, but he sure had a lot of pride! If Prince wanted that, he'd have to get it the hard way.

About that time, Slick showed up with the Coke.

"Here's yore pop, Jerry." Slick glanced toward the back of the lot as he passed the Coke.

"Thanks." Sanger took the drink and handed Slick 50 cents. "Keep the change."

"Thanks." Slick turned to walk away, but stopped and turned back around. "You'd better watch yo'self, Jerry. Them rich white boys over by that GTO keep givin' you bad looks. You hatten ought to hang roun' here by yo'self."

"Thanks for the warning, Slick." Sanger knew he had just received some good advice. "But the gang'll be back before long. I'll be alright."

No sooner than he got the words out of his mouth, he glanced over toward the GTO and saw Prince and his buddies moving in his direction. The most appropriate thing that came to mind was, "Oh, shit!"

"I'll stay and he'p you." Slick's voice was shaking.

"Don't worry 'bout it, Slick." Sanger tried to sound confident. "You know they won't do anything here. They'll want to go out in the country somewhere and circle up the cars for the big fight. By then, the rest of the gang will be here."

Sanger wasn't sure he believed his little speech himself. Oh, he knew the fight wouldn't be planned for the parking lot of the Ranch. Too close to where the cops hung out. What really worried him was whether or not his buddies would show before the motorcade headed for rural America. If they didn't, he could end up in deep stuff surrounded by Prince and all his cronies. If that happened and he kicked Prince's teeth in, then the friends would proceed to hurt him in numbers greater than one.

Sanger stepped out of his car just as Prince walked up. As Sanger expected, Prince wasn't alone. In addition to his usual moronic sidekicks, Sands and Merk, there were two others. That didn't count the crowd tagging along to watch.

"Come to see how the other half lives, Sanger?" Prince had a confident smirk plastered on his face. "Or did you get tired of being a nigger-lover and come seekin' forgiveness?"

It was obviously a Prince-type crowd. They roared with laughter in response to his racist humor.

78

"No, not really." Sanger lowered his voice and spoke very calmly in an articulate tone. "I came because I heard about the celebration."

"What celebration you talkin' about, asshole?" Prince almost spit the question out.

"Oh, you know, Prince." Sanger had activated his grin. "The celebration because your mama and daddy finally decided to get married."

Prince turned quickly to the crowd when a few snickers filtered out.

"You're real funny, Sanger." Prince had started talking before he was completely turned back. "But you'd better be careful. You ain't got nothin' in your hand tonight, and that white trash you call a gang ain't here to protect you."

Sanger held his hand up for Prince and the crowd to see. "If all I had in my hand was air, Prince, it'd be more than enough to handle a bigoted fool like you. Everything to you is black and white. Remove the word *nigger* from your vocabulary and you'd be mute. You're so stupid, you think money buys you class. The fact is, you have less class than anybody I know, and that includes every black person in this town."

"You nigger-lovin' piece of white trash." Prince yelled out in a very loud voice. "I'll kick the shit out of you like I would a lazy nigger. Let's go right now. If you ain't chicken, that is. Git in that beat up heap you call a car and follow me out to the Italian Club. I'll show you what class is."

Well, there it was—the challenge, and not a Coahoma Street Gang member in sight. It was once again decision time. If he went out in the country to the Italian Club, he knew what would happen. One way or another, he'd get the crap kicked out of him. If he didn't go, then everybody'd say he was scared and he'd lose his pride.

As Sanger thought it over, Prince stood a half step away with a smile on his face. Sanger knew what he was thinking. One way or another, Sanger would get his tonight.

Standing there looking at Prince with all the world watching, Sanger thought of something a guy had told him once. "If you're challenged to a fight," the guy had said, "you've got three options. First, you can hit the guy as hard as you can without given him any warnings. Second, you can pretend to be scared and turn away. Then, when his guard is relaxed, turn back around and hit him as hard as you can. Or third, you can turn and run as fast as you can."

Sanger decided for a variation of number two. Better to go to jail than end up being a punching bag for Prince's buddies.

"If that's the way you want it, Prince." Sanger scanned the crowd in search of a friend; there were none. "Then let's do it. I'll meet you at the Italian Club in ten minutes." Out of the corner of his eye, Sanger could see Slick violently shaking his head no.

Prince and his entourage turned to head back for their cars. Sanger took one step in their direction. "One thing first, Prince." Sanger had waited for him to start walking away.

"What is it?" Prince spoke to Sanger while turning. "You decide to chicken out?"

Sanger timed his kick to Prince's turn. Just as Prince turned to face him, he kicked young rich Mr. Prince as hard as he could right between the legs. With his family jewels suddenly propelled abruptly into the cavity occupied by his stomach, Prince hit the ground like 150 pounds of expensively dressed dog meat.

The crowd was taken completely by surprise. About the time they realized what had really happened and started to move toward Sanger, someone started yelling, "Cops, here come the cops, git out of here."

Sanger jumped into his car and turned the switch over. As he did, he furiously pumped the accelerator. He wanted to get the hell out of there before anyone figured out what was going on.

The engine caught and came to life with a roar. Everybody else was fighting to get to their cars. Pulling the gear lever into reverse, Sanger took the time to glance over at Slick. He was standing calmly against a post with a grin on his face. Sanger gave him the thumbs up sign. He knew the police weren't coming. Slick had been doing the hollering.

As soon as he got a block down the highway, Sanger turned right and headed into a section of what the Country Club boys called "niggertown." They'd never follow him in there. They didn't have the guts.

He slowed down as he headed into the black neighborhood. Running over some little kid playing in the street was not how he wanted to cap off his evening.

Wow, this was really his lucky night, Sanger thought to himself. First, Eloisa agreed to meet him; and now, he got to kick the ego out of Jim Prince and got away to boot. Maybe he should go shoot a little dice. Apparently, he was on a roll.

Sanger followed the street that he was on. It meandered its way north and finally intersected Fourth. He swung left on Fourth and made his way over to Coahoma Street. If any of the gang was there, he wanted to warn them just in case some of Prince's friends came looking for him.

He didn't really think that would happen, though. Prince and his friends were afraid to come to Coahoma Street. They liked for everything to be balanced in their favor before making a move.

Jim Prince found out tonight, however, the hard way, that even though everything seems to be going in your direction, circumstances can change in a hurry.

As soon as he made the right turn onto Coahoma Street, Sanger could see that most of the guys were sitting on the curb under the streetlight. Boy, did he have a story for them!

81

# *12*

S anger and Eloisa had been meeting on the rooftop of Eliza Prince School now for well over a month. After the second time they met there, the friendship really seemed to take off. Even though she was black and he was white, they were very much alike.

By now, they had spent endless hours talking about their families, their schools, music they liked, and countless other trivial subjects. They were as comfortable with each other as two teenagers ever had been.

Sanger heard the door to the little room open below. As always, he was a little scared until he knew for sure that it was Eloisa.

"Hi!" Eloisa said as she stepped from the ladder to the rooftop. "Been here long? Sorry I'm late tonight. Mama and Daddy got to watching something on television and were late coming down after supper."

"That's O.K." Sanger thought to himself how pretty she was. "I knew you'd be here as soon as you could. How'd your day go? Anything exciting happen?"

"No, it's been one of my typical boring days at the store." Eloisa did not try to hide the pleasure she felt at being there. "The only excitement we had was when two dogs started fighting over our garbage out back. How about you?"

"Same with me." Sanger looked into her eyes. "Load trucks; sort bottles; sell Cokes; take orders. Same as yesterday; same as tomorrow; just like it'll be next year this time. I don't think that job'll ever change if I work there fifty years like Dummy."

They continued to make small talk like that for another fifteen or twenty minutes before Eloisa changed the subject.

"Jerry, I'm curious. Why is it you're so dark? It's more than just a suntan, isn't it. I bet you stay dark year 'round, don't you?"

"I'll make a deal with you." Sanger laughed. "If you'll tell me why you're so light, I'll tell you why I'm so dark. Deal?"

All of a sudden, Eloisa got a very serious look on her face and seemed to drift away into deep thought.

"Hey, I was just kidding." Sanger realized he had unintentionally hit a hot button. "You don't have to tell me anything you don't want to. The reason I'm so dark is because I'm part Indian and part Mexican. Don't spread it around, though. People might begin to think I'm not a white boy anymore." He smiled to try and defuse the moment.

Sanger and Eloisa both laughed at what he had said. He knew he had stumbled upon a sensitive subject and was trying to soften the issue with humor.

"Now it's my turn, right?" Eloisa was looking at him.

"Not if you don't want it to be." Sanger knew he was on thin ice with this situation. "I'm sorry I asked. I didn't mean to put you on the spot. We can talk about something else if you want to."

"No, it's O.K." Eloisa had made the decision to tell him something important. "I think I'd like to tell you about it."

"Before my grandmother died three years ago, I was over at her house one day. As we were sorting through some old photographs, I asked her if she had any pictures of my grandpa. You see, I had never known him. I had always been told that he had died when my mother was very small.

84

My mother, I was told, was then raised as an only child, with my grandmother never remarrying.

"What my grandmother told me that afternoon shocked me so much that I've never been able to repeat it to another living soul. Grandma told me that not even my mother knew the real story.

"The only reason she told me was because she was dying and she knew it. She said that somehow the story must be preserved as part of our family's history and that she knew she could trust it to me. What I'm about to tell you no one else in the world knows, not even my mother.

"My grandmother told me that my grandfather had died twelve years earlier. She also told me that she and my grandfather had never been married. The true story was that my grandmother had actually worked for my grandfather as a housekeeper and nanny after his wife had died.

"You see, my grandfather was a white man.

"After my grandmother started working for my grandfather, they got closer and closer because she actually lived in the house with him and his little girl. Well, one thing led to another, and before either one of them could stop it, they had fallen in love. You can guess what happened next.

"Everyone just assumed that Grandma had gotten pregnant by some field hand. She made up a story about her lover being killed in a bar in Memphis. Nobody ever questioned it for a minute.

"After she had my mama, she kept on working for my grandpa until he died. My mama grew up knowing him as a very kind white man; but to this day, she still doesn't know the real truth. In his will, Grandpa left Grandma enough money to buy a little house and live comfortably for the rest of her life. No one thought anything of it since she had worked for him so long."

"Why do you think your grandma told you all this and not your mother?" Sanger looked at Eloisa in astonishment.

85

"I asked her that." Eloisa had tears in her eyes as she thought of her grandmother. "She told me that even though she loved my mama, she just couldn't take the chance that Grandpa's memory would be hurt.

"In twenty more years, it won't matter anymore. But right now, it's still too soon. She said that if she told Mama, there was the chance that Mama might try to talk to her half sister. If that happened, there was no telling what trouble would start.

"Grandma made me promise that I would never tell the truth to either my mama or my daddy. She said that it was my secret and that someday I would want to pass it along to my daughter.

"From the way she talked about my grandfather, I know that Grandma loved him very much. To have provided for her and Mama the way he did, even in death, I'd say he must have loved them a lot too."

Sanger was speechless. He couldn't believe the story he'd just been told. It was the strangest thing he had ever heard. He had heard rumors before of wealthy white men who had a white family and a black one, but he had never taken any of it seriously. Not till now, that is.

Sanger wanted so much to ask the obvious, but he just couldn't make himself do it. If she wanted him to know, she'd tell him.

Eloisa must have read his mind. "My grandfather was Chester Cotton; you know, the same guy that started the Princeville State Bank."

Sanger thought for a minute. "You mean to tell me that you and Jim Prince are first cousins?"

"More like half first cousins. That does make us kin, though."

"It would probably just make him mad." Sanger smiled at Eloisa. "I wonder if it would make him try to buy his beer somewhere else."

They both laughed and then just sat there looking at each other.

"You can trust your secret to me." Sanger was moved by her faith in him. "I'll never breathe a word of it to anybody. I promise."

"I know you won't." Her eyes were soft and still glistened with tears. "Even though I never knew my grandfather, I bet you're like him in a lot of ways. I'm sure Grandma would not mind me telling you about him."

As the two of them sat there looking into each other's eyes, Sanger could feel his stomach turn over inside. He was coming to realize that there was something really special about this light-skinned black girl. Something special indeed.

The way he felt when he was around her was unlike anything he had ever felt before. He thought he knew what it was he was feeling, but he just didn't have enough courage yet to admit it to himself.

"I'd better be going." Eloisa interrupted his thoughts. "The time has really passed quickly tonight."

"Yes, it really has." Sanger's mind had been far away. "What about Friday night? Can you make it?"

"You know I can." Her shy smile appeared. "I'll see you then."

To get back to the ladder, Eloisa had to pass close by Sanger. As she did, he reached over and kissed her softly on the cheek. Much to his delight, she didn't draw away. She smiled and looked at him.

"Thanks for trusting me." He held her eyes with his. "I'll never make you sorry."

As she started down the ladder, she looked back at him, "I know you won't."

# 13

Culligan left Coahoma Street a little after noon and headed over to Mississippi Street. It had been two days since he had discovered the Ruber girls in their backyard. He had wanted to go back and see them yesterday, but his father made him go to Tunica and work instead.

It was another miserably hot day. With it being almost August, it was the beginning of the hottest part of the summer. The temperatures were running a hundred degrees or better every day now.

Culligan had been soaked with sweat ever since he left home a few minutes earlier. He knew there was no need to try and fight the heat. It always won anyway. The best thing to do was just try and relax and hope for a little breeze.

Again he was sticking to the alleys in an attempt to avoid as much of the sun as possible. Approaching Mississippi Street, he repeated his trip of a couple days ago and headed right, down the alley that intersected the one he had followed over from Coahoma Street.

Before long, he once again found himself standing behind the outbuilding that sat in the rear of old man Ruber's backyard. As anxious as he was to see Alice and Janice again and ask them more questions, Culligan was still scared to go back in the yard. He sure didn't want to run into the old man back there.

Culligan got closer to the fence and listened. After a few seconds, he could hear the voices of the two girls as they played together in the backyard. He was still amazed at how much they sounded like small children.

Moving closer to the fence like he had done before, Culligan began to make noise as he swept the limbs and shrubs out of his way. The closer he got, the better he could understand what the girls were saying.

"I hear somethin'." Alice stopped playing and listened. "Somebody is in our bushes."

"I bet it's Will." By now, Janice had stopped and was listening. "'Member? He said he was comin' back to play with us."

"Will, are you tryin' to scare us?" Alice was straining to see beyond the fence. "We know it's you."

By that time, Culligan had once again worked himself through the tangled mess surrounding the Ruber's yard and was standing looking over the top of their fence.

"I'm not tryin' to scare y'all." Culligan was struggling to get his pants leg free from a thorn bush. "I'm just tryin' to get through these bushes in one piece."

Having figured out how to negotiate the fence on his previous visit, he made it over the fence very easily this time.

The two girls had on the same dresses that Culligan had seen them in the first time. Just as before, they were still very heavily made up.

"Why didn't you come play with us yesterday?" Janice had her lips puffed out in a pouting gesture. "We brought our dolls outside and everything."

"Yeah, we're mad at you." Alice was pouting too. "If you don't say you're sorry, we're not goin' to talk to you anymore."

"I'm sorry I didn't come yesterday. I wanted to, but my daddy made me go to work with him."

As Culligan talked to the Ruber girls, they stood very close together and giggled while he spoke. Neither seemed really mad at him. Instead, they both appeared very happy to see him.

"Our daddy makes us do things we don't want to do sometimes too." Alice looked at the ground in what appeared to be an embarrassed gesture.

"Yeah." Janice seemed more mad than embarrassed. "Daddy makes us take pills every mornin'. Then at night when he comes home from work, he makes us do other stuff."

"Well, my sisters have to take vitamins and do housework too." Culligan viewed the two with mild amusement on his face. "They're always complainin', just like you two."

His eyes wandered around the yard as he talked to the girls. It had two very large trees growing in it and very little else. There was almost no grass. What little there was seemed to be escaping into the yard from the opposite side of the fence. Other than that, there were a few sprigs that had sprung up here and there through the heat-baked dirt. "What a crummy looking place this is," he thought to himself.

"How old are y'all?" Culligan redirected his attention to the girls.

"I'm 18." Alice pointed her finger first at herself then at her sister. "And Janice is 17. How old are you?"

"I'm 17. Who takes care of you while your daddy's at work?"

"We take care of ourselves." Alice swung her arms as she talked. "We're big girls now. We can even come outside by ourselves."

"Do you go to school?"

"Naw." Janice had stopped swinging her arms and was now picking lint off her dress. "We never been to school. Daddy said he could teach us all we needed to know."

"What do you do all day while your daddy is at the factory workin'?" Culligan felt like he was talking to a couple of kindergarten kids.

"We watch TV." Janice watched her sister for approval as she answered the question. "And we fix lunch, and we do our chores, and now we come outside."

"What do you mean, now you come outside? Haven't you always been able to come outside?"

"Just since last week." Alice's voice had taken on a mischievous tone. "Before that, we always stayed inside like Daddy told us to."

"You mean that you've always stayed inside your whole lives?" Culligan stared at the girls in amazement. "Don't you have friends or relatives that you go see?"

"You're the only friend we've ever had." Janice smiled at him.

"What about the store? Does your daddy take you to the store with him when he goes?"

"We've never been to a store. Daddy just brings stuff home with him after work. We don't need no store."

"Let me get this straight." The two girls listened very intently. "You've never been to school. You never go visit friends or relatives. You never go to the store."

Alice and Janice stood watching Culligan talk. They just smiled and answered no to his questions.

"Then let me ask you one more question. Have either one of you ever been anywhere except your house or this yard?"

They both continued smiling as they shook their heads no in answer to his last question.

Culligan couldn't believe what he was hearing. Standing in front of him were two very pretty girls who had never been out of their house except for the backyard. This was unbelievable. What kind of father would raise his children in that fashion? The old man must be a real nut case.

Knowing what he knew now did make things a little easier to understand. For instance, take the way the girls looked. Alice was about five feet three inches tall and probably weighed 110 or 115 pounds.

Janice was just a shade taller and about the same weight. Both of them had kinda dirty, blond-colored hair. Their complexions were flawless and their figures would make any teenage boy's body turn to stone. That's where their resemblance to regular teenage girls ended, however.

Their dresses and their shoes looked old-fashioned to Culligan. Like something maybe you'd see in an old movie.

And the way they wore their hair. His best guess was that it was real long, but it was really hard to tell because they wore it on top of their heads in a bun like roll. It reminded him of the way his grandmother wore her hair. The only other young girls he had ever seen wear their hair like that were the Pentecostal girls, the "holy rollies." He knew it was some kind of religious thing with them.

The girls' makeup was probably the weirdest thing of all, though. At first glance, they both appeared to be heavily made up. But when you got up close to them, you could see that it was just their eyes that had makeup on them. The rest of their faces was plain. The girls' eyes looked like they had tried to copy the kind of makeup actresses wore on the TV shows—their eyes, anyway.

The best analogy Culligan could come up with was a coon, the furry kind with black circles around its eyes. Alice and Janice looked like two little girls who had been playing in their mama's cosmetics and ended up looking like a couple of blond-headed coons.

"Why do y'all want to come outside in this heat?" Culligan wanted to know more about these girls. "Why don't you just turn on the air conditioner and stay inside where it's cool and watch TV?"

"We don't have an air conditioner except in Daddy's room, and we're not allowed to turn it on while he's at work."

"Well, you could open the windows and at least run a fan or something." Culligan began to feel funny but didn't know exactly why.

"We do have a fan we run sometimes, but we can't open any windows. Daddy put nails in them so nobody could get in."

"Your daddy nailed the windows shut in the house!" Culligan began to form a mental image of the old man. "What about at night? How do you stay cool then? Does the air conditioner in your daddy's room cool y'all's room too?"

"Daddy keeps the door closed to his room at night." Alice's demeanor had become distant and inwardly directed. "Except when one of us is in there at night. Besides that, we don't ever feel the cold. Our room is real hot. We git real sweaty at night."

"What do you mean, when one of you is in there at night?" Culligan's gut did a flip-flop. "Does your daddy make you come into his room every night?"

"No, not every night." Janice was studying her feet intently. "Daddy checks one of us every Saturday night."

Culligan didn't like the sound of what he was hearing. If Alice and Janice were saying what he thought they were saying, then not only was old man Ruber a nut case, he was a really sicko to boot.

Culligan hesitated for a second, but he had to know the truth. "What do you mean, he checks one of you every Saturday night? What exactly does he check?"

"He checks to see how we're growin'." Janice talked but both girls looked at their feet.

With his suspicion peaked, Culligan asked the next question. "How does your daddy check to see how you're growin'?"

"He always does it the same way." Alice spoke in a voice barely above a whisper. "One of us has to go into his room and take off all our clothes. Then we git in bed with him.

"First, he feels all over us to make sure we're growin' O.K., then he pokes us with something sharp a bunch of times to check our insides.

"After he checks our insides, he always rolls over and goes to sleep. Then we git up and go back to our room."

Culligan felt like throwing up. He had heard stories about incest before, but up until now, they had just been stories. No wonder old man Ruber kept the girls shut up in the house all the time. If anyone ever found out what he was doing every Saturday night, they'd put him under the jailhouse.

That'd be too good for the bastard. Culligan felt the need to hit something. A better punishment would be one he heard about from an Italian friend of his.

It seemed the Italian friend had an uncle who got divorced from his wife. Well, it happened that the wife took the uncle's two daughters and went to live with her boyfriend. After a few months, the boyfriend got tired of mama and started giving his attention to the daughters, ages eight and nine.

Following being forced to have sex with the boyfriend, both girls told their father what had happened. After quelling his initial desire for immediate vengeance, their father proceeded to ask some friends of his for help.

Within a few days, the boyfriend found himself out in the woods with a couple of real gangster types. First, they took him deep into the woods where no one could hear him scream, and beat him unconscious.

While he was unconscious, they took a spike and, using a hammer, drove it through his penis into a stump. When he awoke, they were standing there laughing.

After making sure he was fully awake, they poured gasoline around the base of the stump. As one of them lit a cigarette, the other handed the child-abusing boyfriend a knife.

The first one flicked the cigarette to the ground at the base of the stump. The pervert child-abuser had a quick decision to make. Burn or cut himself free! All of a sudden, the silence of the woods was broken by shrill screams. Needless to say, the uncle never heard of the boyfriend again.

Culligan snapped out of his thoughts. Fantasizing about what ought to happen to Ruber wasn't going to help Alice and Janice.

"What do you think about your daddy checking one of you every Saturday night?" Culligan felt pity for these two unfortunate girls. Unfortunate because they had a nightmare life going on.

"We hate it." Alice's face was red and she was clinching her fists . "He's always drinkin' whiskey and he smells bad. It don't hurt anymore, but we still don't like to be checked."

"What do you mean, it don't hurt anymore?" Culligan could barely control his anger. "Did he used to hurt you?"

"When we wus little, it used to hurt real bad when Daddy checked us. Now it don't hurt anymore."

"Have you ever told your daddy that you didn't want to be checked anymore?"

"When we tell him that, he whups us with his belt. And when he's drinkin' a lot of whiskey; he gits his rifle out of the closet and says he's goin' to shoot us. He said two pulls on the trigger would put us out of our misery."

"What do you do when he gets like that?" Culligan had begun to visualize the scene in his mind.

"We run and hide in the closet in our room." Janice seemed to be doing some visualizing of her own. "Someday, we're goin' to git our own gun, and then he'll see."

"Yeah." Alice was even madder than her sister. "We saw on TV how to shoot a gun, and we ain't afraid to do it. Last Saturday, we said we wusn't gonna be checked anymore."

Looking at the faces of the two girls, he could see that in their infantile ways, they were very serious about what they had just told him. He didn't think they really knew how to shoot a gun, though. If they did, they would probably have already offed the old pervert.

"Do you girls know how to use a telephone?" Culligan was desperate for a way to help the girls.

"We call the man that tells you what time it is. Daddy taught us one time when we was little."

"If I wrote down a telephone number for you, could you hide it from your daddy?" Culligan's mind was racing. "Then when your daddy drinks whiskey and wants to check you, could one of you call the number on the telephone?"

"Who's number is it, Will? Is it yours?"

"Yes, it's mine. When your daddy tries to hurt either one of you again, call me and I'll come and help you."

Culligan asked Alice to get him a piece of paper and pencil from the house. Very carefully and in large numbers, he wrote down his telephone number.

"Now call me if you need help." Culligan was scared for the girls. "Remember that I'm your friend and that friends can help each other. I'm goin' to go home now. I'll come see you again on Monday. Do y'all understand?"

"We understand." They smiled at him. "We'll call if we need help."

Culligan climbed back over the fence and started working his way through the wild growth. The two girls stood and waved good-bye.

He had a lot to think about between now and tomorrow night. What would he do if the girls did call him? They could call as early as tomorrow night because today is Friday. Maybe he should tell the gang. At least tell Jerry. He'd probably know what to do.

Culligan headed back down the alley toward Coahoma Street. When Sanger showed up tonight, he was goin' to talk to him about the Ruber girls. If he told the rest of the guys, they might think he just made it up as a joke. He wished it were a joke—for the sake of Alice and Janice.

# 14

It was Saturday afternoon, and John Ruber was in a particularly bad mood. Usually he didn't have to work on Saturdays, but he had to this morning. It had been hotter than hell even at 7:00 this morning when he had punched in. The boss had made him come in and help tear down his milling machine for its preventive maintenance overhaul. It was bad enough a job when it was cool outside. On a hot day like today, it was pure misery. It had taken him an hour to wash off the grease and sweat when he got home.

For the past three hours, he had been hitting his bottle of cheap bourbon pretty hard. Even though it was only five o'clock, he was well on his way to drunken stupor.

Alice and Janice had been hiding in their room ever since the old man had started hitting the sauce. They hadn't seen him like this before. The drinking always meant at least a slapping around, and sometimes an out and out beating. With their childlike minds, they thought that if they hid in the closet, he wouldn't know where to find them.

By 9:00 that evening John Ruber was totally wasted by the cheap booze. He had finished one bottle and was well into the second.

The night was not shaping up well for the girls. Alice and Janice sat on the floor of their closet. The door was closed and they sat in the stifling hot darkness. Neither spoke for fear that their father would hear them and discover their hiding place.

Even with the ever present intense heat, the girls sat and hugged each other. For as long as they could remember, the only love and comfort they had ever received had come from each other. That comfort was more important to them now than the small relief from the heat that would have been gained by not having their bodies so close together.

As they sat quietly in the closet with only their fear to keep them company, the door to their bedroom opened. The girls could hear the squeak of the rusty hinge as it was pushed inward. Slowly, footsteps could be heard moving sluggishly across the room.

They knew instantly that he was in their room and was coming to the closet to get them.

Suddenly, the closet door was slung open violently!

"Whadya doin' in there?" Ruber yelled at the girls in his drunken brogue. "Git yore asses outta that closet and into the livin' room. I want some company while I watch TV.

"Come on. Git movin'!"

He reached in and grabbed Alice by the arm and jerked her into the bedroom. Next, he grabbed Janice and propelled her in the same direction as her sister. Ruber then proceeded to push and shove the girls toward the living room. "Go on. I said git in the livin' room."

Alice and Janice half ran and half stumbled into the living room. Their father was right behind them yelling obscenities and threats.

Ruber pushed the girls down on the battered sofa that sat against the front wall of the living room. He immediately slumped into an overstuffed chair by the door leading into the hall. He just sat there and stared at his two daughters. First, he would look at one, then the other.

"There's something different 'bout you girls." He sat up in the chair and leaned toward them. "I can't put my finger on it, but there's definitely something different about y'all. What y'all been up to lately? Been watchin' those sleazy soaps on TV agin?"

100

"We ain't been up to nothin', Daddy." Being the oldest, Alice had a tendency to always answer first. "We just been here like always."

"Yeah, Daddy." The fear in Janice's voice seemed to grip her by the throat. "We just been playin' like we always do."

As Alice and Janice were talking to their father, he was scrutinizing them from head to foot. All of a sudden, his eyes danced with anger.

"Alice, git over here where I can git a good look at you in the light."

Slowly, Alice got up off the old tattered sofa and made her way across the room to where her father was sitting.

"Here I am, Daddy. Whadya want with me?"

"Come closer, girl." Ruber was visibly angry. "I want to git a closer look at you. Gimme yore arm."

As Alice held her arm out to her father like he had ordered, he grabbed her roughly and pulled her onto his lap. Then he violently ripped the short sleeve off her dress.

"What's this?" He yelled as he examined her arm. "How did you git this suntan line on your arm? Have y'all been goin' outside while I've been at work? If you have, you'll be sorry!"

With a powerful backhand, he hit Alice in the mouth. Before she could be knocked away by the force of the blow, Ruber grabbed her with his other hand. "Let's see just how much time you've been spendin' outside."

Using both hands, he grabbed the front of Alice's dress and ripped it away from her body with all his strength. She was left standing in front of him in just her bra and panties. Standing there in front of her father with hardly any clothes on, tan lines were apparent on both her arms and legs.

Being as simple minded as the girls were, they had never even thought about the fact that they were tanning each afternoon when they went into

101

the backyard. Little did they know what a great price their tans would cost them.

Seeing the tan lines, Ruber hit Alice again in the face with his hand, knocking her to the worn wooden floor.

"What about you, Janice?" Ruber pointed at the other girl. "You been goin' outside, too? Git your ass over here!"

As Janice slowly walked over to where her father was sitting, Alice crawled back to the sofa. She didn't have the strength to get up off the floor where she had landed with the last blow.

When Janice was within reach of Ruber, he grabbed the front of her dress and ripped it from her body. Like her sister, she was left standing in her underwear.

"Look at those tan lines!" Ruber's face was red with rage. "You're just like your no-count sister. Just a couple of crazy bitches runnin' around, who knows where, against my orders."

To cap off his tirade, he hit Janice in the face, too. She landed in a sprawled-out position on the floor.

"Git back over by your sister on the sofa." He kicked at her with his left foot. "And don't either one of you move till I tell you to."

"But what about our clothes?" Alice had spoken from across the room. "We just got our underwear on."

"Forget your clothes! You're not goin' to need them tonight, anyway. When I finish this bottle, both of you are comin' into my room and git checked. It's time both of you got checked at the same time. One of you can watch me while I check the other."

Ruber turned his attention to the television set and to his bottle. Apparently using a glass was now too much trouble. He was drinking straight out of the bottle. As he continued drinking, he yelled at characters on the TV and cursed them repeatedly.

102

Alice and Janice sat huddled together on the old sofa and watched their father warily. Even though the heat was almost unbearable in the room, the two girls shivered in each other's arms.

By 10:00 the bottle was empty and Ruber was trying to get out of his chair. The effect of the liquor on him was very obvious. He could not stand without holding on to the wall.

"Hey, git yore skinny asses over here and help your old man to bed. Remember, I'm gonna check both of you tonight."

The girls were more afraid of their father tonight than they had ever been before. It wasn't the beating. He had given them both worse beatings in the past. It was what he had said about checking them both at the same time. He had never done that before. They were afraid because they didn't know what to expect.

Each of the girls got under one of their father's arms and helped him walk out into the hallway and down to his bedroom. Once in the room, he collapsed on the bed.

He raised himself just enough to reach the controls on the air conditioner. With the twisting of a knob, the air conditioner emitted a shudder and came to life. Within seconds it was blowing cool air into the room.

The girls stood at the end of the bed watching their father, not knowing what to do. They wanted to run back to their room and hide in the closet, but they were afraid of what their father would do to them.

Ruber had dozed off for a minute, but the cool air brought him back around. He rolled over on to his back and halfway sat up on the bed. "Take the rest of your clothes off!" They both just stood there looking at each other.

"Now!" His raised voice slurred the word.

Reluctantly, both girls took off their bras and panties. They were now standing in front of the bed completely naked.

103

Alice and Janice just stared at their father as he struggled out of his clothes. All the time he was wrestling with his shirt and pants, he kept mumbling about a couple of ungrateful bitches.

"Daddy, please don't check us anymore." Alice was pleading. "We're both big girls now. We don't need checkin' anymore to see how we're growin'."

"Yeah, Daddy." Janice had tears rolling down her face. "We don't need checkin' no more."

"Shut up, both of you!" Ruber began to look around the room like he had misplaced something. "I told you what I was goin' to do the next time y'all complained about this. Now you're gonna see that I was serious."

Ruber rolled over to the edge of the bed and tried to get up. All the cheap booze was making it very difficult for him to get his body to do what his mind said. "I'm gonna git my rifle and shoot you two ungrateful bitches."

Ruber was murmuring halfway under his breath. "I'm tired of being tied down by two idiots like you."

Ruber made another attempt to get off the bed. This time he made it to his feet. The only way he could remain in an upright position was to let the weight of his body rest against the wall.

The two girls had, in the meantime, backed away from the bed and closer to the bedroom door. Slowly they were inching their way out into the hallway.

Ruber had by this time worked his way over to the closet and was struggling with the knob in an attempt to get it open.

As the knob turned giving him entrance to the closet, Ruber looked over to where the girls were standing by the door. "Where the hell you two thank yore goin'? Git back in this damn room. I ain't through with y'all by a longshot."

As Ruber reached in the closet, the two girls ran out of the room and down the hall to their bedroom. When he pulled his hand back out of the closet, he was holding a .22-caliber semiauto rifle.

"I'll show those sluts who the boss is around here." He looked at the rifle as if he were speaking to it.

By now Alice and Janice had reached what they thought was the safety of their bedroom. They could hear their father yelling and shouting at them as they pulled the closet door shut behind themselves.

"I'm comin'." Ruber yelled at the top of his voice. "I know where you two retardos are hidin'. You can't fool me. I'll find you."

"I hear him comin'." Janice looked to her sister for help. "He's gonna shoot us with his rifle just like he said he wus gonna do. I'm scared, Alice."

"Don't worry. I'm the oldest and I'll take care of you. If he finds us here in the closet, we'll just push the door open real hard and run away."

"But where we gonna run?" Janice hugged her sister tighter. "He knows all our secret hidin' places."

"We'll run out in the backyard." Alice perked up a bit. "And call Will. Maybe he's even out in the yard now waitin' for us to come out and play. We can ask him to beat up Daddy for us."

The girls sat quietly in each other's arms and listened to their father as he went through the house looking for them. As he got closer to their place of refuge, the cursing and yelling got louder and louder.

Both of them knew that it wouldn't be long now.

Once again, just as they had earlier in the evening, the girls heard their bedroom door open. By the sound, however, they could tell it wasn't pushed open; it was kicked open. This time, though, they didn't remain seated on the floor of their closet.

"Here he comes." Alice's voice broke with fear. "Stand up and do what I do."

"I'm scared," whimpered Janice. "Daddy's real mad at us this time."

"And we're mad at him, too." Alice tried to comfort her sister with her tone. "He'll be sorry he tried to shoot us with his gun."

"I know y'all in that closet agin." Ruber laughed maniacally. "Come on out so as I can see you."

Alice and Janice remained perfectly still and quiet inside their hiding place.

"O.K., then I'm comin' in to git you. And when I git you, two pulls of this trigger is gonna end all my trouble. I told y'all not to question me agin, but you had to do it anyhow. Now you gonna be sorry!"

As Ruber put his hand on the doorknob to the girl's closet and twisted it open, Alice and Janice ran for it.

"Run!" Alice shouted to Janice just as their father opened the door to their hiding place. "Run!" Both girls pushed on the door at the same time with all their strength.

Ruber wasn't expecting any real resistance from the two girls. All their lives, they had done exactly as he had told them to do.

When the closet door flew open in his face, he was taken completely by surprise.

As Alice and Janice pushed the door, it hit their father with a lot of force. Enough force, in fact, to knock him backward into the room.

Because he was drunk, Ruber lost his footing and fell to the floor. The gun went sailing from his hand as he hit with a thud.

When the gun hit the floor, it discharged a round sending the bullet harmlessly into the ceiling.

The two girls were also on the floor, having landed there after their hasty exit from the closet. The momentum of their pushing the door had caused them to also lose their footing.

The thud made by Ruber when he fell was caused by his head hitting the floor before the rest of his body. He was now lying unconscious from the fall.

Alice and Janice jumped to their feet with a start when they heard the gunshot. Immediately, they tried to get away, but their father was between them and the door to the hallway.

"Daddy's in front of the door." Janice looked at her father the same way she would a rattlesnake. "How can we git out in the backyard now? He'll grab us by the leg when we run by him."

As Janice talked, Alice watched their father to see what he was going to do. When he didn't move, she cautiously moved closer.

"What are you doing?" Janice watched her sister move closer to the source of their lifelong torment. "He'll grab you if you git too close. You better stay over here by me."

"He's gone to sleep." Alice had bent over and was looking at her father's face. "Just like he always does when he's drankin' whiskey. He can't hurt us now."

"But he's sleepin' in our room." Janice wasn't convinced the threat was over. "What we gonna do?"

"Let's git the gun and shoot him like we saw on TV." Alice looked at the rifle on the floor. "Then when he wakes up in the morning, he'll be sorry he tried to shoot us."

"Yeah." A big smile had appeared on Janice's face. "That's what we said we wus gonna do next time he tried to check us."

Alice walked over to where the .22 rifle was laying on the floor. Very carefully, she bent forward and picked it up. She walked back over to where her sister was standing. "See, I know how to hold it!"

Pointing to the trigger guard, Alice said, "See this skinny thing inside here. That's the trigger. Remember, Daddy said that if he pulled it two times, it would put us out of our misery. That's all we have to do.

"Pull it two times."

"Will it kill Daddy if we shoot him?" Janice was intrigued. "I want him to go to the hospital and not come home again just like Mama did. Then we can go outside anytime we want to."

"I don't know." Alice was staring at the barrel of the gun. "On TV, sometimes it does, and sometimes it don't."

"Where'bouts do you think we ought to shoot him?" Janice was looking from their father to the gun and then back to him. "We could shoot him in the head like that naughty man did on TV to that girl."

"Yeah, let's shoot him in the head!" Alice moved closer to Ruber with the muzzle of the gun getting closer to him. "I'll shoot him first cause I'm the oldest; then you can have your turn. O.K.?"

Alice placed the barrel of the rifle awkwardly to the side of Ruber's head. As both girls giggled, she squeezed the trigger causing the gun to fire. The sound echoed through the bedroom. It sounded more like a firecracker than a gun.

"It's your turn just like I promised." Alice handed the gun to her sister.

"Thank you." Janice was smiling as she wrapped her hands around the weapon. She repeated what she had just witnessed her sister do. Once again, the gun fired and the two girls giggled.

# 15

This was the first Saturday night in a long time that Culligan hadn't been over on Coahoma Street hanging out with the gang. His mother thought he was sick. His father just thought he was probably waiting for some hot little number to call.

Neither of them was right. The reason he had stayed at home was because it was Saturday night and he knew that Alice and Janice would be having a hard time with their father tonight. He hoped that if things got too bad for them, one of the girls would remember the phone number he had given them and use it.

He hadn't been able to get them out of his mind since they told him yesterday about their father and what he did to one of them every Saturday night.

What a nightmare those two girls had been living for most of their lives. If they had been normal bright teenagers, this wouldn't be going on. They would have told somebody a long time ago and an end would have been put to it.

Unfortunately, they weren't normal girls; they were two physically mature young women on the outside and two ten-year-olds on the inside. Neither of them had a clue as to what their father was really doing to them every Saturday night.

They knew somehow they didn't like it, but they didn't know he wasn't supposed to be doing it to them. To them, his word was law. Whatever he said, they believed. Until they met Culligan, their father was the only contact they had with the outside world other than the television.

Culligan had been pacing around the house all night like a caged lion. He didn't know what to do. When he talked to Sanger the night before, Sanger had told him to talk to his father about what he knew.

Like Sanger had said, the police would never believe something that a member of the Coahoma Street Gang told them. They would, however, believe his father. Somebody had to blow the whistle on old man Ruber, the pervert. If they didn't, Alice and Janice would have to live the horror forever.

"Will." Mr. Culligan was looking at his son in a concerned manner. "What's wrong with you? You've been pacing around the house all night. Some girl stand you up or what?"

"Naw, it's nothin' like that, Daddy." Culligan glanced at the phone hoping it would ring but dreading what that meant.

"It's something else. I don't know if I should tell you or not."

"Are you in some kind of trouble, boy?" His father looked him in the eyes. "Or worse yet, have you gotten one of these little girls around here in trouble?"

"Naw, it's nothin' like that either, Daddy." Culligan was visibly wrestling with whether or not to talk about the girls. "It does have to do with some girls, though. Have you got time to talk about it for a few minutes?"

"If you've got trouble, then I've got time to talk about it. Let's go in the kitchen where we can talk in private."

Once in the kitchen, Culligan's father got a cup of coffee and lit a cigarette. Sitting down at the table, he motioned for his son to do the same. "O.K., let's hear it, Will. What kind of trouble are you talking about?"

"Do you know old man Ruber that lives over on Mississippi?" Culligan was stalling even though he knew the only way to help the girls was to tell his father.

Of course his father knew Ruber.

"Yeah, I know him." Mr. Culligan paused in thought and then started again. "At least I know what he looks like. I doubt anybody really knows him.

"He lives over there in that house all by hisself and don't mix with other folks much. Used to have a wife and a couple of daughters, but the wife died a long time ago and the girls ain't been seen in years. Most folks say he sent 'em off to live with relatives up North."

"Well, he's the problem." Culligan let out a kind of sigh.

"How could he be the problem?" Mr. Culligan had a questioning expression on his face. "You don't even know him, do you?"

"Naw, I don't know him. But I know his two daughters."

"How could you know his two daughters? They ain't lived 'round here in years." Mr. Culligan was trying hard to understand.

Will spent the next 15 minutes explaining to his father how he had met the Ruber girls and what they had told him. He also told his father his suspicions about Mr. Ruber and what he was doing to the girls every Saturday night.

"So, that's why you've been pacin' round the house all night." Mr. Culligan gave his son an understanding nod. "You think one of the Ruber girls might call and need your help.

"What you gonna do if they call and say they been havin' trouble with their daddy? You can't just go runnin' off over there. That old man'll put a shotgun on yore ass 'fore you git halfway up on the front porch!

"I know he will." The dejection was thick in Culligan's voice. "That's my problem. I want to help Alice and Janice, but I don't know what to do. I was kinda hopin' that you'd tell me what to do. Maybe we ought to call the cops or somethin'."

The ringing of the telephone on the wall by the stove interrupted their conversation. Culligan and his father stared at the phone and then at each other.

"Well, you gonna answer it boy or just stand there?"

Culligan hurried over to the ringing telephone. Almost out of breath from the effort, he grabbed the receiver and thrust it to his ear. "Hello!"

There was only silence on the other end of the line. Then Culligan thought he heard giggling in the background somewhere.

"Hello!" Culligan pulled the mouthpiece closer. "Alice, Janice. Is that you? Talk to me. It's O.K. It's me, Will."

"Hi, Will. It's me and Janice on the phone. Can you come over and play?"

"Does your daddy know that you're callin' me?" Culligan was speaking rapidly, afraid they might hang up. "Where is he? Is he at home?"

"Daddy's at home with us." As usual, it was Alice who answered. "But he don't care if you come over 'cause he's asleep."

"If I come over, he might wake up." Culligan took a breath in an attempt to slow down. "Then he'd be really mad at you girls."

"He ain't ever goin' to wake up." Alice seemed very cheerful. "He's gone to sleep forever just like our mama did. Now we can play whenever we want to."

"What do you mean, he's gone to sleep forever, like your mama did?" All of a sudden, bile charged up Culligan's throat forcing him to swallow.

By talking to Alice and Janice for several more minutes, Culligan was able to get the story out of them about what had happened over at their house that night.

"I'll be there in a few minutes," Culligan told the girls on the phone. "When you hear me knockin' on the front door, you come and open it. Don't go outside until I get there. O.K.?"

Culligan hung up the phone in disbelief. He looked at his father with bewilderment etched across his face.

"What's wrong, boy?" His father was shocked by the look on his son's face. "What did those girls say to you? You turned as white as an albino. What did they say?"

"They said they shot their daddy and he was lying on the floor of their bedroom. They want me to come over and play."

"They what?" Mr. Culligan's face turned its own shade of white. "They shot their daddy? They want you to come over and play? Don't those two girls realize what they've done?"

"No, Daddy, they don't. To them, it's probably some kind of game. We'd better get over there as quick as we can—before they decide to leave or something."

"First, I'm gonna call the police and tell them to meet us there." Mr. Culligan already had the phone out of the cradle and was bringing it to his ear.

"Neither one of us is goin' in that house lookin' for a dead man without the police with us! Go crank the car; I'll be right there."

As Mr. Culligan dialed the phone, Will ran toward the front door. Within five minutes, they were headed toward the Ruber's house.

The drive from the Culligan's house to the house on Mississippi took less than three minutes.

Culligan slammed on the brakes and slid to a halt in front of the dilapidated old structure. As he jumped out of the car, he could already hear the sound of a police siren as the patrol car rushed to join them.

His father stopped him before he could go any further.

"Wait here, boy. We ain't goin' nowhere until the police come. That way, they'll know for sure that we didn't have anything to do with killin' the old man."

The police car went into a slight spin as it made the turn off South Edwards onto Mississippi. It skidded sideways to a stop behind the Culligan's car.

Culligan recognized the cop as soon as he stepped out of the car. His name was Burt Fager. Culligan hadn't seen much of him since last summer.

Fager was your typical small town hick cop. Standing about five foot six inches tall, he suffered from some sort of Napoleon complex big-time.

The summer before he had tried to arrest Sanger for setting fire to the railroad tracks. Some black kids had told him they saw a tall, dark white boy do it.

Since it was in the neighborhood of the Coahoma Street Gang and since Sanger fit the general description, Officer Fager decided to haul him in.

Fager got really pissed off when he found out that Sanger had been at Culligan's house all afternoon and that Mrs. Culligan could verify it. He was very disappointed that he had the wrong person. He wanted very badly to throw Sanger in the back of the patrol car anyway. If it hadn't been for Mrs. Culligan, he would have.

She had threatened to call the Chief and complain about his behavior. He finally decided to leave, but not before telling the Coahoma Street Gang what he was going to do to them if they ever stepped over the line.

114

The rest of the summer and ever since, he cruised the neighborhood on a real regular basis.

Culligan was sure glad he hadn't gone in the Ruber house. Fager would probably have tried to blame the whole thing on him. What a jerk!

Just as Fager was climbing out of his car, another police car came screeching to a stop in front of the house. This one, however, wasn't a patrol car. It was an unmarked car used by one of the department's detectives.

The detective's name was Mitchell Roberts. Unlike Fager, he was a very friendly cop that all the gang liked. He had caught them doing little things a couple of times and let them go with a warning. He knew that basically they were all good kids living in a tough place.

Fager waited for Roberts on the curb.

"Hey, Burt." Roberts started speaking as he reached the curb. "What's goin' on here? I was over on Desoto when the call went out. Thought I'd better check it out since I was in the area."

"I don't know." Fager had spotted Culligan and was giving him a dirty look. "I just made it here myself. The dispatcher said to meet the man at this address regarding a possible shooting."

"O.K., you go around behind the house and check it out while I see who this is in front of the house."

Roberts moved away without waiting for Fager to respond.

"Culligan, is that you over there?" Roberts was squinting his eyes in an attempt to adjust to the darkness.

"Yessir, it's me, Mr. Roberts, and my daddy. We're the ones that called you."

Walking closer to the two, Roberts asked them to tell him what was going on.

115

"You gotta be shittin' me." Roberts examined Culligan's face as if searching for another explanation. "That sounds too damn weird to be true. We'd better try to get inside the house and see what's happened.

Mr. Culligan, you stay out here by the car. I want Will to go to the door with me. From what he's told me about the two girls, they probably won't let anybody in the house except him."

The wooden steps leading up on the porch of the old house creaked under the weight of the two of them as they made their way to the front door. Roberts knocked on the door with his knuckles. "Open the door. It's the police."

As the two of them stood in the dark outside the Ruber's front door, they could hear movement on the other side. The girls were there but not responding to Robert's demand.

"You try talkin' to them, Will." Roberts was whispering so the girls could not hear. "Since they called you, maybe they'll let you in."

"Alice, are you and Janice in there?" Culligan's voice was slightly raised but not angry. "Open the door. How can I come in to play if you won't open the door?"

Once again, Roberts and Culligan could hear sounds coming from the other side of the door.

"Will, who's that with you?" Alice had her mouth close to the door as she spoke. "You're supposed to be by yourself. We're scared of the police. We don't want to let them in."

"Let us come in the house, Alice, and I promise that the policeman won't hurt y'all. We just want to come in and visit for a little bit."

Slowly, the front door was eased open. Alice and Janice were standing just inside the house holding hands. They smiled shyly at Roberts and Culligan as they came in.

"Ask them where their father is," Roberts whispered into Culligan's ear.

116

"Show me where your father is." Culligan tried to smile at the girls. "Take us and show us where he's sleeping."

"He's in our bedroom." Janice looked at the detective. "Come on and we'll show you where it is."

Both girls turned and headed down the hallway. Roberts and Culligan followed.

"He's in there." Janice pointed a finger indicating a door on the left.

Before they could stop them, both girls walked directly into the room. Roberts and Culligan were right behind them. What they found was very shocking!

Mr. Ruber was lying on his back in the middle of the room. He didn't have any clothes on. Even a glance at the body was enough to tell that the old man was dead.

Around his head was a pool of dark red blood. It appeared to be draining from several holes and running along the grooves in the floor. The smell was sickening!

"There he is." Janice again pointed except this time it was at her father's body. "Sleeping just like we told you."

"Yeah." Alice shook her finger at the corpse the way a parent would do to a misbehaving child. "He won't bother us any more. Now we can do whatever we want to do. Come on in the livin' room, Will, and let's watch TV."

Culligan and Roberts just stared at each other in disbelief. It was painfully obvious to both of them that the two girls didn't have any idea as to what was really going on. They were in some sort of never-never land that had little to do with reality.

---

117

An hour later, Culligan stood silently by his father and watched as the two girls were led from the house to a police car parked on the curb. For Janice and Alice, their world was about to be turned upside down.

Roberts came walking over to where Culligan and his father were watching the two girls being put into the car.

He stood with the two of them as they watched the car doors close. "Culligan, I'll probably need to talk to you about this in a couple days. First, I want to spend some time with the girls and try to sort through all this confusion."

"What's gonna happen to Alice and Janice?" Culligan watched the patrol car pull away from the curb. "Will they be sent to jail or what?"

"It's hard to say just yet." Roberts' eyes followed the path of the car as it drove away. "But from what you've told me and from the physical evidence we've catalogued so far, I'd say they've got a good shot at self defense.

"I mean, it's hard to explain what the old man was doing in their room at night with no clothes on and a gun in his hand and not think something was a little screwed up about the guy.

"At most, I'd say they might have to spend a little time in the state mental hospital. Regardless, though, it's pretty obvious that they will end up spending the rest of their lives in some sort of institution.

"There's no way those two girls can ever lead normal lives. Old man Ruber closed the door on that possibility a long time ago."

# *16*

S anger was up on the roof of the school waiting for Eloisa.  Tonight he was a few minutes earlier than usual so he had plenty of time to think.

Ever since the last time on the roof when he had kissed Eloisa on the cheek, he couldn't think about anything except her.  It was as if her soul had taken possession of his mind.  Her image seemed to occupy every little crease and wrinkle.

When he was awake, he thought about her constantly.  When he was asleep, he dreamed about her.  He knew exactly what the problem was; he just didn't have the nerve to admit it to himself.

The truth that he knew in his heart would never be tolerated in Princeville, Mississippi.

A little after seven, Sanger heard what had by now become familiar footsteps as Eloisa started to climb the ladder below.  Soon she was climbing through the opening to the rooftop.

Usually when they were on the rooftop, the two of them sat a small distance apart as they talked.  The space had always been sort of an unwritten safety zone between them.  Eloisa had initiated the practice on the first night when they met at the school.  Thereafter, they had done the same because to have done any differently would have made both of them uncomfortable.

Tonight was somehow different, though. As soon as she climbed through the roof's opening, Eloisa moved over to where Sanger was sitting and sat down close by his side.

It was as if all of a sudden, whatever barrier that had existed between them was gone. No longer was there a white boy and a black girl up on the roof. Now there was simply a boy and a girl.

Color was no longer a consideration; friendship and their genuine affection for each other were the only things that mattered.

Each of them felt it, but neither talked about it.

"Hi," she said as she sat down. "Have you been here long?"

"I got here a little earlier tonight than usual." Sanger's smile was a nervous one. "I wanted to have a little time to think before you got here."

"I know what you mean." Eloisa searched his face for a clue to his meaning. "I came up here last night by myself for the same reason. I wonder if we were thinking about the same thing."

"In a way, I hope so; and in a way, I hope not." Sanger looked into her eyes, then quickly away.

"Why do you say that? What exactly were you thinking?"

"Well." Sanger knew he was moving into dangerous territory. "Mostly I've been thinking about you. No, that's not true; the only thing I've been thinking about is you.

"All day, all night; nothing but you. I even dream about you when I go to sleep. That's what I mean when I say in a way I hope so and in a way I hope not. I hope you're thinking about me too, but I know that if you are, then we're starting a long walk on a short pier.

"Princeville's not exactly the best place in the world for a white boy to fall in love with a black girl!"

Eloisa looked at Sanger in shock. She couldn't believe what she had just heard. "Love!" Her voice was soft. "Are you saying that you love me, Jerry?"

Sanger was just as shocked as Eloisa. He couldn't believe that he had said it, either. The words had just kind of slipped out. Sure, deep down he knew that he loved her; he just never figured he'd get up enough nerve to tell her. Now he had admitted it, not only to himself but to Eloisa as well.

Yeah, Jerry Sanger loves Eloisa Jones. So what? Whose concern was it other than theirs? He took her hand and looked into her eyes.

"Yes, I love you." Sanger's voice was barely louder than a whisper. "Ever since the first time I saw you, I've known that you were very special. After I kissed you last week, I realized that my feelings for you had turned to love.

"I'm sorry, Eloisa. I never intended for this to happen. I was attracted to you and just wanted to get to know you a little better. In my wildest dreams, I never figured it would be anything other than a good friendship. I guess I've really messed it up now, huh?"

"Telling a person that you love them doesn't mess anything up." Eloisa was smiling as she looked deeply into Sanger's eyes.

"Especially if the person you say it to happens to love you in return.

"All you've done is say out loud what each of us has been feeling for most of the summer. I'm glad that it's finally out in the open. Now at least we can talk about it and try to decide what we're going to do.

"It's not going to be as easy for us as the characters in my romance novels. We can't just walk off into the sunset holding hands and assume we'll live happily ever after. We've got to talk it through and try to sort out how we feel about things."

"Before we start talking through things," Sanger said, "could we do one other thing first?"

"What do you want to do first?"

"This." He gently took her into his arms. Drawing her further into his arms, he did what he had been wanting to do for a long time now.

He tenderly kissed her on the lips. "Declarations of love should always be sealed with a kiss." The nervousness was gone from his smile.

"You're right, maybe even with two." With that, she took his face in her hands and returned the kiss.

Five minutes later they decided that they had better stop before things got out of hand. Right now, they needed to talk. There would be time for the other later.

"What are we gonna do?" Eloisa was beginning to feel scared. "We're too involved with each other to just turn and walk away. But if we don't, we're asking for big trouble in this town."

"Turn and walk away from you?" Sanger raised his voice just a bit. "Never! They may drag me away, but I'll never go of my own free will."

"Then you think we're gonna have a lot of trouble, too, don't you?" Eloisa's voice cracked just a little.

"Maybe." Sanger tried to be strong. "But I'm free, white, and over eighteen, as they say. I can do whatever I please. If I want to be with you, then that's my business and yours. Nobody else has anything to say in the matter."

"You may be free, white, and over eighteen." Eloisa had turned the fear to anger. "But those rich white folks across town don't view you as one of them. To them, you're more like me.

"Sure, you're white, but they still treat you like a nigger. The only difference is that you're a WHITE NIGGER."

"Well, then." Sanger tried to defuse the moment with humor. "Maybe they wouldn't pay much attention to two niggers in love. I'll just keep this tan and maybe nobody will notice."

Eloisa and Sanger laughed at his joke before they both fell silent.

"I'm scared, Jerry." Eloisa's eyebrows arched. "It's not just the people in town I'm concerned with. What about our parents? They're not going to be real happy with the news! My daddy's gonna go crazy. He doesn't really like white people very much. I can't imagine him making an exception for you."

"You're right. I had completely forgotten about them. My mama and daddy are as bigoted as anybody else in this two-bit town. The thought of a black daughter-in-law won't exactly have them dancing in the street. A dead son would probably have more initial appeal to them."

"What are we gonna do? What are we gonna do?" As she put her head on Sanger's shoulder, he could see the tears starting to form in her eyes. It was almost more than he could bear. He had to figure something out. He couldn't stand to see her this sad and upset.

All of a sudden, it came to him. If this town and their parents wouldn't let them be together, then the answer was simple. They would just leave Princeville!

"Let me ask you a question." He sat up straighter. "Were you planning to go to college somewhere in the fall?"

Eloisa sat up in turn and looked Sanger in the eyes. When she saw that he was smiling, she smiled too. "Well, I hadn't really decided yet.

"My parents have been trying to talk me into going to Chicago and living with my aunt so I could go to the University of Chicago. They want me to go real bad, but I haven't decided yet.

"Why are you asking? Are you thinking what I think you are?"

123

"You know I am. If we can't be together in Princeville, then let's go someplace else. By the time anybody figures out what's going on, it won't matter anymore. We'll be together and nobody will be able to do anything about it."

"You're right." Eloisa's eyes began to dance as she considered what he had just said.

"I could agree to go to Chicago to college. If I did, I'd have to leave in a few weeks. Then you could go pretty much the same time. In a month, we would both be in Chicago—together."

"That's exactly what we could do." Sanger squirmed around some in his rooftop position. "I've saved most of the money I've made this summer so I could go to college myself in the fall. The University of Chicago sounds like a good school to me!

"But how will we find each other after we get there? I hear Chicago is a big place, and it's not like I can walk up to your aunt's house and knock on the door."

"You're right." Eloisa looked around as if the answer was somewhere on the roof. "Chicago is a big place. We need to figure out a place where we can get together. It has to be a place that is easy to find, otherwise we'll spend the first semester on campus trying to find each other."

"I know!" Sanger reached for her hand. "We can meet on campus. How about the student center? It's bound to have one. We just have to find it after we get there."

"That sounds easy enough." Eloisa felt his fingers find hers. "We'll meet at the student center one month from today. What time?"

"How about 4:00 in the afternoon?" Sanger's mind raced as he considered contingencies. "And if for some reason one of us can't make it that day, then we try again every day until we're both there."

"Yeah, every day at 4:00 until we're together." Eloisa felt like shouting for joy. "All we have to do now is get to Chicago."

"I wonder how your grandparents made it all those years without somebody finding out?" Sanger had never felt happier. "To love each other the way they did and not be able to even talk about it had to be very tough on them. I wonder why they didn't run off to Chicago or someplace themselves?"

"Grandma told me that they talked about leaving Princeville once, but they figured it would never work out. My grandpa had too much invested in the town to just up and leave. Besides, he had a daughter to think about. I don't think either one of them figured it would be good for her."

"Did your grandma talk much about the kind of problems she and your grandpa had?" Sanger felt the need to keep Eloisa talking so she wouldn't change her mind. "Wasn't there ever a time when they both had enough and just wanted to say to hell with the town and tell everybody the way it really was?"

"From what Grandma told me, I don't really think so. Even though I think that my grandpa was basically a good man, it wasn't the same way between them as it is with us.

"From what I can tell, he was a different type person than you. Just because he had fallen in love with a black woman didn't alter the way he felt about the overall social system in the South. He still believed that whites were superior to blacks. Even with a black woman as a lover and a black child, he would never have advocated equal treatment. His life was lived with an enormous double standard.

"Sure, he loved my grandma and my mother, but he loved the traditions and customs of the South more. If he had ever had to make a choice, there would have been no contest. Mama and Grandma would have lost."

"You're right about your grandpa and me being different. Regardless of the contest, I'd pick you every time. And if I thought I could change these crazy Southern traditions, I'd stay in Princeville and do it. But the reality is that we're just two teenage kids.

125

"Maybe someday we'll come back to this town when we're older. By then the people around here might listen and be willing to try and bring Princeville into the twentieth century. Until then, we have only one choice if we want to be together; we've got to leave."

"I don't think that I'll ever want to come back." Eloisa looked at the rooftop sadly. "And you shouldn't either. Twenty years from now, I'll still be a nigger to most of these people and you'll still be that white trash boy that grew up over in nigger-town.

We could come back with a million dollars and it wouldn't make a difference; we'd just be rich niggers. I doubt that either one of us will live long enough to ever see Princeville change. We'll be a lot better off somewhere else where the two of us can walk down the street together holding hands and not create a riot."

"You're probably right." The thoughts verbalized by Eloisa made Sanger sad. "Once we leave this place, we'll never be able to come back."

"Do you think your family will ever forgive you, Jerry? Do you think they will ever speak to us?"

"It'll take them a while, Eloisa, but eventually they'll come to accept it. They may not like it, but they'll learn to live with it, especially after they get to know you. It'll just take a little time; that's all. How about your folks?"

"Oh, they'll be about the same as yours. A little time and they'll come around. After all, I am their only child. They'll forgive me eventually."

"It's getting late." Sanger had just glanced at the watch on his left wrist. "We'd better go before your daddy comes lookin' for you."

"I forgot about the time." Eloisa repositioned her legs to get up. "We had better go. But before we do, we'd better decide what to do next. I think we should be even more careful about meeting than we have been. If we got caught now, it could really mess up our plans."

126

"I tell you what." Sanger realized he was still holding Eloisa's hand. "Let's meet two weeks from tonight. By then we should have been able to do enough so that we have an idea of what is going on.

"If we plan it right, then we won't have to meet again after that until we're both in Chicago. It'll be hard not seeing you every week like we're used to; but you're right, we shouldn't take any more chances now than we absolutely have to."

"Before we go, though, there is one other thing." She lit up with a mischievous grin. She reached over and put her face next to his. "I love you, Jerry. No matter what happens or how things turn out, I'll never stop loving you. Please hold me for just a minute before I leave."

"I love you, too, Eloisa. What we're gonna do isn't going to be the easiest thing in the world, but we'll make it. I don't care if it takes twenty years; I'll never give up until we're together. Two people that love each other ought to be able to be together without having to sneak around. We'll make it one way or another."

# *17*

Beth Prince was still in bed at noon the next day. That was her usual routine. She'd sleep until noon, have a shot of vodka to get her day going, and then crawl into a hot bath. By 2:00, she was almost always ready to face another day.

Today was no different. She did have to hurry a bit, though; she had an "appointment" she really needed to keep.

To hell with Jackson and his threats! She'd see anybody she wanted to see wherever she wanted to see them. She didn't give a damn what people thought. As a matter of fact, she kind of took pleasure in what people said behind her back. Her pleasure came from knowing that ultimately it always got back to Jackson and made him look like a fool to his asshole friends. It never really bothered her.

Everybody knew that the family money really came from her. And in Princeville, money was the only thing that really counted. If you had enough of it you could buy anything, even mock respect.

She didn't know which she needed more today, the hot bath or the shot of vodka. It was a real tossup.

Last night's session with Jackson had been one of the worst in a long time. It seemed that every one lately seemed to get worse and worse.

After he had left for the Club, she drank harder than usual, if that were possible. She had barely made it upstairs to her bedroom before passing out.

129

This afternoon she had to have the shot of vodka just to control the shakes long enough to get the bath water running.

Once she was in the steaming tub of water, she began to at least feel alive again. The bath and a couple more drinks would bring her fully to life and prepare her for another blissful day in paradise.

By the time Beth had finished her bath and dressed, she felt almost good. She was looking forward to her appointment this afternoon, especially after last night's session with Jackson. It wasn't so much the sex that she looked forward to as it was the humiliation that she knew her husband would suffer when one of his friends gave him the latest update on her love life.

Yeah, this afternoon was going to be real special. She could hardly wait to get started.

As Beth came down the stairs, Mary, their maid, was dusting the bottom of the banister. Mary was a good enough girl; she just never said much.

Beth figured that was because deep down inside Mary didn't really like her. Since Jackson hired her and paid her every week, Mary's loyalty was to him, not Beth.

Beth had considered firing Mary a couple of times just to make Jackson mad but had decided it would be too much trouble to find another nigger to take her place. After all, Mary came bright and early every morning and prepared breakfast before starting to clean. She also prepared supper in the evening before going home.

Having Mary working for them meant that Beth didn't have to do anything around the house. It was a good thing Jackson had his hired girl because Beth sure as hell didn't intend to ever do anything around there. Besides, that was what the blacks were good for. All her life, she had maids to take care of her.

"Would you like some lunch, Miss Beth?" Mary gave Beth a look as she came down the stairs that barely disguised the disgust she felt for her employer.

"Maybe just a sandwich and a Coca-Cola. Bring it into the den; I need to make a phone call." Beth barked the command much like she would tell the dog to fetch a newspaper.

As Mary walked back to the kitchen to prepare the lunch, Beth went to the den in the rear part of the house. She needed to call and make sure this afternoon's activities were still on.

Beth's first stop in the den was not the phone, however. It was the wet bar to the left of the door. She opened the overhead cabinet door and took down a highball glass. Next, she reached for the half-empty fifth of vodka sitting between the Jack Daniels and a fine French Cognac.

After twisting off the cap, she poured the glass three-fourths of the way full. Holding the glass with both hands, she lifted it to her lips and began to drink. She didn't stop until it was almost empty.

After "freshening" her drink, Beth sat down in the wingback chair by the phone. Picking the receiver up in her left hand, she dialed with the right.

"Hello, Frank? It's me. Can you still make it at three? You remember the place? O.K., I'll see you there."

Beth was smiling as she hung up the phone. With a big grin on her face, she downed her freshened drink   As she did, she held the glass up in a mock toast. "This one's for you, Jackson!"

Beth was still smiling to herself as Mary came into the room carrying the lunch on a tray.

"Here's your lunch, Miss Beth. Can I git you anything else before I do the upstair's cleaning?"

"No, Mary; that's all I need. Oh, by the way, I might be a little late getting home this afternoon so make sure Jim eats supper before he runs off tonight."

"Yes, ma'am, I sure will. Do you want me to tell Mr. Jackson anything when he comes home?"

131

"No, just tell him I said that I might be running a little bit late and for y'all to go ahead and start supper without me."

"Yes, ma'am, I'll tell him. If you don't want anything else, I need to get started upstairs now. You know how mad Mr. Jackson gits if he comes home and his bedroom ain't been cleaned yet."

"Yes, I know, Mary. You run along upstairs; I don't believe I need anything else."

Beth took her time eating her lunch. She didn't have to leave for about 30 minutes yet. It didn't really matter, though. Frank would wait if she were late. He'd be afraid not to.

Frank was afraid of Beth because she had money and he was just poor, white trash. She had met him one day when she took her Cadillac in to be repaired.

Frank was the mechanic who had done the work. Since it was going to take a while to do the job, the owner of the car dealership had told Frank to drive Mrs. Prince home. During the course of driving her home and then coming to get her again, Frank and Beth had the opportunity to talk and become friendly.

After two months of almost weekly problems with her car, Beth and Frank got to be fairly comfortable with each other. She saw in Frank an opportunity to humiliate Jackson in a big way. She knew that Jackson and his buddies put white trash like Frank in the same category as niggers.

If word got around that she was sleeping with one of them, Jackson would be so embarrassed that it would cause him to lose all face with the people around town.

Beth didn't really care what the people thought of her anyway. As soon as Jim graduated from high school next spring, she was going to force Jackson to buy her 50% of the bank and she was heading for California.

Once there, she'd have enough money to start over and do whatever she wanted. She knew, though, that Jackson would never leave Princeville. Regardless of the shame he had to endure, he would always stay. After all, he was a Prince.

In his mind, Princeville was his town. He would stay there until he died!

She had set the hook in Frank one Friday night when Jackson was in Memphis and Jim was visiting a friend over at Ole Miss.

She called Frank's boss at home and told him that her car would not start. She made up a story about having to go out of town and needing the car fixed right away. Could he please send Frank over to check out the problem. She said that it was such an emergency she was more than willing to pay the triple overtime.

Within thirty minutes, Frank was knocking at her door. "Hello, Mrs. Prince." Frank held his hat in his hand as Beth opened the door.

"What's this Mrs. Prince stuff, Frank? I thought we were friends."

"Oh, we are Be . . . Beth. I just didn't want Mr. Prince to think I was being uppity or anything."

"Don't you worry about Mr. Prince or anybody else tonight, Frank. He and my son, Jim, are both gone until Sunday. I'm the only one here tonight."

As Beth spoke, Frank could not help but notice that she wasn't wearing a bra. "The boss said you had a problem with your car and that you needed it fixed right away. What's wrong with it?"

"Nothing, nothing at all." Beth was eyeing Frank much the same way a cat eyes a mouse right before pouncing. "Haven't you figured out yet why I've been having so many problems with my car the last couple of months? Don't you know it was just so I could see you."

"But Beth, I'm a married man. I've got a wife and a house full of kids on the other side of town."

"So what! I'm a married woman and I've got a husband and a son on this side of town. I don't want to marry you; I just want to enjoy a little of your company. Besides, being friends with me could have real advantages."

"Advantages, what do you mean?" Frank was looking at Beth curiously.

"Well, like for instance that shop of your own that you've always wanted. Remember telling me about that?"

"Yeah, but that's just a dream. I'd never get a bank to loan me enough money to start my own business. Nothing that I have is worth enough to be collateral for that kind of money."

"Like I said, being friends with me could have its advantages! You seem to have forgotten that my daddy started the Princeville State Bank. I can get you a loan for whatever amount of money that you need."

"But why would you do that for somebody like me?"

"I wouldn't do it for somebody like you." Beth's smile grew from ear to ear. "But I'd do it for a friend."

By the time Frank left two hours later, Beth and he were the best of friends.

It had been about three months since the friendship had been consummated. Since that time, Beth and Frank had only been together a couple of times. She wanted to be sure the time was right before letting Jackson find out.

Beth took her time getting downtown. She wanted to make sure that as many people as possible saw her.

She had been insistent with Frank that they meet at the Uptowner Inn. It was only a few blocks down the street from their bank.

134

She had convinced him that no one would think anything about seeing her car and his truck there. After all, it was a popular meeting place for people in town.

Frank had told Mildred at the front desk that he needed a room for a friend of his who was coming in late that night. He told her that he would just go ahead and pay in advance and take the key. That way his friend wouldn't be bothered. He'd have his friend leave the key in the room in the morning.

Mildred gave him the key to room 120.

Mildred may have been born at night, but she prided herself on the fact that she wasn't born last night. She decided she would see just who Mr. Frank Wilkerson's friend was.

Frank tried to be casual as he got into his truck. He drove around the block once, then parked across the street from the side entrance to the section of the Uptowner where the rooms were.

He hoped that nobody would pay any attention to his truck. Seeing a service truck downtown that time of the afternoon wasn't really all that unusual.

He was really nervous about this whole thing. Even though Beth was still a nice-looking woman, she sure wasn't worth this kind of risk! If it wasn't for the fact that she had helped him get the money to start his garage, he would already have blown her off.

What if his wife found out; or even worse, what if Jackson Prince found out? He could handle his wife, but he wasn't sure about Mr. Prince.

Frank knew that Jackson Prince could wipe him out with one stroke of his powerful pen. All he had to do was find a way to call in the note on the business.

Even if it weren't legal, what could Frank do? Prince saw the lawyers and the judges out at the Country Club every night. They'd go through white trash like him in a New York second. He wouldn't stand a chance.

This had to be the last time with Beth; he had to find a way of killing this relationship before anybody found out.

The only problem was how to do it and not piss her off so bad that she would cause him trouble. There had to be a way and he had to find it.

As Frank walked through the side gate, he spotted Beth sitting in her car. The stupid bitch had parked in one of the spaces directly in front of the rooms.

She was either crazy or she didn't really give a shit.

Frank walked as directly and as quickly to room 120 as his legs would allow. He quickly put the key in the lock and let himself in.

A minute later Beth knocked on the door. Frank hurriedly opened the door and let her in.

All of this secret activity was not going unobserved, however. Mildred had gone to the back door that led out back to the rooms as soon as Frank had left through the front. She saw the whole thing.

"Well!" She thought to herself. "What do you think about that? One of Princeville's elite ladies slipping around to sleep with white trash." She couldn't wait to tell somebody!

"Beth, this is crazy." Frank raised his hands to make the point. "What if somebody saw us? What if Mildred didn't believe my story about a friend coming to town? We could end up in deep shit, especially if your husband sees your Cadillac sitting out there.

"Hell, if I didn't know better, I'd think you wanted people to know."

"Calm down, Frank. Nobody's going to pay any attention to my car. It's not exactly the only Cadillac in town.

"Besides, I don't really care. All people can do is talk and they're going to do that regardless of what we do. Let's quit wasting time and start having a little fun. We don't have all afternoon!"

"Whadya mean, you don't really care?" Frank's face had turned a deep shade of red in anger. "You may not care, but I sure the hell do! I got a wife and kids to think about. This ain't some game to me."

"Game? Sure this is a game, Frank. It's the latest edition of who's doing whom in Princeville. This week's show is featuring Princeville's elite humping poor, white trash. Be sure and stay tuned for the final results!"

"So that's what this has been about! You bitch. You highbrow, debutante bitch. You just wanted to be the first one on the hill to hump some poor, white trash fool. How did it work? Did you and your bitch friends have a pool or something going? The prize must've been big time considering the money you invested in me."

"Oh, you poor, dumb boy. Do you really think this was for the benefit of my friends? It wasn't! It was for the benefit of that lowlife husband of mine. I wanted to shame him as much as possible. What better way than sleeping with somebody he puts in the same class as niggers?"

"You slut! I oughtta beat the shit out of you. I'd love to see your slimy body floating in the Sunflower River with the rest of the crap."

"Remember who you are, boy, before you get so brave." Beth punched a manicured finger into his chest. "I can have you doing time on the county farm before the sun goes down. One word from me and times will get real hard for you in Princeville.

"You'd better leave now! Oh, and don't worry. Just to show you how grateful I am for all your help with Jackson, I'm going to let you keep your greasy little garage." Her maniacal laugh filled the small motel room.

"Beth, you can't play games like this with people. One of these days, you're going to have to pay. Everybody eventually does. In your case, though, it might be real soon."

Beth was sitting on the bed laughing as Frank walked out the door. "His kind just doesn't understand how low on the totem pole they really are," she thought.

Beth got up and left the motel room. Her destination was the Uptowner Bar. She needed a couple of drinks before heading home.

# 18

It was 3:00 in the afternoon and 105 degrees on the loading dock. Sanger had been completely soaked with sweat since early in the morning.

Since the dock faced east, mornings were usually hotter than afternoons. Until about 12:30 every day, the sun came beating down directly on Sanger and the other men loading the trucks. After that, the heat went from being unbearable to just plain hotter than hell.

It was now in the hotter-than-hell period, and Sanger was taking his third salt tablet of the day. As he washed it down with a drink of water Martin, the Plant manager, walked up.

"Hot out on the dock today, huh, Jerry. How'd you like a little break?"

"I'd pay you for a break." Sanger wiped his mouth with the back of his hand. "We're on our seventh truck and we've still got three to go. We'll be lucky to get through by 7:00 tonight. Look at me! I look like I've been in a swimming pool with all my clothes on."

"Please give me a break!" Sanger held his hands together jokingly in a mock begging gesture.

"O.K., O.K. I get the message." Martin laughed. "I'll give you a break. I need somebody to run 20 cases of drinks out to the Country Club. They're running short and the route truck doesn't work them until day after tomorrow.

"Here's a list of what they need. Throw them on the flatbed and run them out there. The drive should help cool you off a little bit."

"Well, that wasn't exactly the kind of break I had in mind." Sanger's tone turned sarcastic. "But it beats nothing. Thanks!"

It took Sanger about 30 minutes to get the 20 cases of soft drinks loaded on the flatbed truck and ready to go. The only cool part of the job would be the drive to the Country Club and back. And that part wasn't really cool. It was just that he could roll down the windows in the truck and get a breeze blowing over his wet clothing as he drove. It wasn't air conditioning, but it was the closest he was likely to get to it before he went home tonight.

As he was pulling away from the loading dock, Martin came through the Plant and waved at him to wait. "Jerry, be sure and take the truck around back when you get to the Club. They won't allow you to unload the drinks in the front. They specifically told me to have my boy bring the cases in through the back door of the kitchen. The only nonmembers they allow in the front are guests and waiters. As dirty and sweaty as you are today, they'd raise holy hell if you got one of their sofas or something dirty."

"Sure thing, Martin," Sanger answered with the trace of a grin starting to form on his face. "I sure wouldn't want to offend the folks out on Nob Hill.

"It'd be mighty distressing for them, I'm sure, if they had to look at somebody all dirty from an honest day's work. It might cause them to have nightmares about the times back when their ancestors had to work for a living!"

"Just take the drinks to the back, Jerry, and spare me the social commentary."

"Sho boss." Sanger's movements were those mimicking a slave. "I's sho gwine take the dranks to the master's backdough. Us won't offend him; us gwine be a good boy. Yi sir, us be a good nigger."

Sanger glanced in the rearview mirror as he pulled the truck away from the loading dock. Martin was looking at him and shaking his head from side to side in bewilderment.

"Just a couple more weeks of this torment and I'm history." Sanger shifted gears in the truck and pulled out onto Fourth Street without stopping.

As he clutched the truck and tried to shift to fourth gear, he missed and the transmission started to make a grinding noise. After accusing it of having sex with its mother and shifting again, he managed to get it in to fourth gear.

"Away I go." He spoke out loud. "Away to the land of the rich and famous. How much luckier could a guy be?"

The Country Club was located about three miles north of town on Friar's Point Road. Sanger figured that if he drove slowly enough, it would take him ten or fifteen minutes to get there.

He wasn't really in a big hurry. The longer he stayed gone, the more time he'd have to cool off before hitting the loading of the trucks again. Besides, he needed to stay gone at least long enough for Martin to forget his smartass remarks. Someday, he knew his big mouth was gonna get him in a lot of trouble.

After turning onto Desoto Street and driving under the viaduct, the harsh sun was suddenly cut off by the branches of the towering oaks that lined the street for the next few blocks. Sanger slowed the truck down a little to enjoy the temporary respite from the sun's intense heat.

Within a few blocks he started down a steep hill that marked the northern boundary of town.

If you were to park and walk down the hill away from the street, you'd come to a large culvert about five feet in diameter. It connected the local power plant to a drainage ditch. Its purpose and function was to recycle large volumes of water that the power plant used for cooling purposes in its generation of electricity. The culvert did, however, have a secondary purpose.

When Sanger had been younger, he and the gang used to come through the woods to the culvert when it was real hot like today. Because the area around the culvert was heavily wooded, it couldn't be seen from the road. That made it perfect for their purposes.

When the power plant discharged the water, it came through the culvert with a great amount of pressure and speed. As the culvert came out of the hill, it changed from one of five-foot diameter to a half culvert without a top. Without a top, the discharging water rushing through the half culvert took on the appearance of a rushing, thundering river.

To cool off in the heat of summer, the gang would lower themselves into the culvert and lay flat on their backs. When they did, the torrent of water rushing downhill would carry them toward the drainage ditch at a heart-pounding rate of speed.

Sanger couldn't help but laugh as he thought about the good times he had there. He could also remember all the times the cops had run them off.

Cops, though, weren't the only problem at the culvert. One of the really big problems was what the concrete culvert did to the skin on your butt as the water dragged you roughly through it. That particular part of the experience was the namesake for the spot. All the gang called the culvert "Redass."

To battle a case of the Redass, the guys in the gang would take a burlap bag and tie it to their butt much like a diaper. If you tied it on correctly, each trip down Redass took off a layer of burlap as opposed to a layer of ass.

The second big problem to be dealt with each trip down Redass was how to stop yourself before the water dumped you into the drainage ditch. The drainage ditch wasn't really the big problem, though. The big problem was the growth of bushes and thorns that the water passed through before falling the foot or so into the ditch.

To remedy this painful encounter, a log of small diameter was placed across the culvert at the end next to the ditch. When the gang member came rushing toward the end, he would simply reach up with both hands, grab the log, and swing himself up over the edge of the culvert.

Needless to say, Sanger had missed the log a few times and then had to be fished out of the drainage ditch.

"Yes," Sanger thought as he steered the flatbed down the hill and away from Redass. "There were some things in Princeville besides that culvert that could give you a bad case of the redass." He was headed for one of them right now.

Within a couple of minutes, he was braking to a stop at the intersection of Friar's Point Road. Before turning right into the intersection, he looked to the left for on-coming traffic.

As he did, he caught sight of the Jewish Cemetery back toward town and across the road. He'd often wondered why they had their own graveyard instead of using the same one as all the other white people in town.

He figured it had something to do with their religion. Or maybe it was because they didn't want to be planted in the ground next to some redneck who had made fun of them their whole life.

All the Jews that Sanger could think of had a lot of money. At least he thought they all had money. They weren't part of the top layer of Southern society, though. The money could never buy them that position. They were mostly merchants by trade. He could think of maybe one lawyer and one doctor; all the others owned one type of store or another.

For your average redneck citizen, the Jew fell in the social order somewhere between the nigger and the China man. They hated niggers most of all; then they hated Jews next worst, followed closely by China men.

If you were white (even poor, white trash) at least you could still look down your nose at niggers, chinks, and Jews. Damn it was great to be white in Mississippi! It was so great that Sanger could hardly wait to get out. He longed for a place where a person was measured according to personal worth and nothing else.

He turned the truck right onto Friar's Point Road and once again made the transmission grind. Maybe he just wasn't cut out to be a truck driver.

The Country Club was only about another mile down the road. Pretty soon Sanger saw the entrance up ahead on the left-hand side of the road. Turning the steering wheel to swing the truck into the large circular drive, he gazed at the ultimate symbol for power and elitism in his hometown, the Princeville Country Club.

The building itself was magnificent. It had huge white columns that supported the roof in a most stately manner. The remainder was fashioned from red brick and reminded him immediately of a very large and expensive plantation home.

In front of the building were several tennis courts surrounded by green mesh wind screens. Adjacent to the courts and embracing the Club on both sides were lush green lawns shaded by large magnolia trees. It looked like something out of a movie about the old South.

Sanger knew that the back of the Club was surrounded by equally lush golf greens and fairways. There was also a very large swimming pool to keep the members cool.

He laughed as he tried to picture the wealthy clientele of the Princeville Country Club shooting through the culvert at Redass.

His first inclination was to stop at the front door and take the drinks in through the main lobby. He fought that urge, however, and continued to drive around back to the kitchen door.

Grinding the gears again, he pulled the truck past the back door, then put it in reverse and backed as close to the kitchen as he could get. He could smell the food as he climbed out of the truck.

Fighting back hunger pangs, he walked into the kitchen.

"Hey." Sanger raised his voice to get the attention of one of the cooks. "Where do you want the Cokes?"

"Take them to the snack bar out by the pool." The cook turned a steak over on the grill as he responded.

"This is really great." Sanger murmured to himself. "First I got to come around back; now I got to hump these suckers all the way out to the pool."

Sanger pulled the two-wheeled dolly off the truck and on to the ground. He then proceeded to stack four cases of drinks on it. With the dolly fully loaded, he started rolling the drinks toward the pool area.

The pool was about 50 yards from the parking area. Lucky for Sanger, there was a sidewalk all the way for him to roll the drinks on.

He could see that the pool was really packed today. Probably stay that way until the weather cooled down some.

When he got closer, he could see that there were several of his classmates lounging around. No doubt working on their tans and preparing mentally to go to Ole Miss in the fall and spend some more of daddy's money.

"Hi, Jerry." Sanger heard his name called as he rolled the two-wheeler up to the snack bar.

Sanger scanned the row of lounge chairs for the source of the greeting. Finally, he saw her. It was Marty Black, an old girlfriend of his.

She was shading her eyes with one hand and waving at him with the other. From his vantage point, he couldn't tell if the smile on her face was friendly or conniving.

It was probably friendly, he concluded; she was basically a nice kid. Their biggest problem hadn't been between them. Instead it had to do with the distance from his side of town to hers; not the miles, the social gulf.

145

"Hi, Marty. How's the tan coming along?"

"Great." Marty adjusted the top of her swimming suit as she sat up. "How's your summer been going? I haven't seen you around very much. Where've you been keeping yourself?"

"Mostly, I've just been working and hanging around on Coahoma Street. Since I graduated, I have to pay my own way now.

"The working takes most of my time. What have you been up to?"

Sanger knew the answer to that question before he asked it. Like everybody else sitting around the Club pool, her biggest problem every day was deciding what time the sun would be out and which swimsuit to wear. Beyond that and making sure her tan was even, she had probably been up to little else.

"Oh, I've just been lying around the pool and going out to the Ranch now and then." She reached for the suntan lotion and started to apply it to her chest. "Why don't you meet me at the Ranch some time; we could talk about old times!"

"Sure." Sanger couldn't help but glance at her chest. "I'll watch for you.

"Don't work too hard." She added the comment as kind of an afterthought.

"Oh, I won't, and don't you get too much sun. And by the way, be sure and tell your mama and daddy that I asked about them!"

Sanger sent his most sarcastic grin her way.

Marty just smiled as she put the lotion down and rolled over onto her stomach to give the sun a chance at her backside.

Nobody else spoke to Sanger during the next twenty minutes as he made several trips to and from the pool bringing the rest of the drinks. Although he encountered several other people that he knew, they just looked through him without speaking, the way you would a servant or some undesirable you chanced to encounter on the street.

Finally, he was through. With a grunt, he lifted the two-wheeler and threw it into the back of the truck. Exhausted and still very sweaty, he climbed behind the wheel of the flatbed and headed back toward the Plant. Not exactly the relaxing break he had hoped for, but at least it was a change of pace from his usually boring routine.

In ten minutes, Sanger was rolling through the Desoto Street viaduct and back under the railroad tracks.

"My side of town where I belong." The thought passed through his mind as he peered through the windshield at the railroad tracks.

A few minutes later, as he turned off Fourth into the Plant's gravel drive, his most recent case of the redass was starting to clear up.

# *19*

It was another hot day in Princeville and Culligan was once again sitting on the curb under the streetlight in the middle of the afternoon. As had been his habit lately, he was thinking about Alice and Janice.

Since the night they shot their daddy, he had spent a lot of time thinking about them. He had even been to see them several times in jail.

Mr. Roberts had seen to it that they weren't locked up with the rest of the female prisoners. They were being kept in a separate part of the building in just a room.

The Princeville City Jail wasn't exactly set up for situations like theirs. Mr. Roberts had convinced the Chief that it would be a lot smarter to keep them isolated.

He had a couple of cots moved into the room and some spare furniture. He had even brought a television set from his own home for them to watch.

In a lot of ways, it wasn't that much different from the way they had always lived. As a matter of fact, they had seemed very happy and content each time that Culligan had visited them. To them, they had all the comforts of home and didn't have to put up with the tirades of their father any longer.

Since the shooting, the local newspaper had published three or four different articles about the Ruber girls and what had happened to them.

From reading the paper, Culligan knew today was the day the Grand Jury met and heard the case. After they listened to all the evidence and considered the circumstances, a decision would be made concerning whether or not to indict the girls.

Culligan had given a sworn statement about his involvement with the girls and what he knew about the killing. After going down to the police station and doing that, he had no further official involvement.

Mr. Roberts had left orders with the jailers that Culligan could visit the girls whenever he wanted. When he hadn't been working, he had gone to see them every afternoon.

Today, he was really nervous, though. The girl's fate was resting in the hands of the Grand Jury. Whatever they decided would impact Alice and Janice for the rest of their lives.

He sure hoped the girls wouldn't be sent to prison. They'd never survive the Mississippi State Penitentiary.

Culligan had been sitting on the curb for a couple of hours now. He was waiting on word about what had been decided. Mr. Roberts had promised to come by and let him know as soon as it was over.

Sitting there in the heat, Culligan was sweating like a bastard at a family reunion. It didn't matter to him, though. He'd sit there as long as he had to. The only thing that really mattered was Janice and Alice.

Even though he couldn't do anything about it, he was still worried. For some strange reason, the two girls had taken on real importance in his life. In a way, he felt responsibility for them and their fate.

Deep down, he knew that they didn't have anybody else. If they had any other family, they sure hadn't shown their faces during the whole process so far.

Whatever family there was had obviously decided not to get involved in the mess. Their family now was just Culligan and the State of Mississippi.

Considering what the state would do for them, Culligan knew that, in reality, he was it. Nobody else really cared anything about them.

Culligan was jolted back out of his thoughts by the sound of an approaching car. When he looked up, he saw Mr. Roberts' car slowing down and pulling over to the curb.

He knew this was it. The Grand Jury had made its decision. Culligan was about to hear the fate of the Ruber girls. Hopefully, what he was about to hear wouldn't be too awfully bad.

Roberts honked the horn lightly and motioned for Culligan to get in the car. Very quickly, he was standing and moving around to the passenger's side of the vehicle. Opening the door as fast as he could, he immediately started talking.

"What did they do? What's gonna happen to Alice and Janice? They going to prison? What's gonna happen to them?"

"Just calm down, Will." Roberts looked at Culligan patiently and used a soft voice. "I'm going to tell you everything I know. Just give me time!"

"I'm sorry, Mr. Roberts. It's just that I'm anxious to know what happened. I been sitting here most of the day worrying about them."

"Well, you can quit worrying." Roberts had a happy expression on his face. "The girls aren't going to prison. They aren't even going to trial. The Grand Jury decided that they acted in self defense."

"You mean that nothing's gonna happen to them." Culligan visibly relaxed his body. "They're free to go. They don't have to go to jail or nuttin'?"

"I didn't say that." Roberts' demeanor saddened. "I said they didn't have to go to prison. I didn't say anything about them being free."

"What are you saying then, Mr. Roberts? What's gonna happen to them? What did the Grand Jury decide?"

"Well, Will, the jury decided that even though the girls acted in self defense, they couldn't be just turned loose. They're not mentally competent to take care of themselves.

"The Grand Jury recommended that the judge commit them to the state mental hospital until such time they are deemed capable of independent living or until such time as a relative or other responsible party would assume the duties associated with their care and maintenance."

"What does all that mumbo jumbo mean exactly?" Culligan looked confused.

"It means that Janice and Alice Ruber will be sent to the state mental hospital in Jackson tomorrow. They will have to stay there until someone agrees to take care of them. Considering what they did to the old man, I doubt that happens anytime soon."

"You mean they gotta stay in the crazy house their whole lives?" Culligan felt a lump forming in his throat.

"Yeah." Roberts felt terrible about what he was saying. "That's probably what it means. There's really not much choice, though. We can't very well just turn them loose. Who knows what would happen to them?"

Culligan opened the car door and got out. Before closing the door, he turned to look at Roberts. "I appreciate everything you've done for Alice and Janice, Mr. Roberts. Thanks for coming by and letting me know what happened. I'll see you around."

"You're welcome, Will. I'm sorry that there's nothing else I can do. Oh, and Will, if you want to see the girls before they leave, it had better be this afternoon. Come tomorrow morning, they're gone. Take it easy."

Culligan sat back down on the curb. "Well, at least they don't have to go to prison," he thought. "And in the mental institution, they'll be sent to school and taught to read and write.

"Who knows, in a few years with the right kind of help, maybe they will be able to live independently. At least they don't have to put up with their father's abuse anymore, and they'll be together.

"Considering that they have never been out of Princeville before, it could be quite an adventure in their eyes."

Culligan got up off the curb and headed across the street to the alley. It would take him about 20 minutes to walk downtown to the city jail.

That would give him time to figure out what he was going to say to the girls. If he could somehow convince them of what he had been thinking, it would be a lot easier on them. If they accepted everything that was happening to them calmly and didn't get too scared, then the institution might just be the thing they most needed right now.

Culligan sure hoped so!

# 20

It was Friday and Beth was feeling particularly down. It had been about three weeks since the scene with Frank at the Uptowner.

If Jackson had heard about the affair, he hadn't thrown it up to her in one of their fights. She was beginning to be concerned that it had gone unnoticed. That would be just her luck!

If Jackson did know about her and Frank, he was hiding it for some reason. Maybe he had heard about it and was so embarrassed that he didn't even want to talk to her about it.

Whatever was going on, it was mighty damn strange. That afternoon when Jackson had left for one of his frequent trips to Memphis, he was in an especially good mood. As a matter of fact, he had come very close to being pleasant.

So, here she was alone in the house again on a Friday night. Jim had already gone out for the evening and probably wouldn't be back until two or three o'clock in the morning.

What a total bore. To compensate, she was already working on her fourth drink and it was only 6:30. With any luck, maybe she would get drunk and pass out early tonight.

---

Frank's Garage was just about to close for the night. The two mechanics who worked for Frank were already gone. Frank himself was doing some last minute paperwork.

Sometimes, nights like this, when he had to stay late doing paperwork, he wished he still worked down at the Cadillac dealership. At least there he could go home when he finished working on the cars. Here, it seemed like the work just started when the mechanicin' was done.

He'd figured that owning his own business would be a piece of cake. All he had to do was hire a couple of guys to do the work and he would make all the money.

Nobody had told him about the 80-hour weeks or that after the workers were paid and the parts man paid and the rent and utilities paid, there might not be much left for the owner.

After almost three months in business, he was barely making what the Cadillac place had paid him; plus, he had to put in a helluva lot more hours and handle a lot more headaches. The one big headache that kept returning was Beth Prince. At least once, sometimes twice, every night he woke up in a cold sweat worrying about her.

He couldn't help but fear that she would tell her husband about them or tell his wife or tell somebody else when she was on one of her drunken binges. He didn't know how much longer he could live with that constant threat hanging around his neck.

Frank finished the paperwork and put the accounts he had been working on in the desk drawer. As he walked out of the office into the shop, he couldn't help but wonder how much longer he would be able to keep the place. Even with all the headaches, it was still the fulfillment of a lifelong dream.

As a young man he had sworn that he would not work himself into an early grave like he had watched his father do. Not working for somebody else, anyway. If he was going to kill himself working, it would be for himself; not some rich son-of-a-bitch who couldn't remember his name even after 25 years.

No, he had learned from watching his father that the people with the money didn't give a rat's ass about poor, white trash like them.

156

Nobody was going to force him into an early grave, not even Miss hotsy totsy Beth Prince. Maybe she had looked down on folks long enough. Maybe it was time somebody looked down on her!

Frank took one last look around the shop before he opened the utility box and flipped off the lights. It may not be anything but a greasy garage like Beth had called it, but it was his greasy garage. He intended to make sure it stayed that way.

Frank got into his service truck and turned over the engine. He stared off into space as the truck warmed up. Almost 7:30 and still light. Summer days sure were long. He put the truck in gear and pulled out of the parking lot.

The traffic was light on Fourth Street for a Friday night. Frank figured it would probably pick up later. He turned right when he was out in the street. His house was on Coahoma Street so he didn't have a long drive to get home.

Frank pulled into the drive in front of his house. As houses went, it wasn't much to look at. Right now, though, it was all he could afford. He hoped that when business picked up, he'd be able to afford something a little nicer. Maybe he'd even have enough money to get out of nigger-town and move across the tracks.

He worried about his kids growing up around here, especially Mike. It seemed like all he wanted to do anymore was hang around under the streetlight with that gang of his.

Frank could smell supper cooking as soon as he crawled out of the truck. It smelled like his wife, Patsy, was frying fish. They always ate a lot of fish this time of year.

Fish were easy to get and didn't cost much. Usually some old nigger man would come through selling catfish he had caught. They were always fresh and always cheap!

After supper, Frank got up from the table and headed back out the door.

157

"Where you off to this time of night?" Patsy was putting the last of the supper dishes in the sink.

"Oh, I got a car I promised to have out by tomorrow morning and there're still a couple of things that need to be done to it. I'll be home as soon as I can."

"Frank, can't you have one of the guys do that tomorrow morning? I'm worried about you. You haven't been yourself for the last two or three weeks. I think you're worrying too much about the garage. Remember what worrying did to your daddy. I don't want the same thing happening to you."

"I'm going to be all right." Frank shot a weak smile at his wife. He thought about what a good woman she was.

"As a matter of fact, I decided just this afternoon that I wasn't going to worry anymore. I know that everything's going to be alright. After tonight, I promise to ease up some. You'll see the difference."

"O.K., but you promise to be home by midnight; you hear?"

"I promise, Honey; I'll be home by midnight. That'll be plenty of time to do what I've got to do."

---

Jackson Prince usually went up to Memphis a couple of times a month. Since it was only 75 miles, it was no big deal. He always went late Friday afternoon and came back early Sunday morning.

He never liked to be gone later than that. Sunday was church day, and he never missed church.

Jackson was a deacon at the Princeville Baptist Church. It was the biggest church in town. He liked to see and be seen by everybody on Sunday morning. It was the one time during the week when he mingled with people who were less than his equal.

158

At church he would shake their hand and call them brother. On Monday, however, he'd foreclose the loan on their house. After all, being a Christian brother and good business practice had little to do with each other, unless, of course, it worked in Jackson's favor.

Jackson had always told Beth he went to Memphis to unwind. Basically, that was the truth. He did go to unwind. It was the way he did his unwinding that he never told his wife.

She thought she knew the truth, though, and he had always let her think it. Things were a lot easier that way. He didn't really care what she thought about his trips as long as she didn't press the issue.

Beth never knew where Jackson stayed in Memphis; he figured she thought he stayed at some whorehouse or something. He himself didn't really know if such things even existed in Memphis. He supposed that they did, though.

The real truth was that he had an apartment he kept in Memphis. He had it for years. It was one of the first things he had done when old man Cotton died.

He went to Memphis and opened a bank account under a phony business name, then rented the apartment. He told the owner of the apartment that it would be used by corporation employees when they were in town. That way, nobody expected people to be in the apartment every day; but if someone was there, it was no big deal either. It had worked great for a long time now.

If Beth knew that he went there and met somebody from Princeville, she would have gone mad. Especially if she knew that he had been meeting the same person twice a month for all these years. And what would have made her even madder would be to know that the person was actually one of Jackson's employees at the bank.

Jackson never went straight to the apartment in Memphis. He usually went back by the bank for the final reports on the week's business. After that, he would drive out to the Country Club and have a couple of drinks.

He didn't like to arrive at the apartment before dark and chance that someone would see him. This time of year he seldom got there before 9:30 or 10:00. His friend usually made it about the same time, give or take thirty minutes.

At 10:20 that evening, the phone rang in the Memphis apartment. It was answered with a simple, "Yes."

"Hey, it's me." Jackson spoke into the pay phone's mouthpiece. "Been there long?"

"Not long, I just walked in the door." The reply was very affectionate, the way one lover talks to another. "Where are you? Is everything O.K.?"

"I'm fine." Jackson twisted the phone cord in his left hand. "Which is more than I can say for my car."

"What's wrong with your car? Do you need me to come get you or something? Where are you?"

"Don't get excited." Jackson spoke rapidly into the phone. "I just had a blowout. It happened by that little store at the Robinsonville turnoff. I'm calling from the pay phone outside."

"Did you wreck or anything? Can you get somebody at the store to change the tire for you?"

"I didn't wreck and the store is closed." Jackson looked around warily. "I'm gonna have to change it myself."

"When should I expect you here?" His friend sounded like an anxious wife.

"Well, it's almost 10:30 now. By the time I get the spare on, it'll be 11:00 or after. Then I'll need to stop at the Blue and White Service Station in Tunica and see about getting a new tire. I don't trust driving on in to Memphis this time of night without a spare. With any luck, I'll be there by 1:00."

160

"O.K., but if you're not here by 1:15, I'm coming to look for you."

"Don't worry." Jackson chuckled. "I'll be there by then. That'll still leave us plenty of time to be together before Sunday. Honest to goodness, sometimes you're worse than a wife with your worrying."

"Your wife, I'll never be." His friend had a high-pitched voice that sounded naturally sarcastic. "But I can still worry. Now get off the phone and hurry up and fix that tire. Good-bye!"

Jackson hung the phone back in its cradle. He was smiling as he walked back to his car.

---

It was 10:45 and Beth was making her way up the stairs. She was holding on to the stairway banister with both hands. Tonight she had drunk even more vodka than usual. It hadn't helped though. The time was no earlier than she usually made the trek.

The difference would be in the length of time it took her to get going in the morning. Beth finally got to the top of the stairs. She figured she was lucky to have made it so many times without falling and breaking her neck.

She leaned against the wall as she made her way down the hall to her bedroom. She didn't bother to turn on the lights as she entered the room. It was a good thing she had put on her gown earlier; she certainly didn't have the strength to do it now.

She fell face down on the bed and was immediately asleep. Nothing would wake her tonight. She was dead to the world.

At 11:00 the back door to the Prince mansion opened very slowly. Inching its way inward, it made almost no sound at all. It was closed in the same fashion.

Apparently the intruder had been in the house before. He moved through the darkened kitchen without a sound, stepping to one side to avoid the cooking island in the center of the room.

161

He very carefully worked his way across the room to the servant's stairs that led upstairs. They were hardly ever used by anybody except the maid. The family always used the front stairway.

With a gloved right hand, the intruder felt his way quietly up the steps.

At the top of the stairs, he stopped for a full minute and just listened. From the total lack of sound, he figured that Beth must be alone in the house. It was unlikely that Jim would be home so early on a Friday night. He would just now be chasing some little hot number around the Ranch.

The door to Beth's room was wide open. The night-light from the hallway shone into her room. When he looked around the door frame, he could see her lying face down on the bed. She had not even bothered to turn down the covers.

Seeing that she had passed out on the bed, the intruder walked over to her side. He took her by the left arm and turned her over on her back.

Next he reached over to the nightstand by the bed. With his left hand, he opened the top drawer; with his right, he felt for the revolver that Beth kept there. Slowly, he withdrew his hand from the drawer. In it he held a two-inch barreled .38 special.

As he held the gun in one hand, he tried to sit Beth up with the other. Even though she weighed only 110 pounds, he could not control the dead weight with one hand. Finally, he realized he was fighting a losing battle.

Reluctantly, he thrust the revolver into the front pocket of his coveralls. With both hands now free, the intruder sat Beth up and pulled her to the head of the bed.

With a final grunt, he positioned her so that her back was resting against the ornately carved headboard of the four-poster bed. When he released his grip on her, she remained in the upright position. The alcohol had her in a near comatose state. Nothing that he could have done at this point would have awakened her.

Next, he took the gun out of his pocket and carefully placed it in her right hand. He held her hand in his as he pushed her shooting finger through the trigger guard.

With that accomplished, he pulled the hammer of the gun to the cocked position with the thumb of his left hand. Now with both hands wrapped around her one, he raised the barrel of the gun to the underside of her chin.

With the barrel pointing upward toward her brain, he sarcastically said, "Good-bye, bitch," and calmly put pressure on her trigger finger. With a resounding BANG, the gun fired.

Simultaneously, he released his hold on Beth's hand. The force of the bullet's impact caused her hand to fling outward and fall limply by her side. Her body was thrown back against the headboard, then rebounded forward. Beth came to a stop as her body lay sprawled face down on the expensive bedspread.

As he had suspected, blood and gore flew in all directions. Some was even dripping from the ceiling back on the body. He could see blood all over the front of his coveralls and feel its sticky presence on his face.

Quickly, the intruder retraced his footsteps. Before leaving the room, however, he removed his shoes. A quick glance at his front revealed nothing that was likely to fall off.

With a silent click, the back door closed behind him as he melted into the darkness.

---

Frank quietly slipped into bed with Patsy about midnight. As he pulled the sheet up over his body, she rolled over. "I tried to call you about 11:00; where were you?"

"I got a AAA call about 10:30. It was halfway up to Tunica. Some folks from Illinois busted a radiator hose. I just got back. I didn't even go back by the shop."

"Well, I hope you didn't wear those greasy coveralls into the house. Grease'll be all over the place." Patsy's hair fell in her face as she turned sleepily back over.

"You won't have to worry about those coveralls again. When I was working on those Yankee's car, I got battery acid on myself. I knew it would eat holes in them, so I threw them in the dumpster when I was through."

I hope you didn't git that stuff on your other clothes." Patsy fought sleep as she talked over her shoulder. "It'll eat right through them!"

"Don't worry, I stopped and checked. The last thing I want to find is battery acid all over my clothes. I'm dog tired now, Patsy. Good night."

---

"I was beginning to worry, Jackson. It's after 1:00. I was fixin' to come find you."

"I had trouble getting those damn lug bolts off the wheel." Jackson appeared exhausted but yet energized at the same time. "When they use those air impact wrenches to tighten them at the shop, they're hell to get off.

"It must've been 11:30 before I even got back on the road. Then when I got to Tunica, it took forever for those hicks to find a tire the right size. They finally finished mounting it about 45 minutes ago."

"You poor thing! You must really be tired. Do you want anything? How about your clothes? Do they need washed?"

"No, my clothes are fine. Jackson startled his friend with the speed of his answer. "I put on my coveralls that I always keep in the trunk. They didn't do too well, however; I'm not sure they'll survive. Don't worry yourself about them, though. I'll take care of it when I get back to Princeville.

"I could use a drink before I go to bed. It might help me unwind a bit; I'm wound tight as a clock. Would you mind?"

"Of course not.  I'll get it right away."

Jackson sat silently staring off into space as he waited for his drink.

# 21

Mary always hated going to work on Saturday morning. By then she was already worn out from the first five days of the week. Besides that, Miss Beth was always especially hard to please on Saturdays. Mary didn't have to do much figuring to know why.

Every Saturday morning when she came to the house, she always started with the den. There were usually spills on the carpet and one or two empty vodka bottles laying around. It was always especially bad when Mr. Jackson was out of town.

When she didn't see Mr. Jackson's car out back this morning, she knew this would be one of those mornings.

Mary cleaned the den first as usual. Last night must've been real bad for Miss Beth. There were three empty vodka bottles on the bar.

After cleaning the den, Mary headed upstairs to close Miss Beth's bedroom door. Mr. Jackson insisted that she do it first thing every morning. Even though Mr. Jim's bedroom was on the opposite end of the hall, Mr. Jackson was afraid he might come to that end for some reason and see his mother passed out on the bed. He didn't want his son to see his mother like that.

Mary went upstairs every morning and closed the door just like Mr. Jackson said. She did it even though she knew it wouldn't do no good. Everyone in town, even her folks, knew that Miss Beth was a drunk. It was real hard to believe that young Mr. Jim didn't know too.

On the way to the back stairs, Mary threw the empty vodka bottles in the trash. As she dropped them in, she thought to herself how much the empty bottles were like the booze that used to be in them. They both ended up in trash. She chuckled to herself at the joke she had just thought up. She'd have to try and remember it so she could tell a friend.

"Lordy be, these steps is gittin' taller every day," Mary said to herself as she neared the top. Huffing a little, she put her right foot on the top step and went on through the doorway. As she did, she could see Miss Beth's bedroom door. Sure enough, it was standing wide open just like always. "One of these days," Mary thought, "it'll be closed, and I'll faint dead away."

As Mary reached in the room and wrapped her hand around the doorknob, she looked over at Beth to see if she was sleeping in her clothes again.

Jim sprang straight up in bed when he heard Mary scream. By the time she screamed for the second time, he was running down the hall in his underwear.

"Mary! Mary! What's wrong?" Jim could see Mary standing outside his mother's room.

"Call the am' bu' lance boy! Yo mama done been hurt. Hurry up and do it now!" Mary had her hand over her mouth fighting back the vomit rising in her throat.

"Let me see!" Jim tried to push past Mary.

"There ain't time for that now. I told you to call the am' bu' lance. Now go do what I said!" Mary pushed Jim back toward his room.

As Jim ran back to his room to use the phone, Mary pulled the door closed. She didn't really think the am' bu' lance would do no good.

---

Sheriff Dugan's patrol car came sliding to a halt in front of the house as one of the ambulance attendants came running back outside.

168

"I got the call on the way in to the office. What's going on in there?" The Sheriff adjusted his gun belt as he moved forward.

"Looks like Ms. Prince had one too many last night and tried to blow her brains out." The attendant had reached inside the ambulance, grabbed some equipment and was starting back in the house at a trot.

"Then what's the big rush?" The Sheriff had stepped between the attendant and the house.

"The big rush is that she ain't dead yet." The attendant had stopped almost nose to nose with the sheriff. "Damdest thing you ever seen! Half the top of her head is gone, but she's still breathing.

"Johnny's in there right now givin' her oxygen. We're going to move her right away while she's still alive. Maybe they can do something for her over at the hospital!"

Sheriff Dugan ran into the Prince mansion and up the stairs right on the heels of the ambulance attendant. He stood back and watched as the two men worked on Beth Prince. They were wrapping bandages around her entire head. The only parts left exposed were her nose and mouth. When they got through, her head looked like one of those mummies in the museum.

When her head was wrapped, one of the attendants started an IV in Beth's arm. They then lifted her onto the stretcher. After wrapping her in a sheet and strapping her in, the attendants started rolling her out of the room.

"Tell 'em over at the hospital that I'll be there as soon as I have a chance to look around here." The Sheriff raised his voice so as to be heard by the rapidly departing attendants. "And by the way, you boys don't stray too far; I'll want to talk to you later."

"You got it, Sheriff." The reply had come from the top of the stairs as the men headed down.

169

As Sheriff Dugan turned to look around the room, he could hear the stretcher being pulled down the front stairs. A noise in the doorway caused him to turn back around. It was Mary and Jim.

"Y'all two go downstairs and wait for me in the living room. And don't either one of you leave till I say so." He watched as they turned to go. They were both moving like zombies or something. "Probably still in shock," he thought to himself. Who wouldn't be after finding what they found.

Beth's bedroom looked like it had just been cleaned. All of it with the exception of the area around the headboard was very neat. If there had been a struggle, the room certainly showed no signs of it.

The headboard area was a different story, though. Dried blood was everywhere. From the looks of things, Beth had been sitting with her back to the headboard when she pulled the trigger.

The gun was still lying on the floor by the side of the bed. Probably where it fell after she shot herself.

He left the gun on the floor. He didn't want to disturb any more than had already been done by the ambulance attendants.

Sheriff Dugan stepped closer to the headboard of the bed. As he examined it, he could see no sign of a bullet hole. All he saw was blood and what was probably brain cells on the wall.

He noticed that the pattern of the gore seemed to lead upward. He let his eyes follow the path of the gore up the wall and onto the ceiling. As his eyes reached the ceiling, he saw it. The bullet hole was up there where his eyes had stopped.

Beth must have put the gun under her chin pointing up. Then when she pulled the trigger, the bullet went through her head and into the ceiling. With any luck, he would find it lodged in a roof joist.

"Funny," Dugan thought, "most people either shoot themselves in the mouth or in the temple when they commit suicide with a handgun."

Sure, he had seen people who had shot themselves under the chin; but always before, it had been with a rifle or shotgun.

They shot themselves under the chin because they were holding the long gun between their knees. You certainly don't have to hold a gun with a two-inch barrel between your knees!

The Sheriff had seen enough for now. He backed carefully out of the room and closed the door. He'd be back later with one of his men to go over everything in detail.

As the Sheriff came down the stairway, he stopped by the phone sitting on a table at the bottom. After dialing, he placed the receiver to his ear and listened to the rings on the other end.

"Sheriff's Office, Deputy Miller speaking."

"Miller, this is Dugan. I'm out at Jackson Prince's house. There's been a shooting here. I want you to get a hold of Jenkins and y'all haul ass on out here as quick as you can. And bring the lab kit with you."

"Who got shot, Sheriff?"

"It was Mrs. Prince; now git your ass in gear and git on out here." The Sheriff yelled into the mouthpiece then slammed the phone down and headed toward the living room.

Jim and Mary were sitting on opposite sides of the room just looking at their laps.

"Jim, where's your daddy?" Sheriff Dugan had walked over close to the boy.

"He's up in Memphis for the weekend." Jim's voice was hardly more than a whisper.

"When's he coming home?"

"He's always back before church on Sunday morning." Jim never looked up.

"Do you know how to reach him, son."

"No sir, I don't. He goes up there a couple times a month on business, but we never call him or anything. He always says that nothing's such an emergency that it can't wait until he gets back.

"I guess he was wrong, wasn't he?"

"How 'bout you, girl?" The Sheriff switched his attention to Mary. "Do you know how to get hold of Mr. Prince?"

"No sir, I don't." Mary would not look directly at the Sheriff; she seemed to be talking to his feet. "I never knows he's gone till I git here and don't sees his car. I'm jest the maid; they don't tell me nothin'."

"Who found her this morning?" Sheriff Dugan was still looking at Mary.

"I did." Mary's voice broke slightly with fear. "I went up to close her door like I do every mornin', and there she was jest layin' there all bloody and everything."

"What happened to Mama?" Jim jumped up from his position on the sofa.

"Now calm down, son." The Sheriff stepped closer to the boy and put his hand on Jim's shoulder.

"Yore mama shot herself sometime last night. But she's still alive, and they took her to the hospital. What time did you get home last night? Did you hear or see anything funny?"

"I got home about 1:30 this morning." Jim stepped away from the Sheriff's touch. "I didn't see or hear anything funny, though; I just went upstairs and got in bed. Like I always do. Sheriff, I want to go to the hospital and see Mama. Can't you talk to me later?"

"Sure, Jim, you go on out to the hospital; but don't leave until I tell you you can. Understand?"

"Yes sir, I understand. I'm not going anywhere." Jim quickly got up and hurried out of the room.

"Sheriff." Deputy Miller was shouting from just inside the front door. "Where are you?"

"I'm in the living room!"

The two deputies immediately came running into the living room looking out of breath.

"No need to hurry like that now, boys." The Sheriff looked at his heavily breathing men. "The shooting was last night; we got plenty of time now.

"Miller, I want you on the front door. Nobody in or out without my permission. If Jackson shows up, I want to know about it. Understand?"

"Yes sir, nobody in or out; and let you know if Mr. Prince shows." Deputy Miller turned and headed out of the room.

"Jenkins, I want you to take the lab kit upstairs and get started on the bedroom. I'll be up in a few minutes."

"Yes sir." Deputy Jenkins picked up the lab kit and headed toward the front stairs.

Sheriff Dugan and Mary were the only two left in the living room. He turned his attention back to her. "You said that you went up to close Mrs. Prince's bedroom door like you do every morning. Is that right?"

"Yes sir, that's right Sheriff." Mary still talked to his feet. "I goes up there every morning to do it."

"What's your name, girl?"

"Mary Washington, sir."

"Well, Mary, tell me something." The Sheriff's tone was strong but not threatening. "Why do you have to go upstairs every morning and close Beth Prince's door?"

"Because Mr. Jackson told me when he first hired me that every morning he wanted me to go upstairs first thing and close Miss Beth's bedroom door."

"Why does he want you to do that, Mary?"

Mary hesitated before answering. She wasn't sure she should tell family stuff like that to the Sheriff. Mr. Jackson might git mad and fire her.

"I said, why does he want you to do that?" The Sheriff repeated the question with just a hint of anger showing in his voice.

Mary was afraid of white men, especially white lawmen. She didn't want the Sheriff mad at her so she answered the question.

"You mean that Mrs. Prince gets drunk and passes out on the bed every night!" Sheriff Dugan could not mask his amazement.

"Yes sir, as far as I knows. I only comes in six days a week, though. I don't knows who closes Miss Beth's door on Sunday. I guess Mr. Jackson does it hisself."

"Do you have any idea how much she had to drink last night, Mary?" The Sheriff was studying the maid carefully for any hint of lying.

"I throwed three empty fifth bottles in the trash this morning that I cleaned up in the den. I 'spect she drunk most all of what was in 'em."

"Does she always drink that much?" The Sheriff was astonished. "It's a wonder her liver ain't pickled by now!"

"No sir, she don't. Usually, I jest clean up one empty bottle; sometimes on Saturday, though, I has to collect two."

174

"She must've felt she was going to need the extra courage last night." The Sheriff needed to think. "That's all for now, but don't leave, Mary. Why don't you make a pot of coffee; looks like this is going to be a long morning."

Mary got up from where she had been sitting and walked out of the room. The Sheriff just stood where he had been standing. From the looks of things, this was simply a case of attempted suicide.

He could never understand why a person who had as much as Beth Prince would want to kill herself. These rich folks were real hard to figure sometimes.

Dugan turned and walked out of the room. He'd better get upstairs and see what Jenkins had found.

Jenkins was holding the gun carefully by the handle with two fingers. He was looking very closely at the barrel.

"What you got?" The Sheriff had noticed what his deputy was doing.

"I don't really know, sir. Just something funny about this black stuff on the end of the barrel. If I didn't know better, I'd say it was grease from a car. But how would car grease get on the barrel of Beth Prince's gun? Here, you take a look, Sheriff."

As Jenkins continued to hold the gun, Dugan moved forward to take a closer look. "Looks like car grease to me, too." The Sheriff was squinting to get a better look at the gun barrel. "Hold it up a little higher so I can smell it.

"Yep! That's grease from a car. No doubt about it. I'm with you. It sure makes you curious as to how it got on this gun. I seriously doubt that Beth Prince was the kind to do her own auto mechanics.

"Secure this room for the time being, Jenkins. I want you to get over to the hospital ASAP and do a paraffin analysis on Mrs. Prince's right hand. Don't leave that hospital until you get that analysis."

"Yes sir, I'll be on my way in about five minutes."

Sheriff Dugan didn't like the new wrinkle that had mysteriously appeared in his open and shut attempted suicide case. As he walked down the stairs and across the foyer toward the front door, a large question mark was beginning to take shape in his mind.

Did Beth Prince really pull the trigger that sent a bullet tearing through her brain? He figured this one deserved a little more of his attention before shutting the book on it.

# 22

Sunday school started promptly at 9:45 a.m. at the Princeville Baptist Church. Sheriff Dugan was sure of that. He had called Brother Bailey, the preacher, last night to find out.

He had been parked out in front of the church on Catalpa Street since 9:00 waiting for Jackson Prince to show up. Dugan wanted to be sure and catch Jackson before he got inside. It wouldn't be right for him to find out about his wife from one of the people in the church building.

Everyone in town had been talking about the shooting since word of it started to filter out about noon yesterday. If Jackson stopped anywhere on the way into town, someone would surely mention it.

Sheriff Dugan wanted to be the one to break the news to Mr. Prince. He wanted to witness firsthand the reaction to the news. It wasn't exactly that he suspected Jackson Prince of anything; it was just that he needed to cover all the bases.

Princeville Baptist Church was the biggest church in town. It certainly had the building to go with its size. The thing took up the better part of a city block.

Dugan sat in his cruiser and watched the people arrive. One thing about a good ole Southern Baptist church—you saw all types. Well, almost all types; there were, of course, no blacks. The crowd was really starting to get heavy now. There were rich people and poor people and middle class people, all congregating together as brethren.

The Sheriff didn't go to church himself. He felt that it was hypocritical. He never could understand how Princeville's elite citizens thought it was O.K. to associate with the less affluent on Sunday and then treat them like shit the other six days of the week.

Or better yet, he couldn't understand how Princeville's everyday Joe could come to church on Sunday and take the hand of somebody like Jackson Prince, then turn right around on Monday and take the shaft from the same guy.

Naw, it never made sense to him.

As Sheriff Dugan sat watching the arriving church crowd, he noticed a dark blue Lincoln pull into the parking lot. That would be Jackson Prince arriving for church.

Dugan quickly started his engine and wheeled into the parking lot. He pulled up behind Jackson's car just as the front door on the driver's side was being opened. The Sheriff put his car into park and hurriedly got out.

Jackson was smiling at him as he got out. "Hey, Sheriff. You going to bust me for getting to Sunday School late?"

When the Sheriff didn't smile or offer any type of greeting, Jackson's facial expression changed. "What's going on Sheriff? You don't go to church here; why are you here?"

"I need to talk to you, Jackson." The Sheriff was trying to absorb any meaning from Jackson's behavior that would be unexpected given the circumstances. "Why don't you get in the car with me."

"I don't have time right now." Jackson started to walk away. "Sunday School's starting and I'm late. I've got a class waiting for me. I'm their teacher. Can't this wait?"

"No, I'm afraid it can't, Jackson." Dugan stepped in Prince's path raising his voice slightly. "Now get in the car, please. We're going to take a ride. You'll understand the reason for this in a couple of minutes."

"You'd better have a damn good reason for this, Dugan, or I'll have a piece of your ass."

He reluctantly walked around the Sheriff's car and got in on the passenger's side. The Sheriff climbed in on his side and started the engine.

By now people had spotted Jackson and were coming over to speak to him. Dugan needed to get him away from the church quickly!

As fast as the car came to life, the Sheriff stomped the accelerator and sped out of the church parking lot. He drove down Catalpa for a few blocks out of sight of the church; then he pulled the cruiser to the curb and stopped.

"O.K., Sheriff, what's the big mystery?" Prince was staring out the window in an annoyed fashion.

"The big mystery is that sometime Friday night, your wife was shot in the head with a Smith and Wesson .38 special revolver in her bedroom at y'alls house." The Sheriff spoke slowly and deliberately. "Obviously, you haven't been home since then?"

Dugan was looking Jackson Prince right in the eyes as he told him the bad news. He was searching for any hint of the fact that Jackson already new about the shooting.

Jackson Prince just sat there in silence. The news had either shocked him speechless or he was choosing his words very carefully. The Sheriff just sat there and watched.

As he did, Jackson tried to speak but the words seemed to be stuck. All of a sudden, tears started to roll down his cheeks.

"Is she . . . dead?" Prince's words were emitted in a quivering voice.

"No, she's still alive." The Sheriff's eyes never left those of Prince. "The doctor thinks that she has a slim chance of making it if everything goes her way."

179

"How did it happen?" Prince had swiveled his body in the car seat so that he was facing the Sheriff more directly. "Was it an accident or what?"

"Right now, we don't know." The Sheriff repositioned his own body. "Most of the evidence points to attempted suicide, but I haven't ruled out other possibilities yet."

"Other possibilities; exactly what do you mean by that, Sheriff? Do you think that somebody shot my wife?"

The Sheriff just sat there and watched Jackson speak.

"Well, what other possibilities are you talking about? I demand to know! If you think somebody shot Beth, then I want to know. Tell me!"

"I'll tell you what I know on the way out to the hospital, Jackson. Even though you haven't asked, I assume you'd like to go see how your wife is doing."

"Well of course I want to go see how my wife is doing." Prince looked at the Sheriff in a contemptuous manner. "What kind of crazy question is that anyway? Is she conscious; has she been able to say anything about what happened?"

Sheriff Dugan glanced into the side mirror to make sure the street was clear as he eased the car away from the curb and headed for the hospital. He couldn't figure Jackson Prince out from watching him. Either he really was surprised by the news about his wife, or he was one fine actor.

One thing did puzzle the Sheriff, however. Why Jackson hadn't asked immediately to see his wife. Seems like that would have been what most folks would've wanted to do first!

"No, she's not conscious." Dugan applied pressure to the car's accelerator. "She's been in a coma ever since it happened. The doctor says that even if she makes it, it could be months, even years, before she recovers enough to speak. With the kind of brain damage she suffered, she may never be right again."

180

Prince interrupted Dugan. "You said you were going to tell me what you knew about the shooting."

"Oh, yeah, the shooting. Best we can tell, it happened sometime between 11:00 Friday night and about 2:00 Saturday morning. Mary, your maid, found her yesterday morning when she went upstairs to close the bedroom door.

"It's amazing she lived that long! The doctor said that probably the only reason she lived through the night was the amount of alcohol in her system. He said it must have slowed her system down enough to just keep her barely alive.

"Whatever kept her alive, your wife is one tough lady. I was the first officer on the scene. I got the call while I was on my way to work. When I got there, the ambulance was already there and the guys were working on your wife. They're what probably saved her life. They managed to stop the bleeding and get her to the hospital right away."

"What about Jim? I almost forgot about him. How's he taking everything? Where is he?"

"Your boy's O.K. He was shook up at first, but he settled down after a few hours. He stayed over at a friend's house last night. I figured it was best for him not to go home again until you showed up."

"I appreciate you looking after him, Sheriff. I guess he told you that I was in Memphis on business. I just now got back into town. You said you were still investigating other possibilities in the shooting. What makes you think it wasn't an attempted suicide? Were there signs of a struggle or of forced entry into the house?"

"There were no signs of a struggle or of forced entry." The Sheriff slowed for a car turning in front of them.

"When I got there, Mrs. Prince was lying on the bed and the ambulance attendants were working on her. The gun was lying on the floor beside her. Jim told me it was his mother's gun when I showed it to him later at the hospital."

"Then, I guess I don't understand." Jackson didn't really appear confused to the Sheriff. "If her gun was the one that shot her and there was no struggle or break in, why do you think it could've been anything other than an attempted suicide? Seems pretty simple to me."

"Did your wife always keep her gun in the bedroom?" The Sheriff was now concentrating on Prince's tone of voice.

"Yes, always. It had belonged to her daddy. She never took it out of the nightstand drawer as far as I know. She kept it there because he had always told her to keep a gun close in case a nigger broke in on her at night."

"What about you, Jackson? Did you ever use it? Maybe clean it or something for her?"

"Never touched it, Sheriff. As far as I know it didn't need cleaning. To the best of my recollection, the thing hasn't been shot since Mr. Cotton died. I doubt if it's even been out of the drawer.

"Why all the questions about the gun anyway? Are they really all that important?"

"They could be." The Sheriff glanced briefly at Prince. "We found something real peculiar on the barrel of your wife's gun. The best we could make out, it was car grease. Thinking as hard as we could, me and my deputies couldn't figure out how it got there. You got any ideas on the subject, Jackson?"

"Not a clue, Sheriff. The only thing I know less about than guns is cars."

Sheriff Dugan pulled the car into the drive that ran in front of the Coahoma County Hospital. His brakes squealed a bit as he came to a stop.

"Here we are, Jackson. I won't be coming in with you. I've got a little business to take care of. You'll find your wife up on the fifth floor in the ICU. One of my deputies is up there around the clock just in case she

182

comes to. If you need anything, just ask him. He can get you a ride back to your car when you need it, too.

"Oh, there is just one other thing, Jackson. For the record, I need to know where you stayed in Memphis and the name of somebody that can verify your whereabouts."

"And just what the hell record is that for, Dugan?" Anger was clearly evident in Prince's voice and on his face. "Are you trying to accuse me of something? If so, you'd better tell me right now. I'll have that badge of yours shoved so far up your redneck ass it'll look like a taillight."

"Now don't get your bowels in an uproar, Jackson. I just need to know for the record. It doesn't mean I'm accusing you of anything. It wouldn't matter if you were the Governor of Mississippi; I'd still have to ask. Is there some reason that you don't want to tell me?"

"Of course not." Prince was visibly shaken by the sudden line of questioning. "I guess I'm just upset over everything that has happened. I'm sorry I blew up at you. It's just that I was in Memphis going over the details of a really big loan with one of my bank officers. We went to Memphis because it's very confidential and I can't afford to let word of it leak out. We spent the whole weekend holed up in an apartment that a business associate let me have. Do you really have to have all the details?"

"I'm not going to tell anybody your business, Jackson. All I need to know is the name of your bank officer that was with you. I can't imagine that would cause a problem for you either at the bank or with your wife's shooting. Unless, of course, you spent the weekend in Memphis with another woman.

"You weren't with a woman, were you, Jackson? Because if you were, it would look real bad for you."

"No, of course not, Sheriff. I wasn't with a woman. I told you that I was with one of my bank officers. You know that all my bank officers are men!"

183

"Well, I'm waiting Jackson; which one was it?"

"I spent the weekend in Memphis working on the loan with Ronald Beakner," Jackson said. "You can check with him when he gets back. He'll tell you that I got there about 11:00 p.m. Friday night and didn't leave the apartment until this morning."

"O.K., Jackson. I'll call him when I get back to the office. See how simple that was. Once I call Ronald and check out your story, the record will be taken care of. Then nobody can say that I gave you special treatment just because the town happens to be named after you. Right?"

"Yeah, that's right, Dugan. We wouldn't want the citizens of Princeville to think you did me any favors. After all, we know it was the 'common man' element that elected you to office. Just think, if it weren't for them and a bunch of nigger voters, you wouldn't even have this job. We certainly don't want any of them to get the wrong idea."

Jackson Prince climbed out of the Sheriff's car and slammed the door.

"Piss on you, Dugan, and all your nigger supporters, both black and white," Jackson thought to himself as the Sheriff pulled away.

Jackson hurried into the hospital. As he headed down the hall to the elevator, he stopped at the pay phone on the way. Hopefully, Ronald hadn't left the apartment yet. He usually stayed around till about noon cleaning the place up. Jackson hoped Ronald hadn't chosen today to do something different!

"What an asshole," Dugan thought to himself as he drove off and left Jackson Prince standing on the sidewalk. "But at least he was probably an innocent asshole. What better alibi could you have than a mama's boy like Ronald Beakner?

"I mean, what else could a guy be doing in Memphis all weekend with a nerd like Ronald except working. No wonder Jackson was in such a shitty mood. Even though she had a bullet in her head, Beth Prince probably had a better time this weekend than Jackson."

# 23

Sanger had been excited all day. It was Friday and tonight was when he and Eloisa had agreed to meet again. It had taken every bit of willpower that he possessed to stay away from her for the past two weeks.

He pulled the old Ford up to the spot where he always parked. The place was about a block away from the school and around a corner. "After tonight," he thought, "the next time Eloisa and I see each other will be in Chicago. No more hiding and sneaking away to rooftops after that."

As Sanger climbed through the trapdoor leading to the roof, he glanced at his watch. It was 6:35. A few more minutes and they'd be together again. He settled in for the wait. As excited as he was, the minutes would, no doubt, drag by very slowly.

At five minutes after seven, Eloisa came climbing through the opening to the rooftop. She and Sanger were immediately in each other's arms.

"I thought that Mama and Daddy were never going to come back downstairs after supper." Eloisa's body seemed to have a slight tremor caused by her excitement. "Today has been the longest day of my life. I didn't think it would ever end."

"That makes two of us." Sanger continued to hold her. "I bet I looked at my watch every five minutes today. I was beginning to wonder if it was broken; the hands seemed to be moving so slowly."

"Let's sit down." Eloisa took Sanger's hand and coaxed him to the spot where they usually sat. "We've got a lot to talk about and not much time."

"Sure." Sanger eased to his usual sitting place. "You're right; let's sit and talk. Are you going to Chicago; what's going on?"

"Well." Eloisa's body could not hide her feelings. "When I told my mama and daddy I had decided I wanted to go to Chicago to school, they were so happy they called my aunt right then to discuss it with her. They didn't even ask me what had made me decide to do it. I guess they figured that they would leave well enough alone."

"So, what's the deal?" Sanger leaned toward Eloisa in his anxiousness to know. "When do you leave?"

"I'm supposed to leave next Friday morning. Mama went and got the bus tickets today."

"Tickets, as in more than one?" Sanger was confused. "Who's going besides you?"

"I've told you how protective my parents are. You don't think they'd let me ride a bus all the way to Chicago by myself, do you? My mama is going with me and stay for a week to get me settled in. Then she'll come back home."

"In a way, I'm glad she's going with you." Sanger seemed relieved at her answer. "It is a long way to ride a bus. It'll make me feel better knowing that somebody's with you."

"How about you?" Eloisa looked at Sanger with a question in her eyes. "What have you been doing? Are you going to be able to get away too?"

"I think so. I've given the boss notice at the Plant that next Friday's gonna be my last day so I'll be able to leave anytime after that."

"What did you tell your boss was the reason you were leaving? And what about your parents? Have you told them yet that you're leaving?"

186

"I told Martin and my parents that I was heading to California for a couple of weeks before I started college in the fall. They all think that I'm going to school out there. They have no idea where I'm really headed."

"How did you convince them of that?" Eloisa was surprised at the reaction of Jerry's parents. "Didn't they ask you why you were going to college so far away from home or anything?"

"Sure, they asked. But when I told them that I just wanted to see a little of the country, they accepted it. They consider me grown now and know that I can do whatever I want to do. I told them I'd call after the semester started and I was settled in at a school."

"Boy, your family is sure different from mine." Eloisa shook her head in amazement. "My parents won't think I'm grown till after I graduate from college. Even then, it'll still take a while to convince them."

"Yeah, you're right; our families are really different." Sanger let out a small chuckle. "But with five kids, my family will never be as close as yours. Plus, in my family boys are treated differently than the girls.

"I've been pretty much free to come and go as I please since I was in about the eighth grade. I always figured it was that way because Daddy has been on his own since he was in the eighth grade.

"For a Sanger boy, that's pretty much been the coming-of-age time. After that you're treated and expected to act as a man.

"Acting like a man also means paying your own way. About that time, Daddy quit paying my expenses and I had to start picking up the tab. My first regular job was the summer after I finished the eighth grade.

"So, you see, according to family tradition, I stopped being a dependent child over four years ago. They probably figure it's 'bout time I left home and started fending for myself."

"So, when exactly are you going to leave?" She looked at him for the answer.

187

"I figured that I'd spend one last Saturday night with the gang and then leave early Sunday morning. That ought to put me in Chicago sometime Monday if I'm lucky. You never can tell, though, when you drive an old beat up car like my Ford. At any rate, I'll be there in plenty of time to make our meeting at the university on Friday."

Eloisa reached over all of a sudden and hugged Sanger, with all her strength. "I'm so excited; I don't know if I can control myself. Just two more weeks and then no more sneaking around. We'll be together in Chicago."

"That's right," Sanger said between her squeezes. "The first thing that I want to do is take you to the movies."

"Take me to the movies?" Eloisa once again was surprised by him. "Why do you want to take me to the movies?"

"Because." Sanger smiled. "That's always the first date, the movies. It will be our first real date, you know. I want everything to be just right for us. I'm gonna work real hard to make sure that you keep loving me. I promise you that you'll never be sorry for what we're about to do. You can count on that!"

"I'll never be sorry." Eloisa's eyes reflected exactly how she felt. "Whatever happens will be good because it'll happen to us together. If we can get through the next two weeks, nothing will ever stop us from being together again. Nothing!"

As the two young lovers sat there holding hands and looking at each other, they both jumped at the same time.

"Do you hear that?" Sanger was all of a sudden very nervous. "It sounds like a police siren, and it's not far away. We'd better get off this roof and quickly!"

They were both up and moving toward the trapdoor opening before he finished the last word of his sentence.

"Are you sure it's coming here?" Eloisa was trembling with fear. "Maybe it's going somewhere else. Maybe someone had a wreck or something."

"I don't know." Sanger pulled her after him onto the ladder. "But we'd better not take any chances. If we're caught up here together, it could ruin all our plans. Let's go! We've got to get down these steps and out of the building before the cops get here!"

Little did Eloisa and Sanger know, but it was already too late!

As Eloisa had walked around behind the school building earlier, the school's current principal, Mr. Jennings, had been driving from his house to the school. He was on his way to get some paperwork he had forgotten earlier in the day.

Just as Sanger had suspected, there was an alarm connected to the utility room door. He was also right when he assumed that it was silent and that it wasn't connected to anything beyond the principal's office. It was another feature of the alarm system, however, that had created the problem.

The alarm was connected to a light in the principal's office that came on any time the door was opened. It always stayed on for thirty minutes and then an automatic reset turned it off and rearmed the system.

The thirty minute period was built into the system so that if the principal happened to be out of his office when the light came on, he'd see it when he came back in. When the thirty minutes expired and the light went off, then you would never know whether or not the door had been opened. That was the reason Sanger and Eloisa had not been discovered before. If not for the forgetful nature of the principal, they would have gone unobserved again tonight.

When Mr. Jennings unlocked the door to his office and went in searching for the forgotten paperwork, the light was the first thing he had seen. Since the alarm had never gone off during his tenure at the school, he didn't really know what to do.

After getting his composure back, he went through the school building and out the kitchen door so he could check the utility room. He was very careful not to make any noise as he stuck his head through the door to see if someone was inside. As he peered inside, his eyes found the ladder and followed its path upward. When he saw the open trapdoor, he knew for sure that somebody was up on the roof of his school.

After withdrawing his head from the room just as quietly as he had inserted it, he walked quickly back to his office and called the police. He reported to them in a voice filled with panic that there were burglars on the roof of Eliza Prince School .

Jennings then sat down in his chair and waited for the police to arrive. He was much too afraid to go back outside. After all, he wasn't a cop; he was an elementary school principal. The school board didn't pay him enough to apprehend criminals. Besides, who could tell how many of them there were!

Sanger opened the door a crack and looked out. The siren had stopped. He knew that was a bad sign. It meant that the cop was out of the car and probably coming their direction.

Sanger had to think of something real fast or he and Eloisa were about to get caught. Whatever happened to him wasn't important; he had dealt with the police before. Under no circumstances, however, was he going to let the cops get their hands on her. Who knows what would happen to her down at the city jail! Besides, she was too nice a person to endure such an ordeal. Mentally, he could handle whatever happened as long as it just happened to him and not her.

"Eloisa." Sanger was whispering hurriedly. "There's gonna be a cop coming around the corner before too long. He'll be here in a few seconds!

"Now listen and do what I tell you to do! When he gets a little closer, I'm gonna run. When I do, he'll chase me.

190

"When you hear him run by, open the door and run. But don't run toward home; run in the opposite direction and go to a friend's house or something.

"Stay there for a couple of hours and then make up some excuse for your parents to drive over and get you. Whatever you do, don't walk home. The cops will be on the lookout for you."

"Jerry, I can't just leave you!" Eloisa had tears streaming down her cheeks. "He'll catch you and take you to jail."

"That's right." Sanger knew they had real trouble and it was on its way. "As a matter of fact, I intend to let him catch me. There's no way I can get by without him seeing me. He'd just come to my house if I outran him. This way he'll concentrate on me and you can get away."

"But I don't want to get away without you!" Tears had made their way down her face and were running into the edge of her mouth. "How will we ever meet in Chicago now? All our plans are gonna be ruined."

"Not if you get away, they won't." Sanger knew time was running out. "It may take me a little longer, but I'll still meet you. I swear it! I'll be there in time to enroll for the fall semester.

"Please, just trust me and do as I ask. And when you run, run fast and don't look back. I don't want that cop out there to see your face. To him, you'll just be another black girl running away. As long as he can't identify you, you're safe."

Sanger chanced another quick glance out the door and then ducked back inside. "Here he comes, get ready!" Sanger gave Eloisa a quick kiss and got in position to run. "Remember, don't let him see your face. I love you. Also, regardless of what happens to me, I want you to promise to be on that bus next Friday morning. Us being together depends on it."

"I love you too, Jerry. Please be careful. Whatever happens, I'll be waiting for you."

Sanger threw the door open and ran just as the cop was approaching.

191

Eloisa could hear the policeman yell at Sanger to stop and then run after him. Just as Sanger had told her to do, she ran out the door and away without looking back.

As Officer Fager was chasing Sanger, he heard someone run in the opposite direction. Turnin' to look, all he could make out was the figure of what appeared to be a young black girl running very quickly. Since he was closer to the one he was chasing and this one wasn't running nearly as fast as the nigger girl, he kept running.

Just as Fager was losing ground on the running teenager ahead, his luck improved dramatically. The boy fell down.

"What a piece of luck!" Fager closed on the fallen boy.

As Sanger struggled to get his feet back under him, Fager hit him from behind with his baton on the shoulder. Sanger immediately collapsed under the effect of the blow.

"Well, what do we have here?" Fager looked down at Sanger and laughed. "If it ain't Jerry Sanger, real Coahoma Street scum caught in the act of breakin' and enterin'. What a shame!

"O.K., Sanger, on your feet."

Across the street Eloisa was hiding and watching. She looked on in fear as Fager handcuffed Sanger's hands behind his back and roughly escorted him to the patrol car. While she sobbed quietly, the car pulled away from the curb and drove toward downtown.

Slowly, she moved back from the street and worked her way to the alley behind. In less than five minutes, she was knocking on the door of one of her girlfriends.

# 24

**W**ell, I got you this time, asshole." Fager glanced over his shoulder at Sanger seated in the rear as he pulled the patrol car away from Eliza Prince School. "You won't be able to get somebody's mama to lie for you now. You and that nigger bitch broke into the school and were up on the roof. What were y'all doin' anyhow? You take her up there to knock off a little black stuff? Was that what you were doing, Sanger? Like that black stuff, huh?"

"That wasn't a black girl, Fager." Sanger had to lean forward in the seat because his hands were cuffed behind his back. "That was your daughter; didn't you recognize her? At least I think it was your daughter. The other 12 guys who have been with her this week said you were her daddy."

Fager slammed on the brakes and pulled the car abruptly to the side of the street. "You little nigger-lookin' son-of-a-bitch." Fager yelled at the top of his voice. "I'll make you think daughter. I'm gonna drag yore ass out of there and kick the shit out of you. When I'm through with you, your bruises are gonna make you blacker than that black slut of yours. Then after that you're gonna tell me who she was and we're gonna go get her, too. I want both of you at the station tonight."

"This is the only way you can do it, Fager." Sanger was getting back up on the seat after having been thrown on the floor of the car by the hard braking. "With my hands cuffed behind my back. Have you ever hit anybody that was looking or didn't have their hands cuffed? I doubt it. The littlest guy in our gang could take you out with one hand while

193

eating a sandwich in the other one. Without your badge, you'd be dog meat and half the town would be dogs."

Fager angrily threw his door open and got out of the car. In a very deliberate fashion, he marched around to the rear where Sanger was sitting. With a grunt, he jerked open the door.

Using both hands, he reached into the car, pulled Sanger out, and threw him across the trunk. "Now let's talk about my daughter, asshole."

Fager hit Sanger over the right eye with his fist. The first blow was followed in quick succession by several more. Sanger was now lying on the street with blood coming out of his mouth and nose plus a cut over his eye. Fager reached down and pulled Sanger to his feet.

"Is that the best you've got, little man?" Sanger spit blood on the front of Fager's uniform. "Maybe you ought to go get your daughter. She can probably hit harder! The harder it is, the better she likes it; know what I mean."

Fager backhanded Sanger in the mouth, then grabbed him by his hair. As he started to hit him again, a hand suddenly grabbed his and held it.

"What the he . . . ?" He turned to see the person that had dared interfere with him doing his official duty. As his eyes followed the restraining arm upward, he could see Mitchell Roberts' angry face at the other end.

"Another one of your many cases of somebody resisting arrest, huh, Fager?" Roberts stared down at the patrol officer. "I think you've got him under control now. Good thing I showed up to give you a hand. He looks mighty dangerous with his hands cuffed behind his back like that. Without my help, you'd probably had to shoot him or something."

"I was just teaching this Coahoma Street crud a few manners; that's all. His mouth was starting to overload his ass so I closed it for him. Besides, here in nigger-town there ain't nobody that's stupid enough to report it. They know what'll happen if they do."

"And just what might that be, Fager? You gonna beat up everybody in this part of town? I don't think you've got enough handcuffs. If you don't cut this stuff out, one of these days somebody's going to tell our black city councilman about you and it'll cost you your badge."

"Are you threatening me, Roberts? Because if you are, imagine what the other officers would think of you snitchin' to that uppity nigger councilman. You'd have to watch your back for the rest of your life in this town."

"You're probably right, but don't push it too far, Fager. I might just decide that it's worth the price!

"Now, I want you to put Sanger back in the car and take him on down to the station. If he picks up any more bruises on the way, I'm going to personally explain to his 250-pound daddy exactly how he got them. You're gonna have enough trouble with him as it is. I don't imagine he's gonna appreciate those marks on his boy's face."

"But he ain't told me who the nigger girl was that was with him." Fager nervously walked up to Sanger and then away again. "Give me a couple more minutes with him and I'll know the little black slut's name."

"Sure you will." Roberts looked at Fager sarcastically. "Look at him lying there. You've beat the shit out of him, and he's just giving you that evil grin of his. He can take what you've got to dish out all week and still come back for more. You just don't understand these Coahoma Street kids, do you.

"They were weaned on your kind of treatment. The more of it you use, the harder they become to reach. They're not like the pussy offspring of that Country Club bunch you're always kissing up to. These kids are tough!

"They're tough and poor, but that don't make them bad. Other than an occasional fight or a little drinking, I've never known any of them to be in any real trouble. So, you take Sanger to the station and put him in the holding cell. I'll be there in a little bit."

195

"Where you going?" Fager shot a challenging look at Roberts.

"I'm going over to the school and have a talk with the principal. I want to find out what happened and why he called us; the things you should've done before you left. We've got to figure out what kind of charges he wants to file, if any. Plus, I'm gonna see if he saw the girl or knows anything about her.

"I'll be back to the station after awhile. Tell the Chief what I'm up to."

"My way would be quicker." Fager looked down at Sanger. "He ain't as tough as you think he is. I can make him talk."

"You just do as I said," Roberts shot back angrily, "or you'll answer to me. Now get him out of here!"

Sanger sat quietly as Fager drove him downtown to the police station. Just as he had always known it would, his big mouth had gotten him into bad trouble. He'd been lucky the first time. Roberts had saved his ass. He might not be so lucky the second time around.

Even though he knew Fager was afraid of Roberts, he also knew Fager was some kind of crazy. Set him off again and who knows what could happen. Naw, no setting Officer Fager off, not now at least. When he did that again, he'd have his hands free to defend himself.

Sanger had been to the police station a few times to buy licenses for his bicycles over the years, but he had never been in jail before. This particular trip the old police station took on a whole new appearance.

As Fager opened the car door and pulled him out, Sanger looked up at the building. Not much to look at really. Just an old two-story building with a parking lot out front.

The smell of freshly baked bread hit his nostrils as he walked up the steps. He turned slightly and looked at the Wonder Bread Bakery across the street. "May not smell that again for awhile," he thought to himself.

Fager pulled open the door to the station and pushed Sanger roughly through into the lobby. As he stumbled and caught himself, Sanger saw a couple Country Club type teenagers sitting across the room. No doubt waiting for their parents after getting caught buying beer underage. If the teenagers had been Coahoma Street types, they'd have been waiting in a cell somewhere. But instead, they were sitting in the police station lobby gawking at him as he was dragged in. In a few minutes, their parents would come slap them on the wrists and take them home. He wondered where he'd be getting slapped in a few minutes. Somehow, he didn't think it would be on the wrist.

The cop at the desk looked up with interest as Fager hauled Sanger over. "Well, what kind of nasty criminal have you brought us tonight, Fager?"

"Him and a nigger girl broke into Eliza Prince School." Fager had a menacing smile plastered across his face. "While I was running him down, the nigger got away. Roberts is over at the school now trying to find out who she was."

"Looks like he tried to resist arrest." The desk cop smirked.

"Yeah, they never learn." Fager replied with a reciprocal smirk. "You'd think white trash like this would learn that they can't fight with the po'leese."

"What were they doing at the school?" The desk cop was giving Sanger the once-over with his eyes. "There ain't nothing worth stealing over there 'cept a few crayons and some kiddy books. Hardly seems worth the effort."

"My best guess," Fager said as he reached over and pushed Sanger's face, "is that they broke in so as they'd have a nice private place to screw. After that, they'd probably of wrote on the walls and messed the place up.

"You know how niggers are; they trash a place just cause they want to. Sanger here has lived over there in nigger-town so long he's just like 'em. Two niggers in a pod!" Fager and the desk cop laughed at the joke he had made.

197

The Country Club boys just sat taking everything in and whispering to each other. Occasionally, they would look at Sanger then at each other and laugh. They were obviously having a good time at his expense.

"Whatta you want done with him?" The desk cop kind of waved his hand in Sanger's direction. "Want me to send him upstairs to a cell?"

"Naw, just throw him in the holding cell till Roberts gets here. He'll tell you what to do with the crud. As for me, I don't really care. My job's just to bring 'em in and protect the citizens." He and the desk cop laughed again.

"Yeah," said the desk cop. "I know how much you like protectin' the citizens." He then called over another policeman and told him to throw Sanger in the holding cell until Detective Roberts showed up.

As Sanger was having the handcuffs removed and being put in the holding cell, he saw the Country Club boys' parents arrive. They wouldn't be there much longer.

Sanger stood looking at the cop who had just put him in the cell as he closed and locked the door. With the door closed and him behind it, Sanger looked all around the place.

It reminded him of a cyclone fence dog pen with wire on all four sides and the top. It sat at the back of the lobby kind of in a corner. Anybody walking into the station would be hard pressed not to see him.

Now he knew what his beagles felt like every time he put them in their pen. No wonder they howled and barked all night. He felt kind of like howling himself.

Along the back wall or fence (or whatever you wanted to call it) was a wooden bench. The bench was the only form of furniture in the cell.

Sanger walked over and sat down on it. All of a sudden, he was very tired. He figured he had better rest while he had the opportunity because from the way things were shaping up, this night was a long way from being over.

When he sat, his mind immediately brought Eloisa into view. With any luck at all, she should have made it to a friend's house without any troubles.

Thinking back about the way things had happened, he was actually glad that it had been Fager who had caught him. Any smart cop would have put him in the car, then driven around for a while to look for the girl.

Even though Fager didn't exactly qualify as a smart cop, Sanger had decided not to take any chances. That was what had prompted the remark about Fager's daughter. He figured he could survive a little slapping around if it meant for sure that Eloisa had enough time to get away.

Sanger was so lost in his thoughts that he didn't see the two Country Club boys walk up.

"Look, Bill." One of the boys poked the other and gestured with his head toward Sanger. "He kinda looks like a dawg in that cage."

"Yeah, he does," said the second boy. "Kinda like a COON dawg."
"Ha...ha...ha!" they both laughed. "Yeah, a COON dawg!"

"You been hanging 'round with coons too long, Sanger." The first one had walked closer to the cell and laced his fingers in the wire. "You starting to look and act like 'em. Next thing we know, you'll be wanting to bring 'em in the front door of your house 'stead of the back where they belong. 'Specially if you been hosing one on a regular basis.

"Yeah, Sanger, you done went and turned into a white coon. Once word gets around about you, no self-respecting white person will ever speak to you again. As the old saying goes, 'you done went and screwed up royally'."

"Speaking of screwing up." Sanger casually looked up at the pair. "Is it true that both your mamas married their first cousins, got pregnant, and you're their retarded offspring? I understand your smart family members are all patients in the State Mental Hospital's idiot ward. Is that true, or is someone just spreading vicious rumors about you boys?"

"Real friggin' funny, Sanger." They both turned and started to walk away, then one looked back at Sanger. "But we'll see who gets the last laugh. You've had it in this town, boy."

The Country Club clowns had reminded Sanger about Eloisa's aunt, Beth Prince. He had intended to ask Eloisa if she had heard about the shooting, but everything happened before he had a chance. It probably wasn't important, though; it wasn't like she was really her aunt or anything.

Officer Fager had reported to the Chief of Police, Bob Jackson, as soon as he had handed Sanger over to the desk Sergeant. The Chief had left word for Detective Roberts to report to him as soon as he came in. The Chief was doing some busywork when Roberts walked into his office.

"Pull the door to and pull up a chair, Mitchell." The Chief made the order as he looked up and saw Roberts. "What's the deal on the school break-in? Fager's got the whole thing turned into some kind of crime of the century with potential racial implications. He also said the kid attacked him and resisted arrest. Said he had to get a little rough."

"Well, I just came from talking to Mr. Jennings, the Principal over at Eliza Prince Elementary School." Roberts had pulled a straight back chair closer to the Chief's desk. "He's the one that made the original call. It seems that nobody actually broke into the school."

"Well, if nobody actually broke into the school, then why the hell did he call us?" The Chief's demeanor was turning toward anger.

"Well." Roberts automatically sat up straighter in response to the Chief's change. "It happens that they have an alarm over at the school rigged to a utility room door around back of the building. Anytime the door is opened, the alarm goes off. Jennings came to his office and the alarm had been tripped. Since he's a real chicken-shit type, he got scared and called the police."

"But I thought you said that the school wasn't actually broken into?" The Chief's anger had turned into a puzzled look on his face.

200

"That's where it get's a little technical." Roberts knew he had his superior's interest. "They don't keep the utility room door locked. It's an access door to the roof for the fire department. It has to stay unlocked at all times."

"So, what you're telling me is that the two kids just walked through the door and climbed onto the roof." The Chief was obviously concentrating hard. "Does the school have a 'no trespassing' sign on the door or anything?"

"No sir, they don't." Roberts looked directly at the Chief.

"Now, let me get this straight." The Chief's brow was wrinkled with concentration. "First we've got two teenage kids—forget their race for a minute."

"That's right, Chief."

"These two teenage kids wander up to a public building, enter through an unlocked door, go inside, and climb up on the roof." The Chief looked at his bookcase as he talked. "While on the roof, did they commit any vandalism or harm any school property?"

"No, they didn't Chief. Just by looking, you couldn't even tell they had been there."

"Then the best I can tell, Mitchell, their only crime at the school was one of poor judgement. Based on the circumstances, I can't see where they committed a crime. I'd say the school is as much to blame as they are."

"That's exactly the way I explained it to Mr. Jennings." Roberts smiled to himself at the way the Chief had followed the logic as if on cue. "Under the circumstances, he decided not to pursue charges. He's also agreed to find a solution to the door problem, too. I think he just wanted to forget what happened tonight and get home for a drink."

"That still leaves the resisting arrest charge against Sanger." The Chief looked at Roberts for a response. "We can forget about the girl, but he still has to answer for that."

201

"You're right, Chief. Somebody needs to answer for those charges, but I don't think it should be the boy!"

"What are you talking about, Roberts? You gone crazy or what? If Sanger don't answer for the charges, then who does?"

"Let me ask you a question, Chief. Have you ever noticed how many people seem to resist arrest when Fager is the officer involved?"

"Yeah, I've noticed he seems to have a little problem in that area; but so what? What exactly are you getting at, Roberts? Quit talking in circles and just say what's on your mind."

"Well, tonight I heard the burglary call and rolled on it, too." Roberts was picking his words carefully—he didn't want this to come out the wrong way. "I must've been quite a bit further away than Fager because he got there enough earlier than me so that he had Sanger in the car and was heading to the station when I got in the area.

"As I got a couple of blocks from the school, I noticed Fager stopped on the street with Sanger outside the car. He was so involved with what he was doing that he didn't even see me pull up."

"What exactly was he doing?" The Chief had leaned forward with his elbows on the desk.

"What he was doing was beating the crap out of Sanger. If I hadn't grabbed him, he might have really hurt the boy!"

"Was the boy resisting?" The Chief seemed to have already guessed the answer.

"Resisting?" Roberts grunted. "The only thing Sanger could do was block the blows with his face; Fager had the boy's hands cuffed behind his back.

"Fager was beating a defenseless prisoner. The thought of a white boy and a black girl must have struck a sensitive nerve with him. He was half crazy when I stopped him."

"Then you think that we should turn the boy loose?" The Chief had raised an eyebrow in questioning fashion.

"Chief, I think we don't have a case of any type against him. Fager was beating the boy right there on the street. Any halfway decent lawyer could probably find a dozen people that saw it out their windows.

"If anybody should be charged with anything, it ought to be Fager. The man's a maniac, Chief. If you keep ignoring his behavior, one of these days he's gonna kill somebody."

"You're right, Mitchell; I know you are. The man is crazy, and I've known it for a long time. But he has a lot of powerful friends that owe him favors. If I try to get rid of him, I'll end up being the one gone, not him.

"I'll talk to him but I'm afraid that's about all I can do for now. What I want you to do is go get that boy and take him home. On the way you might suggest that he join the army or something. Once word gets around that he has a black girlfriend, life is gonna get real hard for him in Princeville. Try and talk some sense into him."

"I'll try, sir, but I don't know how much good it's gonna do. If that boy don't want to go, I suspect that it'll take a lot to run him off."

Thirty minutes later, Sanger and Roberts were pulling out of the police station parking lot in Roberts' car. It had taken a few minutes to get Sanger out of the holding cell and then several more to clean the blood off his face.

"Thanks for getting me out of there, Mr. Roberts." Sanger looked up at the jail as they turned into the street.

"Well." Roberts looked over at Sanger much the way a father would a son. "They didn't really have much on you. After all, the door at the school was left open and y'all didn't harm any property. The fact that Fager went crazy and slapped you around didn't hurt anything either.

"If you get any more bright ideas like this in the future, just remember how lucky you got tonight. And Jerry, do yourself a favor. Whoever the black girl is, forget her; y'all are just asking for trouble in this town.

"If you're smart, you'll even consider leaving Princeville. After word gets around about tonight, and it will get around, certain people in this town are gonna create a living hell for you. You'll never be able to live this down, not in 20 years."

"Don't take this wrong, Mr. Roberts, but I am planning on leaving Princeville. It's not because of tonight, though. I've been planning all summer to go to California to college in the fall. As a matter of fact, I've already given the boss at work my notice. A week from Sunday and I'm old news in this town."

"That's great, Jerry. I hate for a guy to have to leave his hometown, but in your case it'll be best for everybody concerned. What about the girl? Is she going with you?"

"Oh, you've got that situation all wrong, Mr. Roberts. She and I are just friends. She won't be going to California with me. When I leave this shithole town, I'll be by myself—no company."

"Yeah, I'm sure I have that situation wrong." Roberts tried to speak as sarcastically as possible. "Whatever you do, make sure you're a long way from here when you start. Where do you want me to drop you anyway, at your house?"

"Just drop me on Coahoma Street. That'll be O.K."

They drove the rest of the way without talking. Pretty soon the police car was pulling up under the gang's streetlight.

"Try to stay out of trouble until you leave, Jerry. It'd be better if you stayed on this side of town and away from places like the Ranch. You show up out there and trouble won't be far away."

"I'll stay out of trouble." Sanger gave Roberts a long serious look. "As long as folks leave me alone. I'm not gonna hide, though. I haven't done anything wrong. If people in Princeville don't bother me, then I won't bother them. That especially goes for Fager. But if he comes at me again, my hands won't be cuffed behind my back. I'm gonna give him whatever he asks for.

"Thanks again, Mr. Roberts! You're a good guy. Too bad there aren't a few more like you around. Princeville might not be such a bad place to live."

"This coming week is gonna be a real interesting one," Roberts thought to himself as he accelerated down Coahoma Street. "I sure hope Sanger makes it. He's really a pretty good kid. I just hope he's smart enough to stay away from his black girlfriend long enough for them both to get clear of this town. Otherwise, an interesting week could turn into a nasty one in a hurry!"

# 25

Saturday afternoon at the Princeville Country Club was always a very busy time, especially during the hot summer season. The swimming pool was usually filled to capacity with the younger set, while their parents played tennis or golf.

From the golf course and tennis courts, the parents migrated ultimately to the coolness of the bar. The kids stayed by the pool until the sun had exhausted its tan-producing rays for the day; then they headed home for a quick change and final preparations for the evening.

Today, however, regardless of age or activity, the topic of conversation for all the privileged set was one and the same. By now, everyone had heard about the incident at Eliza Prince School and was discussing their version of probably what had been going on.

Jim Prince was sitting by the edge of the pool in a lounge chair watching a couple of the girls splashing around in the shallow end of the pool. Both the girls were careful, though, not to get the other's hair wet. That would have been considered the ultimate error. After all, they were there to see and be seen, not do something as drastic as actually get wet.

Jim wasn't really thinking about the girls, however. His mind was on his mother and what had happened to her last weekend. Ever since the shooting, he had felt kind of embarrassed when he saw his friends. He must not have been the only one, though, who was embarrassed. His friends were just now starting to come around again and treat him in some sort of normal fashion. Apparently, they all felt as awkward about the situation as he did. No one seemed to know exactly what to say.

Today, he was just enjoying the sunshine and appreciating the fact that things were getting back to normal. In a few minutes, Bill and Charlie would show up and it would be business as usual. They'd sit around and eye-rape all the girls while speculating which ones put out and which ones didn't.

Jim had heard about all the "Sorry to hear about your mother" comments he could stomach. At first, he had been upset by the shooting; then reality sunk in.

His being upset had been nothing but embarrassment at what people would say. If people knew how he really felt about his drunken slut of a mother, they wouldn't have bothered to offer him their condolences. As far as he was concerned, she was an obstacle to the family money that had now been removed. He and his father were better off without her around to embarrass them. Prince was deep in his own thoughts as Charlie and Bill walked up.

"Hey Prince." Bill Sands' shadow was blocking the sun. "What you doing looking at the cherries in the pool so hard? You know that'll make you crazy. Neither one of those little cunts is putting out yet."

Both Bill and Charlie laughed hard as they waited for their buddy to respond.

"Well." Prince seemed to be carefully formulating his response. "Cherry-pickin' season is comin' up. Maybe it's about time we tried a couple to see if they're ripe."

They all three looked at the two girls frolicking in the pool and laughed. The girls noticed the attention being directed their way and waved at the boys in appreciation.

"I guess you heard about your good buddy Sanger by now?" Charlie Merk directed his attention away from the girls in the water and back to Prince.

"Yeah." Prince's face reddened at the thought of Sanger. "I heard. Too bad the cops turned him loose. I bet the city jail'd be a real fun place to spend the night. But at least he's out where we can get to him."

"Get to him?" Sands glanced at the girls as they climbed from the pool. "What do you mean? You got something in mind for him?"

"Oh yeah, I got something in mind alright. Remember, I still owe him for that night at the Ranch when he kicked me in the nuts. I couldn't get it up for a week. There for a while, I thought he had done me in for good. I owe that nigger-loving bastard, and now I'm gonna make him pay—big time."

"Whatcha gonna do, Jim?" Merk seemed anxious to participate in whatever the plan was. "What you got in mind for the asshole? Tell us."

"Not yet." Prince seemed to be enjoying a private joke. "I don't want my plan ruined. But don't worry; I'll tell you later. As a matter of fact, the whole stinking town's gonna know about Sanger and his nigger girlfriend. When I'm through kicking his ass, he's gonna be begging me to let him tell the whole town what her name is. I'm gonna make that white nigger wish he'd never heard of Princeville, Mississippi!"

---

While Jim Prince and his buddies were sitting out by the pool discussing Sanger's fate, his father was sitting at a table in the back of the Country Club bar with a few of his close friends talking about exactly the same thing. The only difference was their approach.

Jackson Prince had spent the last couple of hours sitting in the bar with his friends drinking. He was thankful that the group finally had another topic to discuss other than speculating about who had shot his wife.

Personally, he didn't give a shit about his wife and wished people would shut up about her. The thing about the Sanger boy and the nigger girl had meant some very welcome relief for him. He was now leading the discussion about what ought to be done with the boy so that this type of behavior could be discouraged in the future.

"We got to make an example out of that little nigger-lover!" Ralph Bunsten sat his empty glass on the table. Bunsten was one of five men sitting around the table. He was the mayor of Princeville in addition to owning several local businesses and the newspaper. Besides Bunsten,

209

there was Roy Gilbert. Gilbert was the typical wealthy Southern planter. His plantation took in 6,000 acres of the best cotton land in the Delta. Next to Gilbert sat Mike Dickson. The banking business in town not controlled by Jackson Prince, he controlled.

And rounding out the table was Leland Benton. In addition to being a very prominent local attorney, he also was the local slumlord. It was rumored that he owned over 200 tenement houses located in the black section of town that he rented to poor, black families that couldn't afford better.

Most of his properties lacked working plumbing or adequate water and electricity. Through his connections in city hall, however, he avoided having ever had even one complaint filed by city building inspectors.

These five men were the controlling force in everything that happened in Princeville. Through the city councilmen, most of whom they had bought and paid for, this small group of men made all major decisions concerning the town.

At least once a week they all met there at the Club bar and informally decided the fate of the town. They had been operating in that fashion for years.

When they passed on, their heirs would pick up and continue the process. Contrary to popular belief, the wealth of those five men controlled the town, not the voters. This afternoon they were discussing a very important issue.

Bunsten cleared his throat and continued. "Something needs to be done before the niggers across the tracks get any ideas about where they stand."

"Well, I personally don't see what the big deal is." Gilbert's glass dripped moisture on his khaki pants. "It's not like we all haven't screwed a nigger or two in our time. Me myself, I've sure had my share of 'em."

"It's not the screwin' we're concerned with here." Dickson watched Gilbert brush the moisture away. "I talked to Burt Fager, and he said that

210

the way the boy was protecting the girl, you'd think he was in love with her or something. Fager couldn't even get her name out of Sanger after slapping him around pretty good. Naw, it's more than just a horny redneck we're dealing with here, boys."

"If we let that kind of shit go on in this town," Benton sounded like he was addressing a jury, "then the next thing we know, some white nigger like Sanger will come up with the bright idea of getting married to one of them."

"Yeah." Bunsten was getting agitated. "Then the niggers will start to think they're as good as we are. When that happens, it'll be the beginning of the end to everything our daddies and us have put together in this town. We'll lose control; they're too damn many of them in Coahoma County."

"Y'all are right." Prince was taking charge of the conversation. "We've got too many uppity niggers in this town already; we sure as hell don't need any more. We'd better make an example out of this Sanger boy before anything else happens."

"What about the girl?" Benton's lawyer personality would not allow him to take a backseat in the discussion. "Has Fager found out who she is yet? What are we gonna do about her?"

"He's still working on it," answered Dickson.

"Let's deal with her when we come to it." Prince sounded a bit impatient. "Right now, I think we ought to concentrate on the boy. We know who he is and we can take care of him immediately, while the incident is still fresh in people's minds."

"Ralph, you control the paper. How about a big story on the whole thing? Maybe you could influence the embellishment of it a bit."

"How so?" Bunsten glanced to Prince for an answer.

"Well, you could add a little to the story like 'unknown damage to the school after allegedly having sexual relations on the roof.' You know;

211

that type of stuff so that our average citizen in Princeville is outraged at his behavior. We want to make it very hard on Sanger; so hard, in fact, that he can't stay in town. We need him gone!"

"How about getting him fired from his job then?" Gilbert had joined the feeding frenzy. "Who can get to his boss?"

"I can." Benton smirked. "He works at the Coke Plant, doesn't he?" "Yeah, he does," responded Bunsten.

"Well." Benton appeared very smug. "Consider it done. I know one of the managers in Memphis. He owes me a couple of favors. When Sanger shows up for work on Monday, he'll get the sad news. He's worked his last day in Princeville. Y'all can count on it!"

"Good!" Prince seemed pleased. "And Mike, why don't you have Fager kinda keep an unofficial eye on him, too. You know, have him put a little off-the-record pressure on the boy to leave town. Tell him that we don't want anything official, though. We want the boy gone, not sitting downtown in jail like some kind of martyr for the other nigger-lovers in town."

The group of men sat around for another hour talking about the heat and sports. As they did, the bar started to fill up with all the golfers and tennis players who had wandered in for a little refreshment and entertainment following their afternoon of exercise.

Little did the average patron realize how the fate of a young man had been decided that afternoon. Little did they also realize how their town was really run!

212

# 26

**M**onday evening Eloisa was working down in the store just like she had been doing every night all summer. So far, she thought that her parents still weren't suspicious of anything.

Even Friday night when she had called and asked them to come and pick her up from her friend's house, they hadn't thought much of it. She had simply told them that she had forgotten the time and before she knew it, it was getting dark. Since she knew that they didn't want her out walking alone after dark, she had called and asked for a ride. They even praised her for having the good sense to call.

She couldn't help but be worried about Jerry, though. She had seen how rough the policeman was with him. Who knows what had happened to him when he got to the police station! If there were just some way to find out if he was all right. She knew it would be real hard to get on that bus Friday not knowing if he was in jail or hurt or what. She simply had to find out before Friday.

As if somebody had been reading her mind, the phone started to ring. It was him calling! She somehow knew it. Quickly, she ran over to the phone and scooped it into her hand.

Excitedly, she answered it: "Hello!" For once in her life, she was grateful that they didn't have an extension upstairs. Ever since she had been old enough to use the phone, she had pestered her daddy about not having an extension upstairs. He had told her that one phone was enough and anymore was an expense that was unnecessary.

213

Tonight, she was thankful for her father's frugal ways.

"Hi, it's me," she heard in the earpiece. "Don't talk, just listen. I'm O.K.. They've dropped all the charges and we're in the clear. Just make sure you're on that bus Friday. I promise you that I won't be far behind you. I love you; gotta go now. See you in Chicago."

Before she could say she loved him too, the line went dead. Even if she hadn't been able to talk to him, at least now she knew he was alright.

After placing the phone back on the receiver, she turned to find her father staring at her from the bottom of the stairway. She silently said a prayer of thanks that Jerry had not given her time to say anything.

"Who was that?" Her father was using a voice that she recognized as the one he reserved for periods of anger.

"I couldn't tell." She did not like lying to her father. "There was a lot of static on the line. Maybe they'll call back."

Mr. Jones turned and started back upstairs. Eloisa noticed that he held the day's newspaper tightly bunched up in his right hand. "That was a close one," she thought to herself as she walked back over to her place by the cash register.

---

Sanger hung the phone up carefully as he eased out of the bathroom and back into the hallway. He had taken the phone into the semi-privacy of the bathroom when nobody had been around.

Being that quick and blunt with Eloisa had hurt, but he knew that she would understand. He just couldn't take the chance that someone in his family would catch him making the call and then ask who he was talking to. Not after what had been in the paper today!

The article in the paper had been like the icing on a shit cake. It had simply served as an appropriate end to what had already been a really bad day.

It had all started at 7:00 that morning when he walked in to punch the time clock at work. Martin had been standing beside the clock waiting for him.

As soon as Sanger saw him, he knew he was in trouble.

When Martin opened his mouth to talk, his first words confirmed Sanger's suspicion. "Come on out back, Jerry. I need to talk to you about something!" Martin turned and walked through the door leading to the rear of the Plant. Sanger followed him.

Since the office was just one big room and you couldn't talk without the other people in there hearing everything you said, Sanger figured that Martin was taking him back to the shed where they kept Coke machines and parts. That way he could fire him in private.

As he followed Martin into the shed, Sanger noticed that he glanced around quickly to make sure nobody else was there. Obviously, what he was about to say, he didn't want overheard.

"I got a call last night from Mr. Bildon in Memphis." Martin had a sad expression on his face. "You know who he is, don't you?" Before Sanger had a chance to answer, Martin continued. "He's the big boss in Memphis. He works for the family that owns all the Coke plants from there south through Greenwood.

"Do you know what he wanted?" Again, before Sanger could answer, he continued without a break. "What he wanted was to talk about you. He told me to fire you first thing today. He said he didn't want you on his property another instant. He also told me that if I gave you a good recommendation to anybody else in Princeville, I wouldn't be far behind you in the unemployment line. He was really pissed!"

"Pissed?" Sanger was genuinely surprised. "At me? Why me? I wouldn't know the old fart if he walked into our living room. Did he tell you why? Did he say if Mr. Jenner, the owner, told him to fire me?

"I met Mr. Jenner one time; he was a really nice man. I don't believe he would order something as unfair as this! Bildon did this on his own, didn't he?"

"Yeah, he told me why; and it really doesn't matter who told him or didn't tell him. I do what Bildon says; he's my boss." Martin was fighting a losing battle to control his anger. Sanger couldn't tell if the suppressed anger was directed at him or Mr. Bildon.

"He said that one of his friends had called from Princeville to inform him that one of his white employees had taken up with a nigger girl and the affair was stirring up the whole town. Mr. Bildon told me he didn't have anything against nigras; he just thought they'd be better off with their own kind. He said to tell you that screwin' a nigger was one thing; but then tryin' to protect her like she was a white girl was something else. There wasn't a place at his plant for a white-trash fool like that, he told me. He said you weren't any better than a nigger yourself."

"So then, I'm fired, huh?" Sanger wasn't mad at Martin; it wasn't his fault. "Don't worry about it Martin; you know this would've been my last week anyway. Did you tell old man Bildon that?"

"No, I didn't. He didn't give me much of a chance. He just wanted me to get rid of you."

"So, I'm being fired because of hearsay?" Sanger laughed a not so happy laugh. "You haven't even asked me if it's true. Don't you want to hear my version of what really happened. Don't you find it kinda strange that the police let me go and didn't file any charges?

If I had done everything that people are accusing me of, I'd be locked up for years. The police let me go, but you're firing me. Doesn't that strike you as a bit unfair?"

"Fairness has nothing to do with this," Martin shot back. "If you had been in my kitchen eating supper with me and my family when all this was supposed to have happened, it still wouldn't matter! Mr. Bildon said fire you and that is that; I got no say in the matter."

"Sounds logical to me." Sanger sounded very sarcastic.

"I'm going up to the office and get your last pay envelope together." Martin turned and walked away. Almost as an afterthought, he stopped and faced Sanger again. "Oh yeah, I'm giving you two weeks severance pay. You at least deserve that considering how good a job you've done on the dock. That way you'll come out better than you would've anyhow."

Sanger's eyes followed Martin as he turned and walked away. Instead of following, he sat down on an upturned Coke case. No need standing around the office while Martin did the paperwork necessary for the pay. He'd give him ten minutes and then go up. That way, he could just get his pay envelope and leave.

---

Sanger walked into the room that he shared with his brother and started to pack his things. He figured that his mama and daddy would be about ready to have a talk with him. They had been out in the backyard for over an hour now.

He figured that he might as well be ready to go when they came in and told him to get out of the house. He could see them through the window as his daddy read the newspaper for probably the tenth time. It was almost as if he thought that if he read it enough, the story about his son might actually change.

Sanger was packing the last of the things he needed in an old suitcase his grandma had given him. The sound of the back porch's screen door creaking made his stomach do a flip inside. His parents had finally decided on some kind of course of action.

He sat down on the edge of the bed and waited. He knew that this might be the last time he saw his parents for a long time. Depending on how they took things, maybe forever.

They walked into the room together. As Sanger looked up, his father was closing the bedroom door. When his eyes caught those of his mother, he could tell that she had been crying.

217

As he watched, his father held out the newspaper and said, "What's this all about?" He then tossed it onto Sanger's lap.

Staring up at him Sanger once again saw the headline he had read earlier in the day.

## "LOCAL WHITE BOY ACCUSED OF BREAKING INTO SCHOOL FOR SEXUAL RENDEZVOUS WITH BLACK GIRL!"

"It's not true." Sanger worked hard to stay calm. He knew this was not the time to lose his temper. He had created this problem for himself; his parents were just forced participants.

If he had followed his own instinct that first time he saw Eloisa at the Coke Plant, none of this would ever have happened. No, he wasn't going to take this out on his parents. It wasn't their fault; it was his. He'd simply take whatever they had to dish out and then he would leave. He owed them that. They had always tried to be good parents.

"That cut you came in with over your eye on Friday night, did Burt Fager do that to you when he arrested you?" Sanger's father was looking at him intently. "It says in the paper that he was the one that caught you. Did that sawed off son-of-a-bitch hit you? I'll kill the bastard if he did. He didn't have a right to do that no matter what you done."

"I kinda did that to myself." Sanger tried to sound convincing. "I hit my head on the ground when I fell down."

He hated lying to his father like that, but he knew if he didn't that his daddy would go and kick the shit out of Fager and land in jail himself. His pride would not allow one of his children being abused and not making the guilty party pay, even under the current set of circumstances. It was just the way he was. A newspaper article didn't change that.

"O.K., we'll forget about the eye." His father sounded sincere. "What about the article? Is it true what the paper said?"

"If it were true, do you think the police would've let me go? I don't know where the paper got that stuff. It's almost like they just made it up so as to make me look like some kind of creep or something."

"Forgit about the paper then, Jerry. You tell me what happened. Something was goin' on over at the school or the police wouldn't been called. Let's hear it."

Sanger looked up into his father's face, then his mother's. He had two choices; he could lie to them or tell them what really happened. If he lied, they'd eventually find out the truth anyway. Might as well break it to them now.

"The truth is that I was on the roof at the school and I was with a black girl. We were just talking, and. . . ."

Sanger told his parents the whole story about what had happened at the school on Friday night. The only parts he skipped were Eloisa's name and the slapping around by Fager.

"Are you crazy?" His father seemed flabbergasted. "This ain't Chicago; this is Princeville, Mississippi. White folks and niggers don't become friends, especially when one's a boy and the other's a girl. Everybody's just naturally gonna think what the newspaper did."

"Who is she?" Up until then, Sanger's mother had remained quiet. She was now staring down at him waiting for an answer to her question.

"It doesn't really matter who she is." Sanger tried to downplay the question. "As you can see, I've got my stuff packed and I'm leaving. If y'all will let me stay tonight, then tomorrow morning I'll be gone and you won't be bothered anymore. If you want me gone tonight, I understand that, too. Regardless, by tomorrow I'll just be a bad memory.

"Once I'm gone, the people around town will forget all about what they read. In a month or so, it'll just be old news. Nobody'll care."

Sanger's mother went on in pursuit of an answer to her question as if she had not heard any part of his answer beyond "it doesn't really matter."

219

"It must matter, if you won't tell us who she is. Why do you want to protect her? This way, you've got all the trouble and she's got none. What's so special about her anyhow?"

"She's special to me and that's all that counts!" Sanger felt a trace of anger starting to make its way into his tone.

"Forget about her!" His father interrupted. "And I mean both of you. She's not our problem. We've got to decide what we're gonna do."

"I'll just leave." Sanger started to get up. "Then the problem'll be solved."

"Sit back down! Ain't no son of mine gonna be run out of town lickin' his ass like some wounded dog. You're goin' to stay right here till next Saturday like you intended. You ain't been accused of anything that half the sons-of-bitches in town ain't done a dozen times themselves.

"To hell with 'em and their half-assed paper. All I've ever been able to give you is your pride, and I'll be damned if I'm lettin' you leave home without it. Unpack that suitcase. You ain't goin' no place till the weekend."

Sanger had been secretly hoping that his father would react in this fashion. Now he could stay and make sure Eloisa was on that bus Friday. He could never have left town anyhow without knowing for sure. He would just keep a low profile until she was gone, take care of a couple of matters, then ease on out of town himself.

220

# *27*

Friday at last! Eloisa had thought it would never come. This had been without doubt the longest week of her life. Ever since Monday night her father had treated her as if she didn't exist. It had all started right after the newspaper arrived.

Somehow, he had decided that the black girl in the article was her. He hadn't said anything, though; he had just given her the silent treatment. Her mother hadn't been much different; she had just said what was absolutely necessary as they had gone through the week and made the necessary arrangements for the trip to Chicago.

So, here it was Friday morning and Eloisa was about to leave town for Chicago. She knew that once she left, it might be a long time before she got to see her parents again, especially after they found out about her and Jerry.

She had decided that they had to have a talk before she left. The three of them had always been very close. It just wasn't right for her to leave town and have them thinking the worst about her. They had to be told the truth, whether they believed it or not.

When Eloisa walked into the kitchen, both of her parents were sitting at the table having breakfast. She knew that if she were going to talk to both of them at the same time, it had to be now. In a few more minutes her father would go downstairs and open the store for the day. It was now or never.

She walked directly to the table and sat down. "We've got to talk. You two have been giving me the treatment all week, ever since you read that article in the paper on Monday. I don't want to leave this afternoon with things like this between us."

There was a strained silence at the table before her father finally spoke. "What would make you do something like that? You know how white people are, especially white men when it comes to black women. They only want to use us. He only wanted to use you."

Eloisa's mother looked angrily at her father. "I thought we agreed that we weren't going to bring this up with her. What's done is done. The important thing is to get her to Chicago and away from here."

"She brought it up; I didn't." Mr. Jones threw his own look back at her. "Now that it's up, I'd like a few answers!"

"O.K." Eloisa looked at her mother then at her father. "I'll answer your questions, but you don't have to bother asking them. I already know what they are.

"Answer one is YES! It was me that was at the school. Answer two is that I didn't do anything like you or the newspaper think I did.

"What do you think? That I somehow changed over night. Can't you see that I'm the same person that I've always been. If you need proof, take me to see Dr. Williams. There's still time before we leave. He can examine me and prove to you that I'm still a virgin. If you won't take my word for it, maybe you'll take his."

Again, there was silence at the table. Eloisa's parents looked at each other questionably. All of a sudden, there seemed to be confusion in their eyes.

"Then what were the two of you doing on the roof of the school?" Her father seemed genuinely confused. "And why did the newspaper write what it did?"

"Who knows why the paper wrote what it did." Eloisa sensed the change in her father's demeanor. "Maybe the same person wrote the article that wrote Dr. Martin Luther King is an associate of known communists. Who knows why they write what they do. As far as what we were doing, we were just talking. That's all."

"If you were just talking, then why did you have to sneak up on top of the school building?" Mrs. Jones had apparently decided it was alright to ask the questions.

"Would you have let me talk to him if you had known? Of course you wouldn't. You'd have run him off and not let me out of the house for the rest of the summer."

"But why did you want to talk to him in the first place?" Mr. Jones had a confused look on his face. "He's a white boy. Haven't I told you about white boys?"

"That's exactly the point, Daddy. All I know about white people is what you've told me, and what you've told me has all been bad. I wanted to find out for myself."

"And just what did you find out?"

"The first thing I found out is that white people don't really know any more about us than we know about them. They're told what to believe, and most of them believe it. Very few of them have the interest to want to know the truth.

"Jerry was curious about me, and I was curious about him so we became friends. All we ever did was talk. I swear it. We never did any of the stuff that the paper implied.

"The only reason we met up on the school's roof was because we knew people would talk if we were seen together. So, we found a place where we wouldn't be seen.

"I don't know what happened that made the police come. All of a sudden, that little white policeman showed up. When he did, Jerry made me hide in the building while he ran. He knew the policeman would chase him, and then I could get away.

"He could've gotten away, but he fell down on purpose so the cop would be wrestling with him and I could get away. After I got away, I hid across the street and watched. The policeman was really rough with Jerry, but Jerry never told him my name. Does that sound like a person who just wanted to use me?"

As Eloisa finished her speech, her father just looked at her. All of a sudden, he smiled. It wasn't the first time that his little girl had out talked him. Probably wouldn't be the last. Eloisa smiled back.

"You're right, honey; we should've known better." Mr. Jones looked relieved. "Your word is good enough for me; we don't need no doctor involved.

"I'm still upset about you being involved with that white boy, but I feel better knowing that nothing happened between the two of you. Besides, after this afternoon it won't matter anyhow. You'll be on your way to Chicago, and he'll still be here. Let's just forget it for now."

"Yeah, let's forget it for now." Mrs. Jones' face had lit up with a grin for the first time in almost a week. "We can talk about it on the bus. We'll have plenty of time then. Right now, we need to concentrate on finishing up getting you ready for the trip."

Eloisa's father got up from where he was eating and came around the table to where she was sitting. He gave her a kiss on the forehead as he passed on his way downstairs to open up for the day.

Eloisa felt better about things as she got up and started to help her mother clear the breakfast dishes.

---

Sanger was really getting anxious. It was Friday morning and he had been sitting around the house for most of the week. Except for a couple of walks over to Coahoma Street, he had been right there since Monday. He figured that he had caused his parents enough grief for a while.

224

His game plan was simple. He'd hang around and make sure Eloisa got on the bus, then he'd load up the old Ford and hit the road himself.

Everyone was gone from the house except him, and he was glad of it. Even though no one had really said anything to him about what was going on, the tension was evident.

The whole family seemed to be going out of their way to avoid talking about it. The unnatural environment was beginning to take its toll on everybody. At least when he was in the house alone he didn't have to smile at his family and pretend nothing was going on.

As he was sitting in the living room appreciating the solitude, the phone in the hall started to ring.

Ever since Monday, the ringing of the phone had been a cause of considerable aggravation. Seemed like every bigoted kook in town had called to make some obscene commentary on their perception of what had happened on the roof of the school.

The only positive aspect of the whole thing was that at least they didn't know about Eloisa. He could take whatever their sick minds could dish out as long as he knew she was safe from the abuse.

After the tenth ring, Sanger got up, walked to the hall and picked up the receiver. Apparently they weren't going to give up. "Hello."

"Hi, nigger-lover." The voice on the other end sounded almost jovial.

Sanger had taken about all the verbal abuse he intended to take. Up till now, he and his family had merely returned the phone to its cradle when a crank call was received. Enough was enough!

"Better black than what yo mama's been screwing this week." Sanger spoke casually into the phone. "Is this her week for big dogs or donkeys?"

"Well, I'm glad to see you haven't lost your sick sense of humor, Sanger," the voice on the line said. "Maybe I can change that when I tell everybody who your black whore is. Might make interesting reading on the front page of the paper. Whadya think?"

Sanger thought he recognized the voice on the phone. As the caller had continued to talk, there was little doubt left. Sanger knew exactly who it was. "Is this the way you get your jollies, Prince? Or maybe you're just trying to be nice and called to invite me out to the Club to swim with you and your buddies."

"Yeah, you can bet on it, asshole. You know we don't allow no niggers in our pool, black or white ones. I just called to let you know that I've figured out who your nigger slut is."

"Prince, I don't much like you, but I never really thought you were stupid. You mean to tell me that you actually believe the shit they publish in the paper? All these years of whackin' your wiener has finally caused your mind to snap."

"Well, Sanger, my mind is working well enough to put two plus two together. Eliza Prince School is right across the street from that store where we ran into you. And you sure went out of your way to help that high yellow bitch that was given me the hard time about the beer."

"Prince, are you gonna waste the rest of my morning or is there a point to this? If you think you know something that everybody else doesn't, then tell the world. I don't care. Just leave me alone."

"Do you really want me to leave you alone, Sanger? Is that what you really want?"

"What I'd really like is for you to drop dead, Prince, but I'd settle for you leaving me alone."

"I'll make you a deal, Sanger. You meet me tonight out at the Italian Club about 11:00, and I'll give you my word that I will forget what I know.

"I still owe you for that night at the Ranch. I don't give a shit about your nigger girlfriend; I just want everybody to see what a pansy ass you really are.

"Either you give me your word you'll be there or I'm going to the paper this morning and tell them what I think. You know it really doesn't matter whether it's true or not; they'll print it if I get my father to go along with me."

Sanger knew that Prince was right. The paper would print whatever he said. He just couldn't chance that the story would be printed before Eloisa left town.

"Prince, I don't give a shit what you think you know, but it would be my pleasure to meet you at the Italian Club tonight. You've got my word on it! I'll be there. And, Prince?"

"Yeah, Sanger?"

"Whatever happens tonight—that's the end of it between you and me. It doesn't do either one of us any good to keep looking over our shoulders. This is it!"

"You got it, Sanger. This will end it one way or another. See you tonight, asshole!"

The phone went dead in Sanger's hand. He put it down and walked back into the living room.

Sanger had lived in the South for his whole life, but its ways still baffled him. Here he and Prince were, two people that hated each other, giving and accepting each other's word on something. And the really weird part of it all was that each would keep his word regardless of what happened.

Tonight, they would drive out into the country and meet behind an old building where the local Italian men gathered on Sunday afternoons to gamble.

227

Like countless other guys before them, they would attempt to kick the stuffing out of each other in a fighting circle formed by car headlights. When it was over, nothing would really have been accomplished except for a few bruises and cuts.

Usually, there was never a clear-cut winner, so each would claim victory and go off to the Ranch for one last beer and a silent prayer that they never had to fight again.

Fighting was an unavoidable rite of manhood in the South. To be a man, you fought. Sanger had never actually been to the Italian Club as a participant before. In the past, he had always reacted in a more spontaneous fashion similar to his last meeting with Prince.

Tonight, however, he had to play the game. He had given his word as the only way of protecting Eloisa until she headed North. Even though she would be long gone by 11:00, he had given his word, and he would honor it. That was, after all, the way of the South.

---

Mr. Jones closed the store long enough to take Eloisa and her mother to the bus station. At exactly 3:30, they pulled into the parking lot behind the building. After unloading the luggage and putting it on the curb by the bus, he turned to face the two of them.

"Good-bye, Dear." He hugged his wife. "Call me when y'all get to the house in Chicago. I'll see you in nine days."

Then he turned to Eloisa and put his arms around her shoulders. "I'll see you at Christmas when you come back home. We'll miss you. Now you do what your aunt says and you study hard in school and make us proud of our little girl."

"I will, Daddy. And I'll write every week. Remember that I love you and Mama."

Mrs. Jones and Eloisa stood and watched as her father got back into the car and drove away. Eloisa was sad. It might be a long time before she saw her father again, and he put his arms around her in such a warm embrace, especially once he knew the whole story.

"Honey, you stay here and watch our things while I go inside and make sure everything is alright with our tickets." Mrs. Jones glanced toward the bus station. "I'll be right back."

Thirty minutes later, Eloisa and her mother were seated toward the rear of the bus as it pulled out of the depot and began its long trip to Chicago. Eloisa sat by the window staring out, deep in her own thoughts.

As if sensing Eloisa's serious thoughts, her mother touched her on the arm. "It'll be alright, baby. Once you get to Chicago and start school, you'll make lots of new friends to replace the ones you're leaving behind. The thing to do is to just turn loose the old and give the new a chance."

Eloisa turned and smiled at her mother, then once again returned her gaze out the window. "You're right," she thought to herself. "Jerry and I just need to forget this place and everything that's happened and start over new."

As the bus turned east on Third Street, Eloisa saw an old beat-up Ford sitting across the street. For a brief instant she and Jerry made eye-contact as the bus straightened up and accelerated down the street.

Each of them smiled. At last they were on their way. Eloisa now, and Jerry in a few hours.

# 28

After leaving the bus station, Sanger went back home and spent the rest of the afternoon packing and loading his things into the car. He intended to say his good-byes tonight. By midnight, he planned to be driving north.

At supper that night, his parents tried to talk him out of leaving until morning. They thought he was crazy to want to leave after supper. He prevailed by explaining to them that he wanted to get some driving in while it was cooler.

Since it was over 100 degrees outside and since his old car didn't have an air conditioner, they finally agreed that it probably made sense. He had, of course, failed to mention to them that he wasn't really planning on leaving until much later that night.

After his mama cried and his daddy shook his hand, Sanger backed the old Ford out of the drive and drove away.

His destination was Coahoma Street. He wanted to talk to the gang. Even though he had been over to Coahoma Street a couple of times during the week, he hadn't really had a chance to explain to his friends what had happened.

Each time he had walked over, the guys had been pretty cool toward his presence, then found an excuse to leave.

He knew that they were really pissed. What he didn't know was whether they were pissed at what they thought he had done or at him for not

231

confiding in them what was going on. Whatever it was, he had made up his mind that he was going to clear the air before he left. He owed them that much. They had all been friends too long for him to just drive off into the sunset with bad feelings between them.

Sanger stopped at the stop sign where his street intersected South Edwards. After looking both ways, he eased out into the street and turned left. At the next intersection, he turned left again. He was on Coahoma Street.

Immediately, he could see all the gang sitting around under the streetlight. His brother was even there. They hadn't talked much either during the last few days. Even though they shared a bed, the conversation had been almost nonexistent. Sanger figured his brother was pissed at him too.

The Coahoma Street Gang all stared at him as he pulled the car up close to the streetlight. Nobody said anything as he opened the car door and got out. They just followed him with their eyes as he walked the short distance down the asphalt street to the spot where they were all sitting.

Steed was the first one of them to speak. "Whadya doing here, Sanger? Decide to drop by on the way to visit your nigger girlfriend?"

"Yeah," Travis added. "You sure you can spare the time? We don't want to put you out or nothing."

"Look, I know all y'all are pissed off at me, and I don't blame you much." Sanger tried to not sound angry. "I should've told you what was going on, but I didn't think you'd understand. I guess I really messed things up."

"Messed up?" Culligan had hurt in his voice. "You messed up with a capital M. We've all had to eat a load of shit from every dickhead in town because of you. All the smart asses around Princeville want to know if we're bangin' niggers, too, or was it just you.

"It's hard enough living around here as it is. It shore don't make it any easier having to listen to that kind of crap."

Finally, Sanger's brother spoke up. "Why'd you do it? You know how this town is; people were bound to find out sooner or later. Niggers and whites can't mix around here, at least not like that; you been here long enough to know that."

The rest of the gang didn't say anything; they just sat on the curb and stared at Sanger. He stared back into their faces.

He knew this might be the last time that he saw his friends. Some he knew he would miss more than others. Even though he and his brother had always pretty much gone their separate ways; they were, nevertheless, close in their own special kind of way. They had, after all, shared a bedroom and bed for most of their lives.

Of the other members of the gang sitting there and staring at him, he knew that he'd probably miss Culligan the most. Ever since he could remember, they had been the closest to each other.

Steed and Jake and Wilkerson he'd miss, too, plus Parker and Travis. Hell, he'd miss all of them. They'd been his family for a lot of years now.

He was about to do something that would put him among people that he didn't know and that were probably a whole lot different than he. Chicago was a long way off. He'd always been told that Yankees weren't very friendly and that they would be rude and wouldn't help you. He wouldn't have the Coahoma Street Gang to fall back on anymore.

After today, really since the situation at the school, he was on his own. Whatever happened, he'd have to deal with it. Hopefully he was man enough to handle it!

"I know you guys don't want me around here anymore, and I understand." Sanger's eyes misted a bit; he hoped nobody noticed. "I won't be bothering you much longer.

"Jay probably told you that I'm leaving town tonight. After I'm gone, you won't be seeing me for awhile. I just wanted to try and explain before I left.

"First, I want to apologize, though. I had no right to bring this kind of trouble down on you. The only thing I can say is that I just never stopped to think about what my actions would do to you guys. Since I didn't feel that I was doing anything wrong, I guess I just thought there wouldn't be any problems. I thought I had everything figured out. Obviously, I didn't.

"I'm sorry y'all had to get involved in my trouble. Once I'm gone, maybe folks will forget about me and things will get back to normal around here."

"What exactly have you been doing?" Steed sounded friendlier. "Were you really doin' a nigger up on the school last Friday night? If you were, how did Fager catch you? He couldn't run down a three-legged turtle!"

"Considering the trouble I've caused y'all, I guess you are entitled to know the truth about what really happened." Sanger looked from face to face.

"The answers, however, aren't all that cut and dried. I was up on the school, but I wasn't screwing anybody. There was a girl up there with me. She was a black girl, but we were just talking, that's all.

"We've been meeting up on the school's roof most of the summer. It was the only place I could think of where we could go and not have people giving us a major dose of shit.

"We just wanted to be friends, that's all. All of you have friends that are girls. Because you happen to be friends doesn't mean you're screwing them."

"Our friends ain't niggers, though." Jake's dark face was frowning. "And we don't sneak around and meet them, then lie to each other about what we're doing."

"Well, I didn't exactly lie to y'all." Sanger stuttered a bit. "I just didn't tell you the truth. I was afraid that you wouldn't understand."

"How'd Fager catch you?" Steed was still curious.

234

"I pretended to fall down." Sanger smiled. "I wanted to make sure he was concentrating on me and nothing else."

"You mean to say that you let that little sawed-off shit catch you on purpose?" Parker had stood up and moved closer. "Why did you do that?"

"He did it so his girlfriend could get away." Culligan looked at Sanger for confirmation. "You must think a lot of her to do that, especially with an asshole like Fager."

"I knew I could handle getting caught; I wasn't so sure she could. I just couldn't take the chance. So, I fell down."

"Did you really get those marks when you fell down?" Sanger's brother was talking to him. "That's what Daddy said after y'all had your little talk."

"I don't ever want Daddy to know." Sanger's eyes pleaded. "But our friend Fager gave them to me after he had my hands cuffed behind my back. Y'all know how tough a guy he is."

"Yeah, we know about the sorry, yellow son-of-a-bitch." Jake was scowling.

"What are you gonna do now?" Steed was back to his usual friendly personality. "Are you really fixin' to leave town?

"I was out at the Ranch this afternoon and Slick told me he overheard Jim Prince and his buddies talking about a big fight tonight at the Italian Club. Slick said Prince was bragging 'bout what he was gonna do to you. Are you gonna fight him?"

"Yeah, I am." Sanger sighed. "As soon as it's over, I'm pointing my old Ford west. Prince and I have something to settle between us. I want it settled before I leave."

"Are you crazy?" Jay had jumped to his feet. "You go out to the Italian Club without us, and Prince and his Country Club friends'll kick your ass real good."

"I got no choice at this point. I gave my word that I'd be there. And after what's happened, I don't expect y'all to show up. I'm leaving as soon as it's over.

"Y'all got to stay in this hole. It wouldn't do for you to get involved. Besides, this thing is between Prince and me. It's got nothing to do with his friends. We'll just throw a couple punches, roll around in the dirt some, and then it'll be over. I'll get in my car and drive out of town. Pretty soon, everything will be back to normal."

"Sanger, you'd better forget about Prince." Culligan was angry. "None of us will be there to back you up. You go out to the Italian Club tonight and you'll be all by your lonesome. The best thing for you to do is leave town right now. You can be halfway cross Arkansas before anybody knows you're gone. That way there won't be no more trouble."

One after another the gang members added their agreement with what Culligan had said. The unanimous opinion of the gang was that if Sanger was crazy enough to go out to the Italian Club tonight, he'd be doing it by himself.

When the Coahoma Street Gang members had all had a chance to say their piece, they piled into Steed's car and drove away. None of them looked back at Sanger who was left standing alone under what had always been their streetlight.

As he stood there and watched the best friends he had ever had drive away, Sanger felt more alone than ever before in his life.

"I sure hope I'm doing the right thing," he thought to himself. "However, at this point, it really doesn't matter; I'm committed. Whatever happens, though, I can live with it; as long as Eloisa and I are together. That's really all that counts anymore."

236

# 29

S anger got back in the car and just sat looking around at his neighborhood. He had spent many an hour sitting on the curb under the gang's streetlight.

Looking at it now, he knew that his rear end had probably warmed the concrete for the last time on Coahoma Street. After tonight, he'd be lucky to ever see it again, much less hang out there with his friends.

He glanced down at his watch. It was 8:30. Still another two and a half hours until he was supposed to meet Prince. Plenty of time was still left to make a few preparations for tonight.

Without the Coahoma Street Gang there to back him up, he might need a little extra help. Even though he and Prince had given their word to meet tonight, neither had agreed to any conditions.

That could mean that Prince might decide to fight a little dirty. Sanger needed to prepare for that contingency. He'd have to get a few things ready for his upcoming social engagement.

By 10:00, Sanger was headed out of town toward the Italian Club. He had kept to the back streets as he worked his way out to Highway 61 on the south end of town. As he drove his car through the intersection and continued to the south, he was thankful that he hadn't seen anybody he knew. He didn't want Prince and his buddies to find out that he was going out to the Italian Club so early.

The old building was about three or four miles out of town. For as long as Sanger could remember, the Italian men in Princeville had used the building as a place to gather on Saturday and Sunday afternoons. They'd all come out to get away from their families and do a little drinking and gambling.

Even though everybody in town knew what was going on in the place, it had never been raided or interfered with in any fashion. Apparently, it was just another of the Southern traditions that was unofficially permitted by the local county law enforcement folks.

Sanger was driving on the gravel road that ran in front of the old building. He slowed down as he got closer. In the dark, he didn't want to drive past the Club too far. He was watching closely for another gravel road. It ran along the west side of the Italian Club and intersected the one he was now on.

The brakes on the old Ford squeaked as he slowed down even more and turned left on the other road. He drove for about a half mile and then slowed down again. Up ahead on the left was the entrance to a field road that he was looking for. He slowed down again and turned left.

The field road was just a dirt track winding its way through the cotton field. He followed it for about a quarter mile until it passed through a small stand of trees. That was the spot he had been looking for.

When he was younger, Sanger and his father and brother had come to this area often to rabbit hunt. They had always come this way to park the truck.

He pulled off the field road on to the grass leading up to the trees. Very carefully he drove forward toward the deep shadows they were now casting.

Sanger knew that there was an old home site just inside the tree line. He had often been there while hunting.

If he went slowly enough, he knew he could ease his car between the trees and park it where the old home had originally sat. Once there, it would be completely out of sight. Even someone driving past on the field road would not be able to see it.

Sanger pulled the car up as close as he could to the only part of the house that was still standing, the chimney. He turned off the lights and killed the engine.

The stand of trees that the old home site stood in was actually part of a line of trees that ran all the way back up to the road eventually running in front of the Italian Club.

The trees followed a small creek that ran north and south from the point where Sanger was currently sitting. He had followed its path many mornings while trying to flush a rabbit from among the many brush piles along its sides.

After gathering a few things from the back seat, Sanger walked away from the car and moved in the direction of the creek bed. This time of year it would be dry. He figured that even in the dark, walking up it shouldn't be too hard.

---

The Ranch seemed to be busier tonight than it had been for weeks. Jim Prince and his two buddies, Bill and Charlie, had been there for over an hour now.

They were the center of attention on the back side of the parking lot. Everyone wanted to know if it was really true about the big fight tonight out at the Italian Club.

"Hey, Prince," someone shouted from the hood of an adjacent car. "What's the deal with you and Sanger? Why do y'all have such a hard on for each other? He been hosing one of your babes or what?"

"Shit, man." Merk threw an empty beer can on the ground. "You know Sanger only porks niggers. He don't like white girls."

"That's right." Prince was in his element and happy about being there. "Besides, no self-respectin' white girl would let that nigger-loving bastard within ten yards of her.

"What's between us ain't got nothing to do with women. I just don't like smart ass pricks like Sanger. To talk to him, you'd get the idea that he thinks he's as good as the rest of us. Boys like that got to be put in their place.

"He lives over there in nigger-town, he works loading trucks, and he ain't got a pot to piss in. The only difference between him and his kind and the rest of the niggers they live with is their color. And in Sanger's case, that ain't a whole helluva lot different.

"Tonight, I'm just gonna give him a little lesson in manners. When I'm through with him, he'll be crawling back across the tracks with his tail tucked between his legs."

"Oh, that's it, huh?" came the sarcastic voice from the hood of the other car. "And all this time, I thought it was because Sanger kicked you in the nuts that night."

Everybody within listening distance of the cars burst out laughing. Everybody, that is, except Prince!

"Give me another beer, Charlie." Prince barked the command at his friend. "Come on out to the Italian Club tonight and see who gets kicked where." Prince raised his voice so that everybody could hear. "This time I won't be looking the other way. Sanger won't be so tough when we're eyeball to eyeball."

As everybody moved back to their own cars, Prince barked at Charlie again, "I thought I said git me another beer; you deaf or somethin'?"

"You already had three or four beers tonight." Charlie had concern in his voice. "You keep on drinking like this and Sanger's gonna kick yore ass without breaking a sweat. You better back off till after the fight."

"Who are you, my mama or something?" Prince shouted at his friend. "Give me a beer. We still got plenty of time before the fight. Besides, a few beers ain't gonna keep me from giving that nigger-looking Coahoma Street creep what he deserves. I can take him drunk or sober."

"I sure hope so." Charlie spoke under his breath as he reached into the cooler for another Bud.

---

The Coahoma Street Gang was all gathered down the highway at Abe's Barbecue Drive-In. They had been there ever since leaving Sanger earlier in the evening. Even though they tried to avoid the subject, their conversation seemed to keep drifting back to the fight.

"Sanger's crazy to meet Prince and his bunch out at the Italian Club tonight." Culligan spoke to the rest of the gang who were leaning against the hood of the car. "Even if he does kick Prince's ass, the rest of them'll be on him like stink on shit. He won't stand a chance."

"You're damn straight on that one." Steed leaned forward on his elbows. "But it's his own fault. He should never been messin' 'round with that nigger girl in the first place. If he hadn't, none of this shit would ever happened; and if it had, we'd have been there with him tonight to even up the odds."

"He's still one of us, though." Jake shifted his weight from one leg to the other. "And even though he did something crazy, he didn't do it to the gang. He did it to hisself. Whadya think, Jay; he's your brother?"

"I don't know. He is my brother, and he didn't really do anything to me. If I let him go out there tonight by hisself and he gets hurt, my old man'll still be kicking my ass this time next year."

"So, you're going then?" Wilkerson seemed almost pleased.

"Yeah, I'm going." Jay looked at the others. "He's my brother; I gotta go. But he ain't y'alls, so you do what you want to."

241

"He may not be our brother, but he sure the hell's been our friend for a long time." Culligan straightened his body. "Hell, he's still trying to look out for us like he always has. Telling us he don't 'spect us to show up tonight or nothing."

"You're right." Jake raised his voice to make the point. "He coulda put us all on the spot and asked us to be at the Italian Club tonight. But he didn't. He didn't want to give us any more grief. He's still trying to be our friend, even though we been giving him silent shit all week."

"Well, I ain't seen a decent fight all summer." Steed subconsciously made a fist. "How 'bout the rest of y'all?"

"Me, neither." Culligan answered first, then Jake, then the rest of the gang.

Steed's smile had a sinister twist. "Maybe we ought to just wander on out to the Italian Club 'bout 11:00 then."

They all just smiled!

# *30*

It took Sanger about 30 minutes to work his way back north up the dry creek bed.  By 10:40 he was sitting right inside the tree line no more than 25 yards from the parking lot beside the Italian Club.  Any minute now, he knew that a procession of cars would pull out of the Ranch's parking lot and make its way to the spot he was watching.

Leading that procession would be Jim Prince and his two buddies. Following close behind would be every other car from the Ranch. Whenever a fight was going down, the hangout took on the appearance of a graveyard at night.  There wouldn't be a car left on the lot.

Since he figured to face this thing tonight alone, he had come up with a plan.  As soon as the procession arrived and all their attention was devoted to the center of the parking lot where their car lights were all pointed, he would work his way up behind them.  When he walked out into the light, no one would spend much time looking for his car. Everyone's attention would be on him and Prince.  Even if someone did take the time to look around for the car, they'd just assume he had parked it around in front of the building or something.

If it turned out to be your regular, run-of-the-mill fight, he'd have no big problem.  After it was over, regardless of how it turned out, he intended to walk out of the circle of lights and disappear.  If, however, it turned out to be not so run of the mill, then he might have a really big problem. With everybody after him, he'd never be able to outrun them in his old car.

His plan was to sneak away however he could and work his way back down the dry creek bed. Once safely back in the car, he intended to try and sleep for a few hours until everyone got tired of looking for him and went home for the night.

When he figured he had waited long enough, he would drive east through the back roads. Most people would probably not look for him in that direction.

He planned to head over to Tutwiler, a small town about 15 miles southeast of Princeville. Once there, he planned to drive south and then east to Charleston.

He knew that if he made it that far, he could drive east a few more miles and pick up Interstate 55. Interstate 55 was the major North-South artery through Mississippi.

Sanger knew that if he turned north on I-55 and followed it, he would end up in Chicago. He smiled as the thought crossed his mind. Of course, Chicago meant seeing Eloisa!

---

Jim Prince angrily threw his empty beer can down on the gravel parking lot. It joined several more that had gotten there the same way. "Let's go!" He looked at Merk and Sands who were sitting on the hood of his GTO. "Time to take care of one nigger-lover!"

As Prince fired life into the powerful engine of the GTO, everybody else took the cue. They all ran to their cars as fast as they could. Nobody wanted to miss the biggest fight of the summer.

Prince eased the car forward toward the highway. Other people backed their vehicles out of the way to give him a clear path.

Because of the congestion in the parking lot, it took him a couple of minutes to weave through the mass of cars. Once on the highway, he stomped the accelerator, causing the car to jump forward and start to fishtail. Steering into the slide, he continued to give it gas. Amid the sound of squealing tires and the smell of burning rubber, the evening's main event was set into motion.

By the time Prince and the procession sped by the string of black honky-tonks on the highway, they were exceeding the speed limit by 20 miles per hour. Not a single person noticed the police car backed into the alley with its front pointing their way.

Burt Fager sat in the car watching the procession of speeding teenagers. "Speed on, you little rich shits. Get on out to the Italian Club and give that white nigger from Coahoma Street what he deserves. I'll be by a little later to help finish the job."

Fager had been waiting for another shot at Sanger ever since last Friday night. Finally, he had his chance!

---

Sheriff Dugan was also in his car as most of the local teenagers were speeding toward the night's entertainment at the Italian Club. He, however, was oblivious to the activity. About the time the procession of teenagers was turning south out of town toward the Italian Club, the Sheriff's cruiser was turning north on Friars Point Road.

The Sheriff was himself leading a procession of sorts. He glanced in his rearview mirror and was immediately greeted with three sets of headlights formed closely on his rear bumper. They belonged to three patrol cars following behind. Hopefully there would be no major crime wave tonight; half the scheduled patrol deputies were in the cars behind him.

Tonight's activity might not be the most fun Dugan ever had as Sheriff, but it sure would be close to the top. Tonight, he was on his way to arrest the attacker of Beth Prince.

Solving the attack had not required the consultation of Sherlock Holmes; it had merely required the application of good solid police procedure. Since the attack had not been the result of robbery, burglary, or sexual assault; it had to be for some other reason.

245

Sheriff Dugan had begun to formulate a list of possible suspects the Sunday morning after the attack as he sat in front of the Princeville Baptist Church waiting for the arrival of Jackson Prince.

Who would want to kill Beth Prince? Who would have a motive for such a thing? The most obvious suspect was Jackson Prince. After all, Beth had not been exactly faithful to their marriage vows.

Anyone in town with ears knew Beth Prince was a slut; rich, yes, but still a slut nevertheless. The joke around Princeville was that she would screw a snake if it would hold still long enough. Jackson had put up with that for years, though, why kill her now? Had something changed to warrant such a drastic response? Maybe it had.

Beth had changed her modus operandi lately. According to town gossip, she had switched from sleeping her way through the Country Club membership to sleeping with a guy from the other side of the tracks. Now, that might make Jackson mad. He would consider Beth's sleeping with white trash the same as sleeping with a black man.

It had taken Dugan a couple of days to run down the name of the new guy, but finally he had a quiet conversation with Mildred at the Uptowner Inn. It turned out she had quite a bit of useful information.

With two pretty good suspects, Sheriff Dugan decided to start with Frank Wilkerson. Since Jackson had a rock-solid alibi, Frank seemed the most likely suspect. After all, he wasn't accustomed to the bed-hopping routine out at the Country Club. If he had been used then cast aside by the high and mighty Beth Prince, he might have a tendency to take it a tad bit more seriously.

The day after he talked to Mildred at the Uptowner, Dugan went to see Frank at his auto shop. An hour later he was back to square one. Not only did Frank have an alibi, he backed it up with a AAA service bill listing the time, place, and the name and address of the people in the car. A quick call to the motorists in Illinois verified that Frank could not have committed the attack.

That only left Jackson, but he had an alibi. Dugan had talked to Ronald Beakner, the bank officer, by phone the Monday after the attack. He had confirmed that Jackson Prince and he had been working on bank business in Memphis during the specified time.

Upon replaying the phone conversation in his head, however, Dugan decided that Ronald's response had seemed almost rehearsed. He had decided to talk to Ronald again. After all, it couldn't hurt anything. That's when he had struck paydirt.

Dugan had decided to push Ronald a bit. It hadn't been hard to get the address of the apartment in Memphis. Once he had the address, things began to fall in place.

First of all, a check with the landlord of the apartment complex showed that the apartment was rented to a company called JR Connections, Inc. Since a check with the Tennessee Secretary of State revealed no such corporation registered to do business in the state, Sheriff Dugan knew he might be on to something.

Dugan drove to Memphis and began interviewing all the other apartment occupants who lived close to the one where Jackson and Ronald had stayed. The first interview was with an eighty-year-old widow who had been living in her apartment for 25 years. When the Sheriff asked about the apartment in question, she knew immediately the one he meant.

She told him no one really lived there; it was just used one or two weekends a month by some nice businessmen. The same two men had been coming to the apartment for 15–20 years, best she could remember. She didn't know what they did in the apartment, but they hardly ever left once they got there. She knew that because one of them almost always parked his big blue car right outside her window.

When Dugan asked her to describe the men, her descriptions sounded a lot like Jackson Prince and Ronald Beakner. What could they possibly be doing in that apartment twice a month for all those years?

"Now this is a very interesting piece of information," Dugan thought to himself as he knocked on the door of the next apartment. Maybe those rumors about Ronald Beakner he had been hearing for years were true, but Jackson Prince? He couldn't help but chuckle. What would the good people at the Princeville Baptist Church say if they knew?

The second interview was a bust, but the third paid off. The apartment was occupied by a man, his wife, and newborn daughter.

Sheriff Dugan asked the man if he could think of anything unusual about the night of Beth Prince's attack.

"Yep, I remember that night alright," the young man said with a trace of anger in his voice. "It was the night before my wife went into labor with our little girl.

"When Mary Jean, my wife, woke me up wantin' some banana ice cream, I looked over at the clock. I couldn't believe she wanted me to go to the store at 1:00 in the morning. But if you've ever had a pregnant wife, you know what I had to do.

"Since I was parked right out in front of the building below Widow Neely's window, it didn't take but a couple of minutes to throw on my clothes and make it to the car. It took longer to find the ice cream, though. Ever tried to find banana ice cream at 1:00 in the morning?

"On the way back home I was feelin' kinda tired and thinkin' it was good I had a up close parkin' spot and all. At least I wouldn't have to walk so far. But, wouldn't you know it? Somebody had stole my parking place.

"When I came wheelin' into the lot, there was this big blue Lincoln with Mississippi plates parked there. It made me so mad, I kicked one of the tires on the way by. Why couldn't those rednecks stay where they belong? No offense."

Dugan told the man no offense was taken and thanked him for the information. "Better lucky than good," he thought. He had just gotten really lucky.

It didn't take Dugan long when he got back to Princeville to get a deputy to bring in Ronald Beakner.

Beakner was cool and stuck to the story at first. Sheriff Dugan knew how to remove the chill, though. He had him locked up for an hour in a cell with six black prisoners. Beakner soon decided he would rather talk than entertain his cell mates.

He immediately confessed to the lie and told the Sheriff that Jackson had not gotten to the apartment until after 1:00 in the morning. But he was quick to defend Jackson as he repeated the story about the flat tire and buying the new one at the Blue and White service station in Tunica. He even told the Sheriff about Jackson almost ruining the coveralls he kept in the trunk of his car.

It took another two hours in the cell with the prisoners before Ronald admitted the truth about his true relationship with Jackson Prince. This time the Sheriff couldn't contain himself. He let out a huge belly laugh. It appeared Jackson Prince was really a "Princess." Truth can be stranger than fiction.

Sheriff Dugan's mind snapped back to the present as he led his procession into the drive of the Princeville Country Club. He and one car pulled up and stopped at the front entrance; the other two cars drove around back to the service entrance.

As Dugan and two deputies walked up the palatial steps, through the stately white columns and into the richly appointed lobby of the Country Club, they drew curious stares and whispered comments from the members lounging around. One deputy who was black seemed to be getting more than his share of interest.

The officers turned to their left and headed for the bar. Sheriff Dugan knew Jackson Prince was in the dimly lit room with his buddies holding court. He had called just a few minutes earlier and asked.

Out of the corner of his eye, Dugan caught sight of the other deputies coming through the kitchen door.

Dugan stood blocking the bar's door as he waited for a deputy to tell the bartender to turn on all the lights. When the lights came up, he immediately saw Prince sitting at a table in the back. The other men at the table had names that read like a who's who in town. Even though the Sheriff felt confident in what he was about to do, he still felt a little intimidated by the power sitting at the table. A screw-up now could prove fatal to his career.

Prince looked up as Dugan approached. "You boys members of the Club or just drop by to see how the other half lives?"

The Sheriff just smiled as he motioned at two of his deputies. "Jenkins, you and Miller help Mr. Prince up and cuff him."

Pushing his chair away from the table and holding one hand in front of himself, Prince yelled at the Sheriff. "Cuff me? Now you just wait a minute, Dugan. Nobody is going to cuff me—not in my town!"

"It's not your town, Prince. I know you think so, and so do your friends sitting here. After tonight it might be a little different, though. You're under arrest for the attempted murder of your wife, Beth Prince."

Prince laughed although there was little humor in the sound. "Dugan, you are one crazy redneck. You know I have an alibi for that night; there is no way I could have shot Beth."

"I know all about your alibi, Jackson, and about the flat tire and about buying a new one in Tunica and about what time you really got to Memphis. I know about the little love nest you keep in Memphis and pretty much everything else."

About that time a deputy came in carrying a pair of coveralls. "Found them in the trunk of his car just like you said, Sheriff."

"Thanks, Bob. Put them in an evidence bag and don't let them out of your sight until I personally tell you to," Dugan instructed the deputy as he turned again to face a somewhat pale-looking Jackson Prince.

Leland Benton, an attorney who was sitting at the table, came to Prince's rescue. "Dugan, are you insane? You can't really think Jackson shot Beth, can you? I know you don't really like us because we're successful and you're not. Everyone knows you're just a hick Sheriff who owes his job to a bunch of low-life whites and the niggers around here. But do you really think you can get away with this? We'll have your badge and everything you own. You'd better leave while you still can."

The Sheriff was not intimidated by Leland Benton; he just glared at him. "Leland, you don't really want a piece of this. If you take a bite of this case, the bad taste will still be in your mouth ten years from now. Jackson shot Beth, and I can prove it. Now shut up and have another drink. You'll be glad you did in the morning."

"I'll bite into whatever I choose, Dugan." Benton's face was turning pink on its way to a deep purple color. "You couldn't have any hard evidence. Jackson is our friend and you're not taking him anywhere until I know what you know. I'll have a judge and four lawyers on the phone before you get Jackson in the car. They'll be waiting for you at the jail. Not only will they let Jackson go, they'll take that badge of yours and pin it to your liver. You understand what I'm sayin', boy?"

Sheriff Dugan knew what Benton was saying was true. Putting all his cards on the table while arresting a murderer was not his usual strategy, but Dugan could see he had little choice. Besides, it might be fun to take this bunch down a couple of notches in front of the other Club members. Every member present who could was now squeezed into the bar. The crowd also included most of the waiters and kitchen staff. One did not often have the opportunity for such a show.

Dugan looked around the crowded room and then back at the table. "You guys sure you want to do it like this?"

"Damn straight, we're sure." Benton's face looked like it might explode at any minute.

"O.K. Here it is." The Sheriff visibly stood up straighter like he was facing a judge and jury. In many ways, he was. "Jackson said he got to Memphis about 11:00 on the Friday night Beth was shot. Not true. I have two witnesses who put him there a little after 1:00 on Saturday morning. He told one of the witnesses he had a flat and that caused him to be late. Jackson said he ruined a tire, had to put on the spare, then stopped at the Blue and White service station in Tunica to buy a new tire. Again, not true.

"First, the Blue and White sold three tires that night, all truck tires. Second, Jackson's car does not have a new tire on it. So, where was he during the unaccounted for three hours?

"Then there was the grease on the barrel of Beth's gun. I admit I was stumped on that one until a witness told me Jackson kept coveralls in the trunk of his car. He wore them if he had to work on the car.

"I figure he wore them to keep from being splattered with Beth's blood. A head shot can be real messy.

"He must've had trouble sitting Beth up in bed with one hand occupied holding the gun. He probably stuck the gun in his pocket, used both hands to sit Beth up, then got the gun out of his pocket and shot her.

"What he didn't think about was the grease on the coveralls. Also, he never got around to throwin' them away. Big mistake, Jackson; from the looks of them they did get a little bloody."

"Who is this witness you keep talking about?" Benton asked as he glanced over at Jackson who was visibly shaking by this time.

"The witness," Dugan smiled at Jackson, "is Ronald Beakner. Y'all know him, don't you? He's an officer down at the bank and the person who was with Jackson that night in Memphis."

The Sheriff had been waiting for the right moment to drop the big one. "It seems there is this apartment in Memphis rented by a company called JR Connections, Inc. That's where Ronald and Prince were staying."

"So what?" Benton could see the Sheriff was enjoying this.

"Well, it gets a bit complicated from this point." The Sheriff scrunched up his eyebrows as if in heavy thought. "There is no such company as JR Connections, Inc. Best I can tell now, Jackson is the guy paying the rent, and he's been doing it for a whole bunch of years. As soon as I check a

252

couple of other things, I'll know for sure who pays and how long he's been doing it.

"Beakner says he and Jackson have been using the apartment a couple of times a month for about 17 years now. He also told me the stuff about the flat and what time Jackson really got to Memphis that night."

"Using the apartment for what?" Benton seemed genuinely confused.

"Come on, Benton. You get kicked in the head by a mule or something?" Dugan let the silence hang. "JR Connections, Inc. is just a made up name. *JR Connections* means *Jackson Ronald Connections*. Do I need to draw you a picture?

"Seventeen years ago they probably thought the name was cute. I bet they never thought anyone would find out. Well, the gig is up. Ronald admitted the love affair has been going on since college."

Benton and the rest of the guys at the table were stunned beyond words. The people crowded into the bar were silent for a couple seconds then started whispering wildly.

"It doesn't make sense for Beakner to tell you this stuff, even if it's true." Benton was trying to sound convincing but was losing the battle.

"It makes sense if you don't want to be accused as an accessory to murder," the Sheriff responded in a slightly elevated volume. "After a couple of hours in a crowded cell, I couldn't shut him up. You wouldn't believe all the stuff he was saying."

Sheriff Dugan looked each man at the table in the eyes. "Y'all still want to get involved in this? If so, go for it!

"We're takin' Jackson to jail and throwin' his ass in a cell. Anybody interfering, including lawyers and judges, will be talking to the Mississippi Attorney General by morning.

"Let's go, Jackson."

253

Jackson Prince had visibly aged ten years as he stood to leave the bar. His shoulders were drooped and his eyes never left the floor as the deputies escorted him outside.

Dugan watched as the high and mighty Jackson Prince was put into the backseat of a cruiser. Come to think of it, this was the most fun he ever had as Sheriff.

# 31

"Slow down some, Jim. We don't want the cops to stop us before we even git out of town." Sands looked out the window in search of a patrol car. "We got plenty of time."

"That's right, Jim." Merk had caution in his voice. "We got lots of time. We don't want to git there before everybody else. They might miss some of the fun."

"You're right." Prince eased the pressure on the car's accelerator. "When I start kicking Sanger's ass, I want lots of witnesses. We'll slow down and let the rest of those dickheads back there catch up."

The rest of the procession caught up with Prince just as he turned left off Highway 61. In a few minutes they made another turn onto the gravel road that would take them to the Italian Club. It wasn't far now!

"I don't see anybody there yet." Prince squinted his eyes against the darkness of the night. He hit the brakes of the GTO hard and turned sharply into the parking lot. As the car's lights swept the empty lot, it was evident that they were the first ones there.

"Where the hell is that asshole?" Prince slammed on the brakes and roughly shoved the floor-mounted gear shift into park.

"Maybe he chickened out on you." Sands looked into the darkness of the summer night. "I heard he was going to California or somewhere. Maybe he left already."

"He could be just messin' with you, Jim."  Merk turned to look through the rear window of the car.  "You know, make you think he's not coming, then showing up right at the last minute.  Just tryin' to make you nervous so he'll have the edge."

"He'll be here alright."  Car lights lit up Prince's smug face.  "Him and me got a deal.  Let's get out and wait."

By now all the procession had pulled into the parking lot.  One by one, they pulled up and backed up until all the cars were formed into a large circle.

Each driver left the car lights on so that the entire center of the circle was as light as day.  Jim Prince stood in the center waiting.  He had stripped from the waist up and was now shadow boxing to the yells and encouragement of the crowd.

"This is my crowd and my night."  Prince was basking in the glory of the moment and his private thoughts.  "There's no way Sanger can walk away from this.  Even if he gets the best of me, he's still gonna get his."

Merk, Sands, and a couple more strategically placed friends would see to that.  They had been instructed to step in at the first sign that Sanger was winning.  When that happened, they would kick Sanger around some, then hold him for Prince to finish off.

Even though he had given his word to Sanger that this would finish it between them, he had never given his word that he wouldn't fight dirty. He had known that the Coahoma Street Gang wouldn't be around to help. After what had been in the newspaper, there probably wasn't a person in Princeville (a white person, anyway) that would help Sanger.  He could do whatever he wanted to Sanger tonight, and there wasn't anybody to stop him."

Prince was so deep into his own thoughts that he didn't see Sanger step into the circle of light.  The noise of the crowd brought him back to reality.  When he looked up in response to it, Sanger was standing a few feet in front of him.

The volume of noise from the yelling teenagers made it impossible for the two to speak. Each just stood staring at the other. As they did, the noise level decreased dramatically to one where you could hear a whisper. Everyone wanted to be able to hear the two combatants taunt each other as was the customary routine.

With all eyes focused on the two in the center of the ring, the arrival of the last car went unnoticed. The Coahoma Street Gang unloaded and spread out in pairs. They worked their way through the crowd to the front. They had decided to divide up so they wouldn't attract so much attention. Then if Sanger needed a little assist, they wouldn't be far off. Regardless of where he was in the circle, at least two of them would be able to help immediately.

Sanger walked a little closer to Prince. Prince responded by moving to his left awkwardly. Apparently, he had been drinking a little. "You been drinking too much, Prince, or are you just trying to fool me?"

"Up yours, you nigger-loving, white trash." The words were more slurred than Prince liked. "I can take you any day of the week in any condition. You come to fight or you come to visit?"

"I don't really want to fight you, Prince, especially with you drunk. Isn't there another way to settle this?"

"Sure there is." Prince looked at his friends in the crowd and smirked. "Just get down on your knees and beg me not to hurt you. Do that in front of all these people and maybe I'll let you off the hook. Otherwise, let's get started. I been wanting some of yore ass ever since that last time at the Ranch when you sucker kicked me. How 'bout trying that tonight and seeing how far you get."

As if to hide that particular target, Prince turned sideways and assumed a boxing stance.

Sanger realized that there was no way out of the fight. He simply had to make the best of it. At this point, the most productive course of action seemed to be one of trying to get Prince to do something stupid and leave himself open. Sanger decided to go with that line of thought.

257

"You been wanting a piece of my ass, huh, Prince?" Sanger smiled at Prince mockingly. "What's wrong, you don't like girls anymore? You wanna screw me now? I'm really flattered, but I make it a policy to never let spoiled punk drunks with bad breath play with my ass. You understand, don't you?"

Just as Sanger finished, Prince swung at him with all his strength. Sanger sidestepped Prince as the momentum of his swing pulled him slightly off balance. Almost in the same motion, Sanger kicked him hard in the right kneecap. As Prince stumbled to the gravel, Sanger kicked him in the face.

"This is a little too easy," Sanger thought to himself as his foot connected with Prince's chin. At that same instant Sanger got hit in the back of the head with a fist. Charlie Merk was following his instructions real well.

Sanger knew something like this was bound to happen. When he hit the gravel parking lot, his hand immediately went to his ankle. One of his pre-fight preparations was about to be revealed.

His hand came away filled with a homemade sap. It was the same as he had used on several occasions before.

Growing up in a neighborhood like Coahoma Street had certain advantages. You learned early in life to improvise. The homemade sap was such an improvisation. To make it, you simply take a screen door spring like the one he had used the night he ran into Prince and friends in Eloisa's grocery store.

You bend the spring double and tape the two ends together. Once that's accomplished, you use electricians tape to tape an assortment of nuts and bolts into the cavity created by bending the spring. When all the taping is done, you have a nice weighted sap with spring tension built in.

Sanger rolled over onto his back only to see Charlie Merk reaching down to grab him. As hands grabbed the front of his shirt, he hit Merk on the cheek with the sap.

Sanger quickly rolled out of the way and up to his feet as Merk howled in pain. He figured another of Prince's buddies would be moving in to replace the one now writhing on the ground.

Much to his relief, no one was trying to hit or kick him. What he saw was very surprising.

About the time he looked up, he caught sight of his brother, Jay, hitting Bill Sands in the mouth. A little further away, Jake was holding somebody by the shirt and backhanding him repeatedly.

Steed was likewise abusing another Country Clubber. Culligan had made his way over and was now standing back to back with Sanger. Instead of moving in, however, the crowd was just standing there. Apparently, not everyone was willing to help Jim Prince fight his battles.

Within seconds, the entire Coahoma Street Gang was circled protectively around Sanger. The crowd appeared more scared than anything else. What had started as a little ride for most of them, now had the potential of turning violent.

The whole situation had turned into a type of Mexican standoff—the Coahoma Street Gang against everybody else.

All of a sudden, the tension was broken by the sound of a police siren in the circle. Flashing lights suddenly lit up the Italian Club's parking lot.

Walking out of the darkness with a night stick in his hand was Burt Fager. The crowd was parting as he moved forward toward the Coahoma Street Gang.

"O.K., let's break this up. Anybody still here in five minutes goes to jail. Move it! Move it!

"That doesn't include you, Sanger." Fager had to shout over the noise of the crowd leaving. "You stay exactly where you are. I wanna talk to you."

259

With Fager temporarily distracted by the appearance of Prince still on the ground, Sanger slipped the sap to Culligan who was still standing beside him. "Take this and get out of here before that asshole decides to arrest the whole gang."

"We can't leave you like this." Culligan was watching the short policeman help Prince to his feet. "There's no telling what that creep has on his mind."

"Y'all get the hell out of here while you can!" Sanger could barely be heard over the noise. "I'll handle Fager. I brought along a little antenna persuasion. If I have to, I'll use it on him. I'm out of here tonight anyway. I'll be O.K."

"Portable antenna, huh?" Culligan grinned. "We're out of here then. Be careful; let me know where you end up."

Jay was standing there when Sanger looked away from Culligan.

"I kinda figured you might show up." Sanger noticed blood on his brother's knuckles, obviously Sand's. "I appreciate the help. Y'all better get out of here now!"

"You gonna be alright?" Jay had concern etched across his face. "You want me to hang around for awhile?"

"Naw, you better go with the rest of 'em. Y'all don't need any more grief because of me. I'll be fine.

"Oh, by the way, tell Daddy that I still had my pride when I left town.

"I'll let y'all know where I am."

The crowd was pretty much gone as Sanger watched his brother and the rest of the Coahoma Street Gang walk off.

The last to leave was Prince. He just stared at Sanger as his two friends helped him over to his car. When they pulled out of the parking lot, the only car left was the police cruiser. Its headlights were still directed to the spot where Sanger was standing.

Fager was standing by the car with its trunk open. As Sanger watched, he took off his gun and put it inside. With a slam, he closed the trunk.

Fager slowly walked toward Sanger. He still held the night stick in his hand. As he walked forward, he very deliberately struck his left palm with the weapon.

"As you can see, crud, I'm not wearin' a gun. I don't want to go crazy with pleasure and shoot your ass. I just want to ask you a question. And this time, you're gonna give me the answer. If you don't, I'm gonna use this stick on your head."

"You're always the big bad cop, aren't you, Fager? Without a stick or a gun, you're just like the rest of the shit in this world, smelly but not piled too high."

"Maybe I'll break that big nose of yours first thing." Fager slapped the stick against his right leg lightly. "Just so smelling ain't such a concern for you."

"Come on, Fager. What do you want? We're out of the city limits here. You got no more jurisdiction here than I do. If you don't get in your car and drive off, I'm gonna do to you what I've always wanted to do."

"And what's that, punk? What you gonna do? Talk me to death? Give it your best shot! Then I'm gonna shove this stick up your skinny ass."

"I said, 'What do you want, Fager?' I'm not gonna stand around here all night."

"I'll tell you what I want, dickhead." Fager laughed and pointed the night stick at Sanger. "I want the name of the nigger bitch that was at the school with you last week, and I want it right now."

"You probably want a blow-job, too, but I doubt very seriously you ever had one unless you're a contortionist.

261

"What's the big deal about who was with me? All the charges were dropped. The Chief let me go. Officially, its all over."

"Officially, it may be over." Fager moved a step closer. "But me and some friends still want to know her name."

"And why is that?" Sanger moved a step. "Are they the same friends that had the phony stuff put in the newspaper? Are they the same ones that keep all the lies about blacks and whites going?

"I guess they want to stir the pot a little more so that the good, honest white folks of Princeville will feel outraged by the uppity nigger girl. Is that pretty much the story, Fager."

"Pretty much." Fager's lips tightened into a grin exposing his teeth. "Now, you gonna do it the easy way, or do I git to have a little unofficial fun?

"What's the nigger's name?"

Sanger had been slowly moving toward the darkness as Fager talked. All of a sudden, he ran directly into the night.

"I'll get you, Sanger!" Fager moved around the area of light like a mad man. "You got to come out sooner or later. It's a long way back to town and your buddies ran off and left you without a car. I'll get you!"

"Here I am." Sanger spoke from the edge of the darkness to Fager's left. "I could outrun you wearing a leg cast, but I decided to stay. I still owe you something from last week. And this time my hands aren't handcuffed behind my back."

"I always knew you were a stupid shit." Fager could barely make out Sanger off to his left in the edge of darkness. "Now you done gone and proved it. You should've run while you could. Come on over in the light where I can see you and let's do it."

"Naw." Sanger taunted Fager. "You come on over here if you want me."

"O.K., asshole, if that's the way you want it, that's the way you gonna git it!" Fager ran forward toward Sanger with the night stick raised in the air over his head.

Just as he was within striking distance and had started the downward motion of his arm, he experienced a sharp excruciating pain in the arm holding the stick. As quickly as that pain registered with his brain, another of similar magnitude was felt across his face.

He immediately dropped the stick and clutched his bleeding face. That brief reaction was halted by a very painful explosion emanating from his crotch.

Sanger had been standing in the edge of the darkness for a reason. Since Fager assumed he was unarmed, he didn't want to give away his advantage.

His reason for running into the dark had not been one of escape; instead, it had been a necessary move so that he could remove his portable antenna from the back waist area of his pants unobserved. He had been holding it at his side as he waited for Fager to make his move.

"Portable antenna" was the name of a makeshift weapon that he and the gang had called on a few times in the past when nothing else was handy. It was just a long antenna from a car radio.

When not extended, it was only about a foot long. Because of its small diameter, it could be slipped into the small of the back inside your pants.

Once withdrawn and extended, it became four feet of spring steel. With the end sharpened to a point, it could be whipped violently, delivering a nasty cut each time it made contact with the body. Although not deadly, it was very effective in discouraging opponents.

Sanger had stood in the shadows waiting for Fager to get within range. Once he was, Sanger had swung the persuasion with all his strength. The first target was the arm holding the stick, followed by a backhand slash to the face.

When Fager grabbed his face, Sanger kicked him as hard as he could in the nuts. Just like most real fights, this one had lasted less than a minute. As insurance, Sanger also kicked Officer Fager in the face.

"That's for the girl you seem so interested in," Sanger spoke as he kicked the man kneeling in front of him.

He was contemplating kicking Fager again when his train of thought was broken by a voice.

"That's enough, Jerry. He's through for tonight; might even be through for the week!"

Sanger recognized the voice. He squinted in its direction until he could make out the figure of Mitchell Roberts standing in the edge of the light.

"What are you doing here, Mr. Roberts? Y'all gonna start patrolling this part of the county?"

"I stopped at the Ranch about ten minutes ago to see why it was so deserted on a Friday night." Roberts walked closer. "One of the black carhops told me what was going down. He said you were gonna need some help.

"Kid said his name was Slick. Friend of yours?"

"Yeah, he's a good friend of mine. You won't mention his name to anybody, will you? I wouldn't want your buddy there to hassle him."

"You don't have to worry about that, Jerry. What I'm more worried about right now is you. When word gets out about what happened here tonight, certain people in this town are gonna have a real big problem with you."

"Well, if you're not taking me to jail, I'm leaving town tonight. As a matter of fact, I'd like to leave right now. There's nothing to keep me here anymore."

"There's no reason to take you to jail, Jerry. If I did, then Fager would have to explain what he was doing out here in the first place. Then he'd

264

have to explain how a big tough cop like him let a kid like you mess up his face like that.

"I suspect he'd prefer just not to see you anymore. How you leaving? You got a car around here someplace?"

"It's right down the road." Sanger gestured with his head. "Give me an hour and I'll be far enough away from Princeville so that I'll never be a problem to you again."

"Oh, I suspect we'll be at the hospital at least an hour getting that gash in Fager's face sewn up." Roberts seemed to derive pleasure from the thought.

"Looks like he'll be carrying around a little souvenir from you for the rest of his life. If I were you, I'd remember that and stay away from this town for a long time."

"Once I'm gone, I may never come back." Sanger seemed to retreat inward. "The hatred I saw tonight will always be with me as a reminder of Princeville. It's hard to imagine a reason strong enough to bring me back to this town.

"Thanks for all your help, Mr. Roberts. I never have understood why you took a liking to the Coahoma Street Gang, but I appreciate it. Before I leave, could I ask one last favor?"

"Sure, Jerry, ask away."

"Would you swing by Coahoma Street tonight and tell the gang what happened and that I'm O.K. I had a tough time getting them to leave me here with Fager tonight. I don't want them getting worried and doing something stupid."

"Sure, I'll swing by there as soon as I drop Fager off at the hospital. See you around, Jerry. Just make sure it's not around here."

"You can count on that, Mr. Roberts. I'll see you!"

Sanger faded into the darkness surrounding the Italian Club as Roberts helped Fager to the car.

He smiled to himself as he made his way back down the creek bed. "I've made it! I've finally made it out of Princeville!"

# *Conclusion*

The twelve months following Sanger's departure from Princeville were ones of poetic justice for the Prince family. Mrs. Prince died having never come out the coma.

Following the fight at the Italian Club, Jackson Prince was in jail for shooting his wife. Within six months, he was on death row at the state prison. His son, Jim, was well on the road to drinking his way through the family fortune.

Culligan was visiting the Ruber girls every month at the state hospital. He and the rest of the Coahoma Street Gang were still hanging out under the streetlight.

Officer Fager returned to duty with an increased sense of hatred and cruelty. Many thought it had something to do with the ugly scar he now had on his face. People speculated as to its origin, but no one knew the real story. No one that would tell, that is.

Eloisa and Jerry were together in Chicago. They took the same classes, walked around campus holding hands, and went to the movies on Saturday night. People seeing the young couple didn't give them a second glance. Life was good!

## ABOUT THE AUTHOR

Jerry Moorman grew up in a small cotton-farming community in Mississippi. Currently, he lives in Western Colorado with his wife and daughter.